Teres

C000017191

TAKES YOU

NICOLA C. PRIEST

Thanks For
Supporting
ous!

NC
Priest
x:

Thanks For Supporting ous!

Jessa +

Takes You
An Eternal Love Novel
by
Nicola C. Priest

OTHER BOOKS BY NICOLA C. PRIEST

THE HEARTLAND SERIES

Heart & Soul

Mind & Soul

Jason Harper Series

Perception

Standalone Books

Somewhere Love Remains

Chase the Knight

Takes You

Copyright © Nicola C. Priest 2018

Cover Illustration by Francessca Wingfield

Editor: Stephanie Farrant at Bookworm Editing Services
All rights reserved. No part of this book may be reproduced or transmitted
in any form or by any means, electronic or mechanical, including
photocopying, recording, or by any information storage and retrieval
system, without written permission from the author, except for the
inclusion of brief quotations in a review.

This book is a work of fiction. Names, characters, businesses, places, events
and incidents are either the products of the author's imagination or used
in a fictitious manner. Any resemblance to actual persons, living or dead,
or actual events is purely coincidental.

This book is dedicated to everyone who has ever lost someone they love.

Stay strong. They will always be with you.

MYALYF

ACKNOWLEDGMENTS

I never know who to thank when I write a book so I'm going to keep this short and sweet.

To my wonderful PA's Jade and Tracy, thank you ladies for all of your help over the last few months. You've been a godsend and I can't wait to continue working with you into the new year and beyond.

Earlier this year, I went to a music event. It was during this event that I heard the song that inspired this book. As soon as I heard it, I knew the story behind the song would make a wonderful book, so I approached the singer/songwriter to ask for consent to use the title and base my book on the lyrics of the song.

To my delight, he said yes.

Mr Dean Roberts, I can't tell you how much your agreement means to me and I can only hope that I have done your wonderful song justice in this book. Thank you for saying yes to my request. As promised, the first paperback is yours.

PROLOGUE

*N*o, it can't be me.

I can't quite believe the person looking back at me in the mirror is really me. The pretty hair adorned with crystals and pearls, and the made-up face with pink, glossy lips and dark, smoky eyes have become a thing of the past in recent months. They're unfamiliar to me now, so seeing them again feels... I don't know.

Weird.

Like the hair and the face, the dress hugging my body is one I didn't ever think I would have the chance to wear. The mix of pearls, crystals and chiffon is way prettier than I feel most of the time, so looking like this is a novelty to me; one I know will wear off before the end of the day.

My friends and family are all waiting for me to make my big appearance, and my dad is standing right outside that door. I bet he looks really smart in his charcoal grey, three-piece suit, with ice blue tie and matching handkerchief in the pocket. Any minute, I'll call out to him that I'm ready to go. But am I really ready?

They say your wedding day is meant to be the happiest day of your life. It's the day you pledge your love to the one you will spend the rest of your life with. That's what I intend to do today, in front of all those people closest to me. While I have no doubt this is going to be a wonderful day, it is also going to be one of the saddest.

I bet you're all wondering why, aren't you? I guess I should explain why I feel this way. It kills me to admit it, or even think it, but the reality is that today could very well be the last day I get to see my new husband before I leave him for a better place.

I love him with all my heart—have done since I was sixteen and he eighteen—but fate has intervened over and over again, trying to force us apart, and this time, it might have succeeded. No matter how much I love him, I can't put him through this pain any longer. It's breaking my heart to see him hurting, but it's something I have no control over.

Not anymore.

My name is Crissie Walker, and I hope you're sitting comfortably, because this is my story.

CHAPTER 1

Crissie

May 2006
Chester, England

"*O*h my god, he's walking over."

"Shut up. No, he isn't."

"You wanna bet?"

"He's definitely coming over. God, he's so hot I could jump him right here."

Is it really my friends who are talking right now? You'd think we were a bunch of pre-teens with the amount of giggling going on, not a bunch of supposedly mature-ish sixteen-year-old young women.

So what if Caleb Roberts is heading our way? It is a free country, after all; he can go wherever he wants. Head in whatever direction takes his fancy. I am not bothered he's walking over here. Nope. I'm not bothered at all. Oh shit, he really is walking over here.

Oh, who am I trying to kid?

The guy is sex on legs, and he is coming over right now. He's the guy all other guys strive to be like, and the one all the girls would love to be with. His crystal blue eyes are sparkling with a hint of mischief, and his soft lips are tilted up in a sexy smirk. His almost black hair is ruffled in a way that makes me think he's not long climbed out of bed, and his square jaw is covered in a light smattering of stubble.

He looks much older than his eighteen years, and I've heard he's used that to his advantage on more than one occasion. Not that I listen to rumours and gossip, you understand. What he does in his spare time is his business and doesn't matter to me in the slightest.

Yeah right. You just keep telling yourself that, Crissie.

I glance over at him again and see that sexy smirk is still plastered on his face. It's almost as if he can read my mind, and he's amused at what I'm thinking. If it wasn't for the fact I don't want to look like a complete idiot, I'd lick that smirk right off his too good-looking face.

If I lick him, that makes him mine, right?

I can hear my friends whispering and giggling, and part of me wants to turn around and shush them, but it's the part that's watching Caleb close in on my position that's winning out. He's only a few feet away from me now, and that smirk turns into a full-blown grin when he comes to a stop in front of me.

Say something, Crissie. He's just a guy. He's not going to bite.

I can sense my friends are still behind me, and I know they're all practically drooling over Caleb. Every girl I know would love to receive even the slightest bit of attention from this guy, and my friends are no exception. Come to think of it, neither am I. So why the hell am I just standing here gawping at him like a lovesick schoolgirl? Oh yeah, that's right.

I am a lovesick schoolgirl!

"Hey."

He speaks, and he's speaking to me!

"Crissie, right?"

All I can do is nod, knowing there is a stupid grin on my face as I realise Caleb Roberts is actually talking to me —and he knows my name! For six years, he hasn't paid me the slightest bit of attention. I wonder what's changed? Oh yeah, I lost weight, swapped my glasses for contacts, and, as if overnight, boobs appeared.

"I'm Caleb," he says with another smile, and I speak for the first time.

"I know."

Good grief, he must think I'm completely dumb. What is it about this guy that makes me turn into a babbling idiot? *Say something else. Anything else.*

"Do you want something?"

That smirk is back on his face, and for some reason I feel my cheeks flame red. It was an innocent question, but one I now realise could mean any number of things, and it's those other things Caleb is clearly thinking of, which he confirms with his next statement.

"There are a number of things I want, actually, but none of them are fit for public display."

"Oh." It's all I can say as I resist the urge to fan my heated skin.

Jesus. Why am I reacting like this? He's just standing in front of me. He hasn't even touched me, yet there are butterflies taking flight in my stomach, and I'm pretty sure my heart is about to beat out of my chest. Just the sound of his voice is doing funny things to my insides.

That voice is delicious enough to make any girl want to do anything to be with him. Doesn't matter if he's their first or not. I can't imagine being with Caleb to be anything other than amazing.

I'm not naïve enough to believe Caleb is still a virgin. In fact, if what Ellie McIntosh says is true, he definitely isn't. She's told everyone who will listen about the escapade she and Caleb had in the sports shed a few months ago. According to her, Caleb is like an animal in the sack, and, to use her words, he was the best she's ever had—which, by the way, is a lot.

Anyway, I don't want to think about Caleb and Ellie. He's still standing here looking at me, clearly amused by my response and my sudden inability to put together a coherent sentence. What is it about him that intimidates me so much? His age, maybe? As he is two years older than me, we didn't have much to do with each other when he'd been at school. In fact, if it weren't for his sister being in my year, our paths would probably never have crossed.

I have no idea what to say to him. Trying to make casual conversation—something I don't usually have a problem with—is seemingly impossible right now, so I'm pleased when he doesn't seem to have the same issue.

"You've finished your exams now, right?" he asks curiously.

"Yes, I had my last one this morning." *So far so good,* I think to myself. *Just keep going.* "I'm all done with school now. Just got to come back for the results in a couple of months," I tell him

"How do you think you've done?"

I look at him for a moment, seeing that he seems genuinely interested in how I've done on my GCSE's. I know he failed all but one of his, but that didn't stop him going out and getting a job. If there's one thing I know about Caleb, it's that he's not afraid of hard work. The place he's working at right now is putting him through his qualifications to become a mechanic whilst he has on the job training, something his little sister can't shut up about.

Lizzie Roberts idolises her big brother. He can do no wrong in her eyes, and part of me is jealous she has that kind of relationship with him. Being an only child, I never got to have that kind of sibling relationship. I have plenty of cousins I grew up with, but none of them are as close to me as a brother or sister would be.

"Honestly, I'm not sure. I need to get at least three B's to get into the college I want. Guess I'll have to wait and see." I give him a small smile, my heart jumping when he returns it with one of his own. Suddenly, I'm feeling bold and decide to ask him what I'm thinking. "You didn't come over to talk about my exams, did you, Caleb?"

Tilting my head slightly, I hear a nervous laugh slip past his mouth, and he lifts his arm, his hand going around to scratch his neck. Yeah, I've seen that move before. My question has thrown him off balance. He now looks a little unsure of himself, which I find both endearing and a little amusing.

"Actually, no, I didn't." He glances behind me, and I know he sees my friends watching us; they wouldn't be trying to hide it either. Subtle as sledgehammers, that's what they are. They'll all be standing there, blatantly staring, wondering what on earth has triggered this unexpected conversation between me and the guy all my friends have a massive crush on.

I keep my eyes on him as he looks back at me, dropping his arm down to his side, the smile back on his face.

"Are you planning on going to the end of school party on Friday?"

I'm unable to keep the surprise off my face. Of all the things I expected him to say, that wasn't one of them. For the last few years, when school finishes for the summer break, everyone gets together to throw a massive party for the graduating year, their friends, and family.

Truth be told, I hadn't actually decided whether I was going or not, despite having been looking forward to the party all year. Although, depending on what Caleb says next, my decision might have been made for me.

"I hadn't decided yet. Are you?"

"That depends."

Really? I can't help but voice the thought that's swimming through my mind. "Depends on what?"

"On whether you'll go with me?"

I roll my eyes when I hear one of my friends not so quietly whisper, "oh my god", and then I remember to breathe. Has Caleb Roberts really just asked me out? I must be imagining this whole encounter. Any minute now, I'm going to wake up in my bed and this will all have been a dream, because there's no way a guy like Caleb would ask me out, not to a place where he'd actually be seen with me.

Looking up at him, I see he's waiting for an answer from me. I want to shout a massive 'yes' right in his smiling face, but something is holding me back.

It's just one word, Crissie. Just three little letters. Y. E. S. Just open your mouth and say the word.

"Excuse us for a minute, Caleb." It's my friend Pippa that I hear behind me, and before I know it, she's grabbed my arm and spun me around, dragging me a few feet away from Caleb. Now, instead of Caleb's handsome face, I'm looking at the three faces of my friends. They all look horrified that I've not given Caleb an immediate answer, and I can see the questions on the tips of their tongues.

"What the hell, Crissie? The guy—and not just any guy, I might add—has asked you out, and you're just standing there gawping at him? Say yes, woman!"

"She's right," my friend Tasha pipes up. "You can't possibly be thinking of saying no?"

"If it were me, I'd have said yes and would already be out shopping for a new outfit," Missy says, the grin on her face making me smile as her eyes flick over my shoulder towards Caleb.

As I stand there looking at them, I realise they're all right. What am I thinking? Turning around, I see Caleb in the same position I left him. My brain wants to move, but the message isn't getting to my feet, not until I feel a gentle shove against my back that propels me forward.

Within seconds, I'm stood in front of Caleb again, and I see the question in his eyes. Deciding I can't just come out and tell him yes, I smile as a thought pops into my head.

"I don't think I can go with you, Caleb," I say and see his smile fall before I continue. "Unless you go to lunch with me today."

Yeah, I'm surprised too. I've never been this bold around guys, especially not one of the most popular guys that ever went to our school. His expression is unreadable, and I begin to think I've pressed my luck. That is, until the smile returns to his face and he laughs.

"You almost had me there," he says as he reaches out and briefly touches my arm. Was that a spark I just saw? "Lunch it is. Where do you want to go?"

"I'll let you decide." I smile up at him, and for the first time I realise just how tall he is. I'm by no means short at five feet eight, but I only come up to his chest. He has to be several inches above six feet, with broad shoulders and a trim waist. His love of sports is evident in his physique and the way he carries himself. God, he's hot, and I begin to understand why all the girls want to be with him.

The look on his face tells me he's pondering where we can go for lunch, and I see the moment he thinks of somewhere as he looks me in the eyes, smiles, and grabs my hand. "I know the perfect place. I hope you like pasta."

"I love it."

"Great. Let's go." Before I can respond, he pulls me along beside him, and all I can do is follow as I throw a wave over my shoulder at my friends, wishing I could see the expressions on their faces. Caleb Roberts is holding my hand and taking me to lunch. Me. Not the most popular girl, or the prettiest girl.

Me!

Caleb leads me over to the new Ford Focus his parents bought him for his birthday, and, like a gentleman, he opens the passenger door for me.

"Milady," he says as he gives me a small bow and a sweep of his arm.

I can't help it; I laugh as I climb in the car, only now understanding what people mean when they go on about a new car smell. I know Caleb hasn't had the car long as his birthday was only a couple of weeks ago. The scent of leather and polish fills my nose, and there's not a speck of dust to be seen. If I didn't know any better, I'd think it was the first time he'd driven it.

The opening of the driver's door pulls me from my musings, and I turn my head to see Caleb climbing in next to me. He fastens his seatbelt and looks at me, a huge grin on his face.

"So, I take you to lunch, and you'll go to the party with me?" I can hear the uncertainty in his voice as he seeks confirmation, and I realise he's just a normal guy. Because of his popularity, I'd always had him up on a pedestal, believing him to be confident and sure of himself. Looks like he has the same worries and insecurities as everyone else. I smile at him and nod.

"That's the plan," I say as I fasten my seatbelt. "Let's go. I'm famished."

Caleb grins at me again as he puts the key in the ignition and starts the engine. Pretty soon, we're heading into town, and I still can't quite believe I'm going to lunch with Caleb Roberts. My friends will be so jealous.

When did I become 'that' girl?

CHAPTER 2

Crissie

"You have to go with the red. Red makes you more appealing to men, or so I've heard."

"No, you absolutely have to wear the blue. It matches your eyes, not to mention his. His eyes are so dreamy."

"Actually, scrap the red one. I think you should go with the silver. It's simple and understated, but makes you look hot at the same time."

Oh my god! My head is spinning. I knew inviting these three on a shopping trip to help find my outfit for this evening's party was a mistake as soon as the invite left my mouth. So far, I've tried on close to a dozen dresses, and they haven't been able to agree on any of them.

The three of us are all crammed into a large dressing

room at the local shopping centre and there are dresses hanging up, covering every space against the wall, in every colour and style imaginable. None of them felt right to me when I tried them on, and I want to cry at how difficult it is to find something to wear.

At this rate, I'll end up going to the party in jeans and a t-shirt, which is not what I want to wear on my first official date with Caleb Roberts. I've always believed that when you find what you're looking for, you just know it, which is why I know when I find the right dress, it'll all but slap me in the face and scream 'buy me!'.

"Guys, please, you're not helping. I'm nervous enough about tonight without all of you arguing about what I should wear." I tug my jeans up my legs and fasten them at my waist before slumping down onto a nearby chair. I'm about to give up completely when Pippa come barrelling back into the changing room, fighting with the curtain and clutching a mass of black fabric in her hands.

"I think I've found it; the perfect dress for you to wear tonight. If Caleb's jaw doesn't drop when he sees you in this, then the guy needs a good slap."

I laugh at Pippa's words as she thrusts the dress towards me. It's hard to see what it's like on the hanger, but I dutifully slip out of my jeans and t-shirt and take the dress from my friend. It takes several minutes to pull the dress over my hips and fasten it at the back, but I have to admit, Pippa was right.

The bodice is fitted and makes my waist look

impossibly tiny. It has a sweetheart neckline that shows off a hint of cleavage and little cap sleeves. The skirt flares out over my hips and stops a few inches above my knees. The fabric is soft and silky, and I have never felt prettier.

I was right. This is the one. I just know it.

"I figured you could wear your black ballet pumps with it, the ones with the sparkles along the sides," Pippa says as she fastens the last button at the small of my back. "Caleb is going to love it."

I smile at my friends as they all nod, finally in agreement that I've found the dress to wear for my first official date with Caleb Roberts. I look back into the mirror and turn, glimpsing the back of the dress for the first time. I now see why it took so long to fasten. Instead of a zip, there are about two-dozen tiny buttons that start at the small of my back and go up to stop just between my shoulder blades.

"You can wear your hair down for once as you always have it in that damn ponytail. Straight or curly, either will look fab with this dress. Blonde hair and black clothes always go really well together. You'll look epic."

I look at my reflection and imagine my hair in a cascade of curls around my shoulders and down my back. The overall effect is just what I'm looking for, and Pippa is right: Caleb is going to love it. At least, I hope he will.

I feel the doubts begin to creep in, yet again. Ever since Caleb dropped me back home after our lunch date two days ago, I've been wondering why he asked me. With so many other girls, including many his own age, why ask a girl two years younger than him? A girl who is by no means the prettiest one out there. What is it about me that Caleb likes?

I take a deep breath and tilt my head, my hands smoothing down the skirt of the dress. Suddenly, I feel the need to be alone.

"Hey, could you guys take all of these dresses back outside? I'll change and join you in a few minutes."

The girls all nod and grab the dresses currently hung up around the room before vanishing through the curtain. I close it after they've gone and sit down, staring at my reflection in the mirror.

Why am I only now feeling nervous about tonight? We had a lovely time on our lunch date. I was a bit quiet to start with, unsure what to say or ask, but after about ten minutes, we were talking about all sorts of things, and we found we had quite a bit in common.

I'm just being silly. Caleb wouldn't have asked me to go out with him if he didn't want to go with me. Would he? No, I need to stop second-guessing myself, and Caleb, and just buy the dress, go home and get ready for tonight. Yes, that's what I need to do.

After a lot of manoeuvring and twisting, I finally unhook the last button on the dress and step out of it, putting it back on the hanger. Retrieving my clothes from the floor, I quickly get dressed and grab the dress before leaving the changing room.

As I look around for my friends, I hear them before I see them. Rounding a corner, I stand and watch as they argue over what's going to happen between Caleb and I tonight. My eyes widen in amusement when I hear Missy say we'll have the make-out session to end all make-out sessions, and I have to admit the thought is rather appealing.

I feel myself blush when I hear Pippa question, in a not so quiet voice, whether or not we'll actually have sex. Seriously? I'm only sixteen. I'm nowhere near ready for that kind of stuff. Kissing is one thing, but actually getting it on with someone and seeing their private parts... No way—not to mention, ewww!

"Have you decided, Miss?"

I turn to see the sales assistant smiling at me and hand her the dress I'm carrying. "Yes, I'll take this one, please. I'm sorry about them," I say, indicating to my friends. "They can get a bit carried away sometimes."

She peers over my shoulder to see my friends laughing and giggling, and smiles at them. "Oh, don't worry, dear. It's not the first time we've seen an excitable bunch of girls in here. I take it this dress is for something special?"

I follow her over to the till as I ponder my response. Is the dress for something special?

"I suppose so." I look at the assistant as she scans the dress and begins to fold it for me. "It's my first official date with a guy I like tonight."

The assistant's face lights up as she smiles at me. She's

an older woman, probably in her forties, if I had to guess. She has chocolate brown hair that's pulled back into a messy bun at the nape of her neck. Her green eyes are kind, and I feel like I can trust her. Weird I know, but she gives off that kind of vibe.

"You look nervous, sweetie."

"I guess I am a little bit. I'm just not sure what to expect." I hand over the cash as she grabs a bag from under the counter and puts the folded dress inside. Seconds later, she's handing me my change.

"How old are you? Fifteen, sixteen?" I confirm the latter and she continues, "Sweetie, you're still a baby. All you need to do is to have fun, and don't do anything you don't want to do. I have a daughter the same age as you, and I know there is a lot of pressure on girls to do certain things. Just remember that if it's something you're not one hundred percent sure about, just say no, honey. Any guy who's worth being with will understand you're not ready and will wait until you are."

I nod and smile at her as she hands me the bag. How many times has my mum used that phrase when I've gone out with friends? *Just say no.* It's been drilled into us at school as well. Not that I expect to have to say no. Nothing will happen between Caleb and I tonight—well, nothing that will result in my having to say no. I just don't think Caleb is the kind of guy to ask me to do anything like that, not on a first date anyway.

Stuffing my change in my pocket, I turn around and

18

see my friends still huddled in a group. They're not talking now. Instead, they all have their heads down while their fingers fly on their mobile phones. I screw up my face, almost wishing I had one of the devices too. They were all given one on their sixteenth birthdays, but my parents took the stand that I couldn't have one until I could afford to pay for it myself.

You're going to be waiting a long time, Crissie.

Unless I get a part-time job at weekends. With college and housework, there's no time in the week for a job, meaning it's going to be a while before I'll own a mobile phone. Sighing, I walk over to my friends and get their attention.

"Crissie, you're never gonna guess what's happened!" Pippa almost screams at me. "Josh Summers has asked me to go with him to the party!"

I puff my cheeks as I release a long breath and look over my shoulder, seeing the sales assistant looking in my direction.

"We're going to need another dress."

CHAPTER 3

Caleb

"I still don't get why you asked her. There are loads of girls who would kill to go out with you. Why did you have to pick one of my friends?"

"Give it a rest, would you, Lizzie?" I shake my head at my little sister, looking at her in the mirror as she sits cross-legged on my bed behind me. She's been on at me for the last forty-five minutes, ever since I stepped out the shower. I literally had to push her out of my room so I could get ready, but I knew she was out there, just waiting until I was decent before she could barge back in.

Women! Now I understand what my dad's been going on about for the last few years.

Son, you're too young to understand now, but when you get older, you'll realise just how much hard work women are.

Boy had my dad been right. I love my sister, I really do, but right now she is being a royal pain in the ass and getting on my last nerve.

"I'm just saying. Of all the girls out there, you ask her," Lizzie whines.

"What's it to you who I go out with, Lizzie? It's not like it's any skin off your nose, is it?"

Lizzie shrugs as she picks at my quilt cover. I shake my head again as I finish fixing my hair. I've never really been bothered what people think about me or the way I look, but tonight, I actually care about what someone thinks. I care what Crissie thinks. Lizzie and I are lucky to have been blessed with attractive parents, and that has filtered down to our genes too.

I've never had a problem getting women, but I always seem to attract the kind who just want to be seen with me to make their friends jealous, or the ones who only want to jump into bed. The lack of self-respect they have is scary, and, needless to say, those girls aren't the kind I want in my life.

I know Lizzie usually has a string of guys after her, too —some of them are my friends—but she's so innocent that she's oblivious to their attention. Part of me wants her to stay innocent, but I know that'll never happen. The only thing I can hope for is that she waits for the right guy to come along before taking that big step.

I have a feeling Crissie is just as innocent as my sister. While I don't know her well, I know she's not the kind of girl I usually attract, which I think is why I find her so fascinating. All her friends make eyes at me, and even though I've seen her smile at me every now and then, she doesn't go all out to make me notice her, which only makes me notice her more.

Yeah, I know, that doesn't make much sense, but the fact she *hasn't* been trying to get my attention is what's made me want to get to know her better. She strikes me as a girl who has no idea how attractive she is to the opposite sex; including me.

"Do you want a lift to Penny's?" I ask my sister as she looks up and meets my eyes in the mirror. "I don't mind—it's on my way to Crissie's." When she nods, I continue, "Best go get your stuff together, then. I'll be leaving in five minutes."

Lizzie jumps off my bed and out the door, leaving me alone—at least for the next few minutes. I look at my reflection and nod, happy with what I've chosen to wear for tonight's party. The dark jeans and black polo shirt are casual but smart at the same time. I grab my black loafers and slip them onto my feet, just as Lizzie comes back to stand in my doorway.

The look on her face tells me she's still not happy, and I sigh as I straighten. "Seriously, Lizzie, I don't see what the big deal is with me going out with Crissie. It's not like you two are close or anything."

"Yeah, well, you're a guy, so I wouldn't expect you to

understand. If you start going out with Crissie properly, my life will be over."

I roll my eyes at her dramatics and grab my wallet and keys, before walking towards the door to my room. Lizzie has to back up to let me out, and I fight my laughter as she huffs and puffs her way along the hallway and down the stairs. Dad was right; women are hard work. At least my little sister is anyway.

She's out the front door before I even reach the bottom of the stairs. I see my mum sat at her laptop, her glasses perched on the tip of her nose as she squints at the screen.

"Hey, Mum, I won't be back too late. I'm going to drop Lizzie off at Penny's on the way."

"Okay, honey," she says without looking up from the screen. "Have a good night."

I smile and shake my head. Ever since Dad got her that laptop, she's been glued to it. The only time she moves is when nature calls or she needs to eat, and even then, it's only for a few minutes at a time. We haven't had a proper homecooked meal in over a week, and, while it doesn't bother Lizzie or me, my dad is starting to get a bit fed up of microwave meals.

He's tried his hand at cooking, but three times this week alone the smoke alarm has sounded when he's left something in the oven for too long. It wouldn't surprise me if he wound up hiding the computer when she's sleeping, just so we can get back to some normality.

"Are you coming, Caleb?"

I hear my sister call me from outside and leave the house, seeing her leaning against my new pride and joy. The sleek, black Ford Focus was a gift from my parents for both my eighteenth birthday and to celebrate passing my driver's test on the first attempt, something none of us thought I would do. I've only driven it a handful of times, and I still smile whenever I look at it. That might seem silly to some, but to me, this car is my baby, and its mine. Lizzie thinks that when she's passed her test, I'll let her drive it. Yeah, there's not a chance in hell that's going to happen.

"Off the car, Lizzie. I don't want you to scratch it with that bag of yours." I point to the black bag she's got slung over her shoulder, referencing all the metal chains that hang from it. She pushes off the car with a huff and glares at me.

"You know, I think you care more about your stupid car than you do anything else."

"Oh, I don't think I do; I know I do," I reply with a grin as I reach out and ruffle her hair, knowing it'll annoy the hell out of her.

She swats at my hand and let's out a very unladylike grunt as she tries to get away from me. I'm laughing out loud now as she dives into the back of the car as soon as I unlock it.

I jump when I feel my mobile phone buzz against my

hip and pull it from my pocket. I still can't get used to having this damn thing, especially when it's on vibrate.

The small handheld device was my first purchase when I got my first wage packet from the garage where I work. I figured, now that I'm working, people needed to get in touch with me.

To date, the only people who have my number are my parents, two of my friends, and my boss, and so far, all the activity has been text messages. No phone calls have been made or received. I mean, why call when you can text?

I open up the text message and see it's from my boss, letting me know he doesn't need me in this weekend. I shove the phone back in my pocket, wondering why he bothers to let me know. We never work on a weekend, haven't done since I started at his garage almost eighteen months ago.

There are only three mechanics there, including my boss and his son, Patrick, and work is steady. We have enough to keep us going throughout the week, but not so much that it warrants us coming in over the weekend. I asked him why we needed three mechanics a couple of weeks ago, telling him that Patrick and I would be able to cope. He wasn't getting any younger, so I figured some time off would do him good. He just shrugged, saying you never know when a big contract would come in.

Seeing that my sister is getting impatient, I round the car and climb in. We're at Penny's house within a couple of minutes, and she wastes no time clambering out of the car and hurrying up the driveway, where she is met by her friend and vanishes behind the front door with not even a goodbye or a thank you.

I know I'll see her later, and she'll be all cutesy and irritating as usual, despite her hurry to get away from me now. She'll spend the next hour or so getting ready and then they'll sweet talk Penny's mum into dropping them off at the party. While the party is open to all family members of those who've just completed their final year, the parents rarely attend, and I doubt this year will be any different.

The only reason I'm going is because I'm Lizzie's brother. If it weren't for being related to her, I wouldn't have had the perfect excuse to ask Crissie to go out with me. I mean, I probably would have asked her at some stage—the girl intrigues me—but this party presented itself at just the right time.

Putting my pride and joy into gear, I pull away and head towards Crissie's house. My mind goes back to our lunch date two days ago, and I smile as I remember how nervous she was. It took me a while to get her to open up to me, even just a little.

I know she's an only child and is very close to her parents. She has a huge extended family; I think she said she has upward of forty cousins, mainly on her father's side, as he is one of eight children himself. She has always lived in Chester and can't think of anywhere else she would rather live.

In that respect, I'm the same. I've always lived in Chester and love the history of the place, but my family is nowhere near as huge as hers. There's just Lizzie, our parents, a handful of extended family, and me. Lizzie is a pain in my arse most of the time, but I wouldn't change her for anything.

Taking a left at the traffic lights, I know I'll be at Crissie's place any minute. I slow the car as I peer at the house numbers, coming to a stop when I see the house she told me to look out for.

You can't miss it. It's the one with the two huge conifers either side of the door and a statue of a lion by the front gate.

Yes, there's a lion all right, and it's bloody huge! I recall when she told me about the statue, and it did seem she was a little reluctant to tell me. Now I know why. That thing would embarrass the hell out of me if it was out the front of my house. All we have is a few rose bushes—my mother's pride and joy—and a perfectly manicured lawn —my dad's handiwork.

Smiling, I grab my wallet and keys and get out the car. Walking round to stand on the pavement, I look at the house and see the curtain move, and I instantly know I'm being inspected, probably by one of Crissie's parents.

Suddenly, I feel very self-conscious, and as I look up at the house, I hope Crissie will just appear and save me from going inside. After a few minutes, when that doesn't happen, I know I'm going to have to grow some balls and go in there.

They're her parents. Nothing to be afraid of.

Yeah right, who am I trying to kid?

CHAPTER 4

Crissie

"Crissie, your young man is here."

"He's not my young man, Mum. He's just a friend."

"A very attractive friend."

I turn from the mirror and see my mum leaning against my bedroom doorframe, her arms folded across her chest, a small smile on her face as she watches me. Trust the first thing my mum mentions about Caleb is how he looks. I want to object, to tell her she doesn't know what she's talking about, but I can't bring myself to do it. Clearly, I'd be lying, and my mum would know it.

"Don't tell me you've not noticed how handsome that young man is?"

"I guess he's okay." Shrugging, I glance back to the

mirror and check my makeup for what must be at least the tenth time. I don't have to look at my mum to know she's still smiling at me. I'm her baby girl and this is my first official date. How could she not smile. Although, I'm surprised she hasn't given me *the talk* yet.

"I'm so proud of you, honey." I hear her voice break, and I look over at her, seeing her swipe a tear from her eye. Oh no, no, *no*. It's taken me forever to get this makeup right. I will not cry and ruin it.

"No crying, Mum. If you cry, I'll cry, and if you ruin my makeup, I'm moving out." My words work, and I watch my mum straighten, take a deep breath, and smile again. She walks towards me, and I stand as she takes both of my hands in hers.

"I know you're sixteen, and you know all this anyway, but please be careful tonight." *Here comes the talk.* "I've put a little something in your bag, just in case, but go out there and have fun."

That was the talk? It wasn't too bad.

My mum squeezes my hand and kisses my cheek as she grabs my bag, securing the strap around my wrist. Curiosity gets the better of me, and I flick the clasp and open on the small silver clutch bag, my face flaming red when I see the square, foil packet.

"Mum, I'm not going to need that. It's a first date."

"I know, honey, but I'd rather you keep it, just in case." My mum sighs and pulls me into a hug. "You're growing up, Crissie. You're a young woman now, but you'll always be my baby girl."

I know she's crying again, and I pull away as she quickly turns from me, swiping at her eyes. I smile as I check my appearance one more time, before I hear a knock on the door. I'm about to leave my room when I hear the door open, and two male voices begin to speak.

Shit! Dad has answered the door. This isn't going to be good. Most dads are protective of their daughters, but mine takes it to a whole new level. If I don't get down there quick, Caleb is going to do a runner and never look back.

Hurrying out of my room, I stop at the top of the stairs, and as if we were in one of those cheesy American movies, my eyes connect with Caleb's and the next few minutes are like they're going by in slow motion.

I begin to walk down the stairs, my eyes never leaving Caleb's as he smiles at me. I can vaguely hear my dad still talking, but it's far off in the distance as my feet hit the hardwood floor. I stop briefly, taking in my date's appearance, and, if I didn't know any better, I'd say my mouth just started watering.

Perfectly styled dark hair, black polo, and dark jeans are what greets me, along with bright, blue eyes and extremely kissable lips. I know I should say something, anything to get things moving, but all words have failed me. The guy really is handsome, and for tonight at least, he's my date.

"You look beautiful." I hear the words pass his lips, but

it takes several moments for my brain to realise he's talking to me, and as soon as I do, I feel the blush on my cheeks as I give him a small smile.

"Thank you, Caleb. You look..." Shit, I can't say he looks good enough to eat. What can I say? "Nice." *Yeah, well done, idiot.* He looks so much better than nice.

Caleb's smile widens as he takes a step closer to me and extends his hand. I look down at it briefly, before I reach out to take it, immediately feeling better when his fingers close around mine.

I know my parents are just a few feet away, but right now, right here, no one else exists but Caleb and me. I could easily get lost in this moment, until Caleb breaks the spell by speaking with my parents. "I'll be sure to have her back no later than midnight, Mr and Mrs Walker."

"Thank you, Caleb," my mum replies. "You two have a good night."

Again, my feet don't want to move until Caleb gently tugs my hand and we head towards the door. I force my brain into gear as we descend the steps and walk down the path towards his shiny Ford Focus. When we reach it, Caleb turns to me and looks me up and down, and I can see he's smiling. Suddenly, I've never been happier about a dress purchase.

"You really do look beautiful, Crissie. I love the dress."

I blush again at his words and can tell he has taken a step closer to me. I lift my chin, so I can look at his face, and

I gasp at what I see. The smile is gone, and his usually bright eyes are dark as he stares down at me. I can't look away. His gaze has me under his spell, and, even though we're stood on the pavement and my parents are probably watching us, there is only one thing running through my mind.

Kiss me.

It's as if Caleb can read my thoughts as his head lowers and his lips gently press against mine. My head begins to spin, and I feel like I'm floating as my hands fly up and grip his arms to keep me upright.

This is it. My first kiss.

Caleb's hands come up and hold my face, his thumbs gently stroking my cheeks. I can feel the tension in his arms as I squeeze his biceps, taking a step closer until I can feel his body against mine. I want nothing more than for him to kiss me in the same way I've seen in the movies, but he makes no move to change our position, keeping hold of my face as he breaks the kiss.

His expression is softer now. The brightness has returned to his eyes and there's a soft smile on his lips. It takes what seems like a long time before my breathing evens out and I am able to return his smile.

"I hadn't planned on doing that until later this evening," Caleb says as he releases my face and lets his hands slide down my arms to take my own. "I hope you don't mind that I kissed you?"

The uncertainty I heard in his voice the other day, at

school, is back, and I know he is looking for reassurance that he hasn't moved too fast.

"I'm still here, aren't I?" I reply with a smile. "Shall we get going?"

Caleb beams at me and lifts my hands to his mouth, placing a kiss across the knuckles. When he releases me, he unlocks his car and opens the door. As I climb inside, I stretch my arm out to stop him closing it.

"Just so you know, Caleb, I'm glad you didn't wait until later." I'm amazed at how shy I sound, considering I just let him kiss me on the street, outside my house, in broad daylight, but I'm feeling brave, and that's something I have a feeling Caleb has brought out in me.

Smiling again, Caleb leans down towards me and whispers, "So am I." He quickly presses his lips to mine before closing the door, leaving me alone with my thoughts until he jumps in the driver's side and sets off to the party.

CHAPTER 5

Present Day

*P*eering at my reflection, I smile. I remember that day like it was yesterday. The nerves. The excitement. Seeing Caleb all dressed up.

That kiss.

That kiss was so sweet and gentle, and, probably because it was our first, it will always be my favourite of all the kisses we've shared over the years.

The feelings I experienced as I stood there looking up at him, as he held my face like I was some kind of precious cargo, was something I didn't understand at the time. Now, twelve years later, I know exactly what it was that caused my pulse to race and my heart to beat almost right out of my chest.

Love.

My sixteen-year-old self had fallen in love with Caleb Roberts right there on the pavement outside my childhood home. It took me a while to realise that was what I was feeling. I tried to deny it many times; convinced myself I was too young to fall in love. In fact, it took me almost three months before I could admit to myself, and to Caleb, that I loved him, but when I did finally believe it, everything changed for us.

The declaration we made to each other on my seventeenth birthday will always be my fondest memory of our time together. That night, we made love for the first time, and it was sweet and romantic, and Caleb stole my heart again with how gentle he was. I had expected it to be painful, but there was no pain.

All my friends had told me that the first time you have sex, it's painful, but there was none of that with us. It was only two people coming together as one. Two people showing how much they love each other by trusting the other with their body and soul.

It was in that moment, right then as we lay together, I knew Caleb was it for me. There would never be anyone else I could love as much as I loved him.

Things really couldn't get any more perfect.

CHAPTER 6

Crissie

August 2006

*M*y eyelids flutter closed as I fight to stay awake. My body is screaming at me to let it rest, but that's the farthest thing from my mind. All I want to do right now is just lie here, wrapped in Caleb's warm embrace as my heart rate comes back down to normal.

I breathe in deeply and then exhale, Caleb's unique, spicy scent overwhelming my senses. My head is resting against his chest, my hand on his stomach as he gently strokes my back. His touch is gentle, and it's making me relax completely against him, helping me to even out my breathing.

Opening my eyes, I smile as I spy the bare skin of Caleb's stomach beneath my fingertips. I flex my fingers and see the muscles contract under my touch as his arm tightens around me, making me shift closer to him. I feel him place a soft kiss against my hair, before he sighs deeply. His free hand reaches over to take mine, linking our fingers together, then resting them on his stomach.

I can't quite believe everything that's happened between us tonight. When Caleb asked me to come round to his new flat for dinner, I thought we'd end up with takeaway pizza, or maybe a microwave meal. Caleb cooking for me wasn't something I had expected.

Up until tonight, I didn't even know he could cook. Apparently, his mum had insisted he learn for when he moved into his own place, and he had certainly listened to her instructions. The coq au vin and herby mashed potatoes he'd prepared for us were delicious. He'd even gone so far as to light some candles, providing a romantic atmosphere, or so he said.

I don't know if it was the atmosphere, the sweet words he'd said to me as we watched TV, or the impromptu dance to one of Cal's favourite bands, Lonestar, in the middle of his living room that inspired me to tell him how I feel, but whatever it was, the moment felt right.

I hadn't planned on telling him I love him tonight. I'd been terrified he wouldn't feel the same and decide to end things there and then, but he hadn't. Instead, he'd just looked me right in the eyes, smiled, and told me he loved me too.

All I could do was look at him as the tears slipped from my eyes, before he gently kissed them away. His tender actions tugged at my heart, and I'd wrapped my arms around his neck and told him to love me. After asking me several times if I was sure, I finally convinced him I had never been more certain of anything. Caleb had led me to his bedroom and proceeded to do as I'd asked.

Now, we're lying here, as naked as the day we were born, and I have never felt so happy. My heart is full to bursting, and I know that's because of the man whose arms are wrapped around me.

"I never knew it could be like that."

I hear Caleb's words and shift slightly so I can look up at him, seeing him peering down at me. "What do you mean?"

"So special. So overwhelming. The connection between us was so strong. I've never felt anything like that before. It's like you were meant for me."

I feel my skin flush at his words as I tilt my face up and place a kiss against his jawline.

"Well, I have nothing to compare it to, but it felt pretty special to me too." I see him smile slightly, but it doesn't reach his eyes. "What's wrong?"

"I wish I'd waited like you did. I mean, I've only been with two other girls, but right now it still feels like it's two too many." He returns his eyes to mine, his expression sad.

Pushing up onto my elbow, I pull my hand from his and cup his cheek. The beard he has only recently decided to grow is rough against my fingers.

"I don't care about that, Caleb. It's all in the past."

"I guess you're right. It's the past. You're my future, Crissie."

For the second time that night, tears begin to stream down my face. How can it be possible to have such strong feelings for someone after only three months? My heart feels like it's about to burst with how much love I have for this man.

I'm his future, and he's mine.

All I can do is look at him, the lump in my throat preventing any further words from leaving my mouth. The tears slip silently down my cheeks as Caleb leans in and presses his lips to mine. I close my eyes and move my hand behind his neck, pulling him forward so I can hold him against me. I need him as close to me as possible right now, if only for reassurance that he really is here.

I tangle my fingers in his hair and tug, hearing his answering groan as he shifts position, pressing me into the mattress. My body comes alive as I let myself get lost in Caleb Roberts.

CHAPTER 7

Crissie

"Good luck today, honey. Call me when you know."

"Will do, Mum. Love you."

"Love you, too, Crissie."

I smile at my mum as I leave the house and practically skip down the path towards the waiting Focus. Caleb is leaning against the car looking delicious as ever in black jeans and a white t-shirt that shows off his athletic physique. I'm slowly getting used to my reaction to him. It's one that never gets old and always puts a smile on my face.

He pushes off the car as I get closer, and before I have chance to say anything, he pulls me against him and his mouth covers mine. The kiss is over before I have chance to react, and it steals the breath from my lungs. All I can do is smile at him as he opens the car door for me to climb inside.

I take a few deep breaths as I wait for him to join me and see the smile on his face is equally as big as mine.

"Morning, Miss Walker."

"Good morning, Mr Roberts."

I'm grinning like an idiot at the moment. You wouldn't think we'd been together just over three months now. Every time I see him it's like the first time. I still get the butterflies in my tummy and the quickened pulse, and don't even get me started on how I react when he touches me. He seems to be able to play my body like a conductor leads an orchestra; with ease and skilled control.

"Ready to go get those results?"

"As ready as I'll ever be," I respond, knowing my nerves are apparent in the sound of my voice. Caleb obviously hears it too, because he reaches over and grabs my hand, squeezing gently.

"I'm sure you've breezed through them. You've done all the hard work, now you just need to go get that piece of paper to show the world that Crissie Walker is going places. I believe in you." Caleb's words wash over me, erasing my nerves and leaving me feeling calm and relaxed. His confidence in my abilities soothes me, and I nod at him. Squeezing my hand again before he releases it, Caleb starts the car and puts it into gear before pulling away.

We are at my old school within five minutes, and I can see all my former classmates crowded together, waiting for the doors to open. I take a deep breath and gaze at them through the car window, the nerves Caleb had earlier banished beginning to resurface. I feel Caleb's hand on mine again as I turn to look at him.

"You'll be fine. I'm sure you've done great." I see him look behind me, and then his gaze shifts back to me. "You should get going. I think some people want to see you."

Furrowing my brow, I turn to see Missy, Pippa and Tasha all waiting for me, and I smile at them as they all wave. Ever since I started seeing Caleb, they've managed to rein in their obsession with him. They all still think he's hot and have called me the luckiest bitch alive more than once, but they respect that I'm with him and have toned down the inappropriate comments—at least, they have when I'm with them. God only knows what they say when I'm not there.

"I'll call you when I know," I say with a smile, but he shakes his head.

"Oh no, I'm waiting right here."

"But I could be a while. Apparently, they're doing it alphabetically this year, so I'll be towards the end."

"Don't care. I'm not going anywhere. I'll be parked right here, waiting for you when you come out." He grins at me, and I sigh, wondering what I did to make him fall for me. Leaning across, I kiss him lightly on the lips, stopping myself from laughing when I hear the wolf whistles from my friends, who are still waiting outside the school gates.

"I should go. I'll see you later." I quickly kiss him again before grabbing my bag from the backseat and getting out the car. I watch as Caleb pulls the car into a nearby parking space and shuts off the engine. He makes no move to get out of the car. Instead, he turns to wave at me, blowing me a kiss that I pretend to catch.

I'm grinning like the Cheshire cat when I turn and see my friends, who are all staring at me with goofy smiles on their faces. I secure my bag across my body and walk towards them. They're all looking at me, none of them saying anything, before Tasha breaks the silence.

"I know I've said it before, but you are one lucky bitch."

I link arms with Tasha and glance over my shoulder at Caleb, seeing he's still watching me, a smile on his handsome face. It's then I realise just how right my friend is.

~

"Crissie Walker?"

I approach my old form teacher and she hands me the white envelope that contains my future. She smiles kindly at me, keeping a firm grip on the envelope, before leaning in to say, "Good luck, Crissie. Of all my pupils, you are the one I see doing great things."

"Thank you, Miss Grant." I smile back at her as she releases the envelope, and then I walk back over to my friends. Even though they've had their results for a while now, they've not opened them yet. We all agreed to open them together, and now I've got mine, that moment is here.

We look at each other and then back to the envelopes in our hands. Why am I so nervous about this? I revised for all my exams. I came out of each one feeling confident that I'd done enough to get the grades I need to get into college. So what's the problem?

"Okay, after three. One, two—"

"Hold on, Pip," I say, stopping my friend's countdown. "I know we said we'd do this together, but would you guys mind if I leave you to it?"

"Yeah, if you want," Missy replies. "Is everything okay, Cris?"

I nod and smile at my friends, before stuffing the envelope in my bag and hurrying out of my former classroom. Within a minute, I'm back outside in the fresh air and I see Caleb's car parked in the same spot he was in when I left him to come inside.

He stayed. He didn't leave me.

I mean, he told me he would wait for me, but part of me had expected him to get bored and drive off somewhere to wait for my call. I wonder what he's been doing for the last ninety minutes. For some reason, the fact he's still here brings tears to my eyes. I know it's a stupid reaction, but I can't help it. Before I know it, I'm crying in the middle of the school car park.

My vision blurs with tears. I try and blink them away, and before I know what's happening, a pair of strong arms wrap around my body and a familiar scent engulfs me. I circle my arms around his waist and just hold him as he gently strokes my hair. I can feel the tension in his body as I lift my watery eyes to his face, seeing the concern in his furrowed brow and the hard line of his mouth.

"What is it, baby? Are they bad?"

I try and smile at him but fail miserably, which only makes him look even more concerned. Why am I still crying?

"No, I've not opened them yet. I wanted to open them with you. You're still here?" I'm not sure whether it's a question or a statement as I peer up at him, tilting my head into his hand as he pushes a strand of hair behind my ear.

"I told you I'd wait for you. Is that why you're crying— because I waited for you?"

He's confused; I can hear it in his voice. I feel silly for crying over something so trivial. I know I should explain it to him, but truth be told, I don't think I can.

He waited. No one has ever done that before.

Suddenly, the words become easy to say. "No one has waited for me before. I know that sounds silly—it does, even to me—and I can't explain the tears. I know my parents love me, but there was always something they had to rush off to, so wherever I went, I had to find my own way home or someone else would have to bring me home. Seeing you parked there, where you were almost two hours ago... it just hit me that I have someone now who's willing to wait for me."

Caleb just nods and pulls me back into his arms, holding me against him tightly. I take a few deep breaths and the tears begin to subside as we just stand there in the middle of the car park. I can hear people walking past us, some happy and excited about their results, others the complete opposite.

I know I should open mine. That envelope is burning a hole in my bag, and I promised I'd call my mum and let her and Dad know as soon as I found out. I'm surprised they've not driven over here to find out what the delay is. Impatience is a family trait we are all blessed—or cursed —with, depending how you look at it.

After a few minutes, Caleb releases his hold on me and takes my hand. "Come on, let's go back to my place. I can sort us some lunch and you can open that envelope. I bet your parents are chomping at the bit to find out how you've done."

I laugh and follow Caleb to his car. We've only been together three months and already he knows what my parents can be like.

When we're both buckled in, Caleb drives us to his flat, and less than ten minutes later, we're sat on the sofa. I have the envelope in my hands, staring at my name neatly printed in the clear window.

This envelope contains a piece of paper that will decide how my future will progress. I haven't given any thought to what I'll do if I don't get the grades I need to get into college. My placement is dependant on me achieving at least three B grades, which must include Maths.

Just open the envelope, Crissie. You're never going to know if you just sit staring at it.

Taking a deep breath, I begin to rip open the envelope, being careful not to tear the contents. When I have the folded piece of paper in my hand, I glance over at Caleb, who is watching me closely. I can tell he's trying to figure out what's running through my mind, while at the same time, trying to be supportive. Thank God he's here with me.

Turning back to the piece of paper, I unfold it and read the neatly typed words, and it's in that moment, the future I had planned, changes forever.

CHAPTER 8

Present Day

I fix my hair for what must be the tenth time in the last hour. It looks fine, but ever the perfectionist, I'm always finding something wrong with it. Not just with my hair, either; with everything. As well as being a perfectionist, I learned pretty early on that I'm also a pessimist.

I always find the negative in any given situation. My brain goes to the worst-case scenario, and no matter what anyone tells me, it won't budge. I've tried to change my way of viewing things, but I've had no luck so far. I'm twenty-eight now, so I can't see it changing anytime soon.

People are used to my negative ways now. My natural

pessimistic streak is why I found it so difficult to understand what Caleb saw in me. I'm by no means beautiful, and I have a tendency to speak before I think, but he stuck by me all these years. Even when I tried to push him away, insisting that he shouldn't wait for me.

That is one conversation I will never forget.

CHAPTER 9

Crissie

September 2006

I knew I hadn't done enough. Even though everyone around me kept telling me I'd be fine, deep down, I knew. My chance at going to college went out the window when I failed to get the GCSE grades I needed to get on my chosen course.

Two B grades and eight C grades just wasn't enough to do the A Levels I want to do. The college offered me alternatives, but none of them are what I want, or need, if I want a career in Forensic Science, and I refuse to settle for second best.

Then, a week later, the phone call came.

Ever since I was old enough to know what a college

was, I've dreamed of attending one particular college and heard older siblings of my friends raving about it all the time. As I knew their entry requirements were ridiculously strict, I never expected to get it, but applied anyway.

As expected, I never heard anything back, not even an acknowledgement of my application. I took that as a sign it wasn't meant to be and put it out of my mind.

Until today.

To say I was surprised to hear from them is an understatement. Apparently, due to a poor acceptance rate on my chosen subjects, they had adjusted the eligibility criteria, which meant my grades were now good enough for them to offer me a place.

Now, I'm never usually speechless, but that phone call came as such a bolt out of the blue that all I could do was thank them. They said they'd send all the information to me via email and I had up until the end of the week to decide, as the course started the following week.

That was three hours ago, and I've thought of nothing else since—unless you count how I'm going to break the news to Caleb. Having to decide between my boyfriend and my career isn't something I ever thought I'd have to do, especially at only seventeen.

I know he'll be over the moon to hear I've been offered a place at college, but when we live in Chester and the college is near Birmingham, that might put a proverbial spanner in the works. I know exactly what he's going to say, though. He'll tell me we can make it work and that we'll still see each other at weekends and during holidays, but I'm not sure I want that.

I love him and don't want to lose him, but I can't expect him to wait for me, or ask him to make the two-hour trek from Chester to Birmingham every time I want to see him, or him me. I mean, it's not like Birmingham is just down the road. Yes, it's only a two-hour drive, but still... After a while, that can become tiresome, and the last thing I want is for him to get fed up with me and the effort it's taking for us to see each other.

I know relationships aren't easy—I'm not that naïve— but they shouldn't be super hard either, and us being so far apart isn't going to make our relationship any easier. My mum thinks I should take the college up on their offer. She knows how I feel about Caleb, and she's confident we will survive the travelling and distance, but just the thought of not being able to go round to his place whenever I want, doesn't sit well with me.

At the moment, we're seeing each other almost every night. In fact, he's on his way round to pick me up right now. We're going to the cinema and then back to his place. Tonight is going to be the first night I'm sleeping over.

Regardless of what's going on with college, thoughts of spending the night with Caleb have turned me into a nervous bundle of excitement. It made me so happy when my parents finally decided they were okay with me staying at Caleb's.

My parents aren't stupid; they know we're sleeping

together—despite how adamantly my father refuses to admit I'm no longer his little girl. My overnight bag is packed and waiting by my bedroom door. Now all I need to decide is when to tell him about college.

I could tell him when he picks me up, but that has the potential to completely ruin the evening. Or I could wait until we get back to his place, but then he might not want me to stay over. I know the reasons against both ideas are purely selfish; I want a nice evening with my boyfriend, and I want to stay over at Caleb's house. I want to lie happy and content in his arms while he holds me close to his side.

After I weigh up my options, I decide to tell him the next morning. A few more hours aren't going to make a difference. Besides, I've still not received the information from the college. Until I receive that with the specifics I need, it's not a foregone conclusion that I'll be going anyway. No, I'll wait until I have all the facts before saying anything to Caleb.

Happy with my decision, I glance at myself one more time in the full-length mirror, pleased with my choice of outfit. The dark jeans are simple and the off-the-shoulder pink top I bought earlier today is cute and will keep me cool in the unusual autumn heat.

I slip my feet into my baby-pink ballet flats before I hear my mum call from downstairs, "Crissie, Caleb's here, honey."

I smile at the mention of his name and grab my

handbag and overnight bag before leaving my room and descending the stairs. I kiss my mum on the cheek and shout a goodbye to my dad, who just grunts from his position in front of the TV. I smile at him and shake my head as I open the front door, meeting Caleb halfway down the path.

I rise to my tiptoes and kiss him lightly on the lips as he takes my overnight bag from me and grabs my hand. As we walk towards his car, I'm amazed at how, after nearly four months, his touch still sends shivers through my body. Part of me hopes it's always like this between us.

Every time I'm near him there's a spark and it makes me want to see him every day. It's probably what I'll miss the most if I decide to accept the college placement.

I put that thought from my mind as Caleb releases my hand and tosses my bag onto his backseat. As I climb in the passenger side, I glance around the interior of his car. Maybe I should start taking driving lessons? I'm seventeen now, so I can apply for my provisional licence. Driving lessons don't come cheap, but I'm sure if I get a part-time job, I'll be able to afford them.

It's definitely something I should consider, especially if I do go away to college. Caleb and I could split the travelling then, maybe it wouldn't be as bad. Yes, that's something I will look into when I've decided what to do.

We're at the cinema complex within fifteen minutes. I've no idea what we're here to see; Caleb just said his friends had been going on about it for days and he wanted to see what all the fuss was about. He doesn't even let me see the tickets. He just buys them, leads me to the queue to get popcorn and drinks, and then we go through to take our seats.

Caleb seats us right in the middle of the cinema, central to the huge screen in front of us. We put our drinks in the cup holders set in the arms of our seats, and he holds on to the tub of popcorn, placing it in easy reaching distance for me.

"So, are you ever going to tell me what we're here to see?"

"You've just got," he pauses as he checks his watch, "twenty minutes to wait."

I frown at him as he grins at me. He's really dragging this out for some reason. We've watched dozens of movies since we started seeing each other. Action, romance, thrillers, even some westerns. In fact, I think we've watched all genres except horror. I draw the line at horror.

Ever since I was six years old and walked in on my mum and dad watching Dracula, I've not been able to watch horror movies. The sight of Christopher Lee with blood dripping from his mouth and those horrible bloodshot eyes glaring at me through the TV screen has put me off those kind of movies for life. I shiver as the image pops into my head, and Caleb looks at me.

"Are you cold?"

"No, I'm good. Just remembering an old movie and the

reason why I hate horrors." When Caleb's face falls, I know instantly why. "This is a horror movie, isn't it?"

He nods, and I sigh. There goes our evening at the cinema.

"I'm sorry, Cris. I had no idea you didn't like horror movies. We can leave and do something else." When Caleb starts to move, I grab his arm and still him. This irrational fear has been with me since I was young. If I'm ever going to get over it, I need to pull up my big girl pants and stick it out. Who knows, they're probably not as bad as I remember.

"No, we can stay." I smile at him as he looks at me with concern.

"Are you sure? I don't want you to stay if you really don't want to."

"I'm good. I promise." He visibly relaxes in his seat and smiles, before leaning over and kissing me lightly. He settles back and gets comfortable just as the lights begin to dim. Reaching across, he takes my hand.

"You can hold on to me if you get scared."

I look at him, before I burst out laughing, my earlier apprehension about the movie forgotten.

CHAPTER 10

Crissie

*W*ell, the movie wasn't all that bad. A story about four young warlocks battling against another warlock, who holds a three-century year old grudge, isn't the type of horror movie I'm scared of. It was actually not a bad movie, and I can see why all of Caleb's friends were going on about it.

As I relax into Caleb's sofa, he busies himself in the kitchen, making us a drink. I can hear the clinking of cups and the jangle of cutlery as he gets everything he needs to make a hot chocolate for himself and a tea for me.

I stare at the empty screen of the too-huge-for-the-room, flat screen TV and grin as the 'boys and their toys' phrase pops into my head. Looking around the room, I can clearly see Caleb has made this place his home. It's definitely a man's place, with only a couple of items I'd consider girlie—probably brought round by Lizzie when she visited during the week.

She's still a little cool on the idea of me dating her brother, but I think she's getting there. At least we can have a conversation now without her pouting at me.

I hear Caleb muttering to himself in the kitchen, something I've realised he does a lot when he's in the middle of something. It's almost like he's talking himself through the stages of whatever he's doing, and it can be comical at times, especially when he doesn't realise he's doing it. Like now.

"Kettle on. Teabag in the cup. Sugar in the cup." He pauses for a moment, wondering what he's missed, and then it comes to him. "Milk!"

He says it a little louder than he intended, and I call out to him. "Did you say something, Cal?"

I wait for his response, which comes when he sticks his head around the doorframe, peering into his living room. "Nope, all's good. Do you want to pick a movie and get it ready? The drinks are almost done. You can pick this one as I picked the last one."

He grins at me, and I know he's referring to the movie we watched earlier. I've a feeling that film could be the first and last horror movie we watch together.

Standing up from the sofa, I walk across the room to the bookcase Caleb has placed in the alcove next to the fireplace. He has dozens of DVDs to choose from, and I think I'm going to struggle to find a movie neither of us has seen.

I recall a conversation we had a few weeks into our relationship, where he told me he buys a new DVD each week. I'm assuming he has watched them all, otherwise what's the point in buying them?

I tilt my head to the side, reading the names on the spines of the DVDs. To say he has an eclectic taste in movies wouldn't be accurate. There is every genre I've ever heard of represented on this bookcase. I'm beginning to think I won't find one, then I spot it; a film I have loved ever since I first saw it when I was eight years old.

Reaching out, I take the DVD off the shelf and smile, jumping when I hear Caleb's voice close behind me.

"Lizzie must have left that here as I don't recall buying that one." I turn and face him, accepting the mug of tea he's holding in his hand. "What's it about?"

"You've never seen *The Princess Bride*?" I ask him.

"No. Is it any good?"

All I can do is stare at him, unable to believe he's lived for almost nineteen years and not seen what has to be my favourite film of all time, bar none.

"Oh, Mr Roberts, you are in for a treat." I put my mug down on the coffee table and insert the disc into Caleb's DVD player. When the TV screen flickers to life, I grin as the familiar introduction appears. Grabbing Caleb's hand, I pull him over to the sofa and we both fall into the cushions. I tuck my feet under me and lean into him as his arm goes around my shoulder, holding me to his side.

"Let's see what I've been missing, then," Caleb says as he puts the remote control in my hand, and I push the play button.

~

*A*lmost two hours later, I'm grinning like a mad woman as the end credits roll on *The Princess Bride*. Watching that movie again sent me back to my childhood, and I found myself repeating the lines more than once. I turn to Caleb, eager to see what he thought of the film. He stayed silent through most of it, and right now, his expression isn't giving anything away.

"Well? What did you think?"

Caleb turns to me and just stares. God, did he really hate it that much? I've never met anyone who doesn't like this movie. Even my dad likes to watch it, saying it reminds him of when I was a little girl and we used to watch it together when I got back from school. I smile at the happy memories as Caleb continues to just look at me.

"My name is Caleb Roberts. I am your boyfriend. Prepare to squeal."

I open my mouth to ask him what he's talking about, but before I can, I'm flat on my back and Caleb's fingers are digging into my ribs as he tickles me. My legs are pinned to the sofa as he straddles my thighs, so there's no way I can move, and when one of his hands grips my wrists and holds them above my head, I'm completely at his mercy.

I try and twist out of his grip but he's too strong, the fingers on his free hand running across my ribs. I do as he said I would and squeal when he hits a particularly sensitive spot on my right side, bucking my hips to try and throw him off. This just makes him tickle me harder, and my breathing comes in sharp gasps between the laughter I'm trying to supress.

"Caleb," I scream as his fingers continue to torture me. I tug at my hands, but he holds them firmly, and pretty soon, my eyes are watering, tears streaming down my face as I'm no longer able to contain my laughter.

Then, he suddenly stops and looks down at me. I peer up through watery eyes, my breathing still erratic, and see his expression is one of wonder and awe. I tug my hands again and this time he releases them, shifting so both of his hands are on the sofa, either side of my head. My legs are still pinned beneath his weight, but right now, I'm in no hurry to move him.

I take several deep breaths to even out my breathing, and swipe at the tears on my cheeks. My heart is beating a fast, steady rhythm as I stare up at Caleb, who's just looking down at me. We say nothing for what seems like an age, just peering at each other. I'm still pinned to the sofa, but moving is the farthest thing from my mind

"Caleb?" I whisper.

"Hmm," is his response.

"Are you ever going to kiss me?"

His expression remains the same for several moments, before he tilts his head and smiles down at me. "As you wish."

When his lips touch mine, I'm lost.

CHAPTER 11

Crissie

I could get used to this.

Waking up next to Caleb this morning is something I know I'll never tire of. Four months together, and already I want to spend every night with him. After last night, and the knowledge I didn't have to get up, get dressed and go home, it's something I want to repeat night after night.

Right now, I'm curled up on the sofa in my bathrobe while Caleb makes us breakfast; bacon and egg sandwiches for him, sausage and tomato for me. I can smell the bacon sizzling in the kitchen and it's making my mouth water.

As I wait, my mind drifts to the conversation I know I need to have with Caleb. I told myself I'd do it this morning, not wanting to ruin our night out, but I don't think I can. Even though I don't think he'll have a problem with me going away to college, I don't want to do anything that could put any kind of strain on our still new relationship.

All kinds of possibilities run through my head, and I make a decision. I'm not going to tell him. What he doesn't know won't hurt him. Right? I'll get a part-time job until I can find something more permanent. Maybe I can take a year off studying and reapply next year. I know a few of my friends are doing that; I don't see why I can't do the same thing. I'm not going to give up my dreams; I'm just going to delay them for twelve months.

"Here you go," Caleb says as he walks through from the kitchen to sit next to me. He hands me the plate, and I inhale deeply, my stomach growling, causing Caleb to laugh.

"If you were that hungry you should have said earlier," Caleb says as he picks up his sandwich and takes a bite, the brown sauce he favours dripping down the front of his chest. I watch the sauce as it leaves a trail on his bare skin, jumping when I hear Caleb clear his throat. I bring my eyes up to his, which are watching me with amusement.

I feel a little embarrassed at being caught staring, and I swallow nervously. My hunger for food has been replaced with my hunger for the man sat next to me.

"Keep looking at me like that, Cris, and I'm going to be

having something else for breakfast, and I'm sure it'll taste a whole lot nicer than this sandwich."

My pulse spikes at his words, and all I can do is turn from him and take a bite of my sandwich. Why does it affect me so much when he talks like that? Part of me loves the reaction his words bring out in me, but the other part is embarrassed by them. It could be my inexperience, I guess. Will I ever get used to Caleb talking to me like that?

He's not afraid to tell me how he's feeling or what he wants. Most of the time, all I can do is nod and smile, as I'm unsure how to respond to his suggestive words. I guess I should be happy a guy like Caleb wants me the way he does. I'm just so unaccustomed to someone speaking to me the way he does that I never know how to react.

I hear his chuckle as I tuck into my sandwich, willing my racing heart to go back to normal. That's no easy feat with Caleb sat next to me, bare-chested and looking as edible as scraps to a starving man. I really need to get us talking about something else to try and get my brain out of the gutter.

"So, what do you want to do today?" I ask as I risk a sideways glance in his direction.

"You mean, apart from you?" My eyes widen at his words, and I pause mid bite. I know he's teasing me—well, only half teasing me—and as usual, I have no clue how to respond to him. "Sorry, Cris, I don't mean to tease, but I love to see that expression on your face. It's a mixture of shock and embarrassment. It's so cute."

I narrow my eyes at him, trying my hardest to look pissed, but I know I'm failing as I can't stop the smile spreading to my lips.

"Anyway, today. I hadn't really thought about it. Is there anything you want to do?"

There is something I want to do, but I don't think he'll be up for it. Everything I know about him tells me his response will be a *hell no,* or words to that effect, but I guess I'll never really know unless I ask him.

"Well, my parents gave me some money for passing my exams. I was hoping to go out and spend it at Cheshire Oaks?" I finish my sandwich and look at him, seeing him considering my suggestion.

"Okay. Sounds like a plan."

"Really? You don't mind going shopping with me?" I ask him, trying to keep the disbelief out of my tone.

"You thought I'd say no?" he asks curiously.

"Well, shopping and guys doesn't normally mix, so I guess I just assumed…" I let my sentence trail off and wait for his response, which comes almost immediately.

"Cris, I'll do anything with you. If you want me to come with you and carry all your shopping bags, then I'm there."

I put my now clear plate on the coffee table and take his from his hands to do the same. Uncurling my legs from under me, I move to stand, and before I can change my mind, I straddle Caleb's lap, his hands going to rest on my hips.

"I knew there was a reason I love you," I tell him as my arms wrap around his neck.

"Oh yeah? Just the one reason?"

Giving him my brightest smile, I lean in and proceed to show him all the ways I love him.

~

Caleb

Not long after we've left my flat, I'm pulling up outside Crissie's parents house. She needed to come home to pick up her exam money, and, after we enjoyed a quick breakfast and then each other, we're finally here.

It's only fifteen minutes to Cheshire Oaks, but Crissie didn't want me to drive. Her excuse was that she didn't like me driving her everywhere, but I have a feeling there's another reason; one she's not telling me. She's never had a problem with me driving before, so why now?

"I'll just be a minute," she says as she jumps out the car, and I'm quick to follow her. "You can wait in the car if you like?" she suggests, but I shake my head.

"I'll come in with you. I want to say hi to your parents."

Nodding, Crissie holds out her hand, and I take it as we both walk up the path towards the front door. Crissie has the door open within seconds, and then we're stepping into her parents' living room.

"Hey, Crissie. Hey, Caleb. What brings you two here?"

"Hey, Mum, I just need to grab my exam money. Caleb is coming shopping with me." She smiles at me again, that smile that makes my heart skip a beat, before she releases my hand and heads off up the stairs.

"She loves to shop, you know, Caleb. I hope you're wearing comfy shoes."

"Yes, I'm all prepared, and if it gets too bad, I can just wait in the car."

Mrs Walker laughs at me and gently pats my shoulder. I like Crissie's parents. It's clear they love their only daughter, and the house they live in has provided Crissie with a loving and safe home. I shall always be grateful to them for that.

"You're going to drive, then? Thought you might have taken the bus. It runs pretty frequently into Cheshire Oaks. I assume that's where you're going?"

"Where else would a teenage girl with money to spend go?"

"Good point," she says with a smile, a smile that matches her daughter's.

"Crissie didn't want me to drive, though. For some reason, she seems really hung up on me driving everywhere. I keep telling her I don't mind, and she usually relents, but I have to admit, it's bugging me why she suddenly has a problem with it." I can't quite believe I'm telling Mrs Walker this. I don't think Crissie would appreciate me talking to her about her problem with my driving. It's never been a problem before this morning, which is partly why I think it's more than her just not being comfortable with me driving all the time.

"I wouldn't worry, Caleb. She's probably just thinking about all the driving you'll have to do when she goes off to college in Birmingham."

Say what now? College? Birmingham?

"I'm sorry, Mrs Walker, but what do you mean when she goes to college in Birmingham?" I see the expression on her face change instantly, and I have a feeling she's told me something she wasn't supposed to. The question is, why hasn't Crissie told me?

"Oh, Caleb, I'm so sorry. I thought she'd told you. She said she was going to tell you this morning. I just assumed..."

It's clear Mrs Walker feels bad about what she's done, but before I can reassure her it's okay, Crissie reappears at the foot of the stairs. She looks between her mother and me, and as soon as she sees the expression on her face, I can tell she knows something isn't right. "Is everything okay, Mum?"

"Everything's fine, Cris," I say before her mother can respond. "I was just telling your mum about the movie we watched last night. Seems she's not a huge fan of horror movies either."

I see Crissie nod, her brow furrowed as she takes in what I've said. "You sure you're okay, Mum?"

"I'm fine, honey. You two go and have a nice day."

I hold out my hand to Crissie, and she takes it without hesitation, her eyes still on her mum. Something tells me she doesn't believe my explanation about the horror movie, but she doesn't say anything as we leave the house and return to my car.

I'm in two minds whether to say anything to her about Birmingham. On the one hand, I want to know what's going on and why she's not told me. On the other hand, I don't want to cause any tension between Crissie and her mother.

Indicating as I pull away from the pavement, I decide I'll give Crissie until the end of the day to tell me what's going on of her own volition. If she's not said anything by then... well, I don't know what I'll do. But one thing's for certain: there must be a reason she's not mentioned anything to me. I hope above all else that it's not because she wants to end things, because if it is, I'm pretty certain my life will never be the same again.

CHAPTER 12

Crissie

*S*omething's not right.

Ever since we left my parent's house this morning, Caleb has only spoken when I've asked him something. Something happened between him and my mum when we were at home. I knew something wasn't right when Caleb said my mum must hate horror movies. She loves them. Give her the choice of any movie genre and that would be the one she would go for.

Could my mum not be as cool with me sleeping over at Caleb's as I thought she was? That would certainly cause her to be a little off with him, but not him with me. I dismiss that idea immediately and glance across at him. He's walking beside me, holding my bags in one hand and my hand in the other.

I hate this. I need to find out what's going on with him and why he's suddenly gone cold on me after the wonderful night we shared together. Checking my watch, I see it's almost two p.m.; a perfect time to stop for lunch.

Knowing Caleb loves pizza, I lead him to a little pizza place I've been to a few times before with friends. He doesn't question me, just follows. I ask for a table for two, which we're quickly seated at and told someone will be back to take our orders in five minutes.

Caleb picks up his menu and scans it, and I try and do the same, but I can't concentrate. I need to know why he's being like this. Usually the banter between us is easy and non-stop, but he hasn't initiated a conversation since we left my house this morning.

"Cal, is there something wrong?"

He puts down his menu and looks at me intently. "Why would there be anything wrong?"

"Oh, I don't know. Maybe because you've not said two words to me since we left my parents' house unless I've spoken first. That crap you spouted about my mum hating horror movies was bullshit, so are you going to tell me what's going on, or do I have to guess?" I keep my voice as low as I can, aware there are other people within earshot, but it's clear from my tone that I'm more than a little irked by his sudden bout of silence. I keep my eyes on him and see him lean back in his chair and sigh. His expression changes from hard to soft in a nanosecond, and he looks... almost lost.

"Were you ever going to tell me about college and Birmingham? Or would I have found out when I went to pick you up one day and you weren't there."

What? How does he—my mum. She must have told him, but why? Why would she do that?

As if he can read my mind, Caleb speaks. "Don't blame your mum. She thought you'd told me. I mentioned about you not wanting me to drive today, and she assumed it was because of all the driving I'd have to do when you go to college in Birmingham. Apparently, you told her you were going to tell me this morning. So why didn't you?"

Damn it, I knew I should have said something to him. Why did I try to hide it? We were having such a lovely time until my mum opened her mouth. No, like Caleb said, I can't blame her. This is all on me.

I look into Caleb's blue eyes and can see he's waiting for an answer, but I've no idea what to tell him. I decide to go with my heart. "I don't want to lose you."

I can barely look at him as I say the words, and I'm saved—at least for the moment—when the waiter comes back to take our orders. I'm aware that Caleb's eyes never leave my face as he orders his pepperoni pizza with a diet coke. I glance at him as I order the same and see something different in his eyes. He actually looks pissed.

"Please tell me you're not serious? You really think you'd lose me if you went off to college?"

"Well, we've only been together for four months, and if I go to Birmingham, we'd hardly see each other. It wouldn't be fair of me to ask you to wait for me while I complete my studies. Besides, none of this matters anyway. I've decided not to go."

"Like hell you're not!"

My eyes widen at his words as the waiter brings our drinks over and, as if sensing the tension, mutters that our food will be with us shortly and leaves.

"I'm not having you miss out on college because of me, Cris. You were devastated when you didn't get the grades you wanted, so how can you even think about turning this down? Having a career in forensics means the world to you. You can't give all of that up because of me."

"I'm not giving it up. I'm going to take a year out and reapply next year. Loads of my friends are doing it, so why can't I?" I know I'm on the defensive, but I can't think of any other way to be now. I knew he would try and convince me to go—that's partly why I decided not to tell him—and I'm being proven right.

"Okay, and what if you reapply next year and don't get accepted? Will you put it off for another year and try again?" He pauses before reaching over and taking my hand. "You can't take that risk, Cris. This might be the only chance you get to go to college, and I'm not going to let you pass it up. Not because of me."

"But what if you get sick of not seeing me and find someone else? You're funny and handsome and kind... I can't expect you to wait around for me to come back."

And there it is, the reason why I'm so hesitant to leave

him. I'm scared—no, I'm terrified—he'll find someone else, someone prettier and sexier, if I'm not around.

"Give me some credit, Cris. I'm not that kind of guy. I love you. You could be going to study in America and that wouldn't change how I feel about you. You're my girl, Crissie; nothing will change that, especially not a two-hour drive down the motorway. I'm not going anywhere, and you need to start believing that."

Oh, I want to. I really, really want to believe we can make things work, but everything inside me is screaming that it won't. I mean, how can it? He's a guy and he has needs. Needs I won't be there to fulfil.

"Do you trust me, Crissie?"

"Yes," I reply without hesitation.

"Then trust that we can make this work. Have some faith in our relationship. We're great together, Cris, and a little bit of distance isn't going to make any difference to how I feel or how we are together."

I listen to his words and take a deep breath. I can feel my eyes welling up, and any minute now I'm going to be sobbing into my diet coke. It's only the arrival of our pizzas that drags me back into the moment, and I quickly swipe at my eyes to eliminate any stray tears.

Dare I believe him? Is there a chance we can make this work, even with the distance between us?

I repeat those two questions over and over as we eat our lunch in silence. I can feel Caleb watching me, and I'm acutely aware I've not said anything since his last statement.

Can we make this work? God, I hope so. I've never wanted anyone the way I want Caleb, and I would do anything to make him happy. Despite my negative tendencies, deep down I know it's the same for him.

Taking the last bite of my pizza, I push the plate to the side, seeing Caleb has already finished. He's looking at me, a question on the tip of his tongue.

"Have you made a decision?" he asks quietly, and as soon as he asks, I know my answer.

"We should probably get back. I've an acceptance email to write."

CHAPTER 13

Crissie

<u>Present Day</u>

*O*nce we'd returned to Caleb's flat after the pizza, I'd logged into my email account and found an email from the college waiting for me. It contained all the information about the A-Levels I'd chosen to do and instructions about what I needed to do next in order to confirm or deny their offer.

Caleb had insisted I print it all out and read through it before committing to attending, which we'd done together. He had seemed really impressed with the facilities, and by the time we'd gone through everything, he was adamant there was no way I could turn down the offer. He was so enthusiastic about it, for a moment I'd thought he might sign up to a course himself.

He had also pointed out I would need to find somewhere to stay while I was studying. As luck would have it, he had a cousin who lived just a fifteen-minute walk away from the college, and after a quick phone call, he arranged it so I could stay with her for the duration of my studies.

Luckily, Elise Roberts wasn't a complete stranger. I'd met her a few times when she'd come up to visit her family in Chester. She had studied at the same college and loved the area so much she'd decided to stay there. Her life was in Birmingham now, as was her boyfriend of almost five years and her job as a legal secretary.

Sighing, I smile as I realise how often my thoughts drift back to the past and all the good times Caleb and I enjoyed. Even though the journey from Chester to Birmingham was only two hours, he had kept me entertained, despite me in hysterics most of the time.

We'd had our very own karaoke contest in the car, with him winning hands down. I couldn't hold a tune for toffee, but it turned out Caleb had an excellent voice. Even now, I still love it when he sings to me, but he doesn't do it often enough for my liking.

As I hadn't been due to start at the college until the Tuesday, Caleb and I had decided to travel down on the Saturday. We had agreed to take a look around the area, so I would know where I'd need to head on my first day. We'd spent most of the weekend exploring and had just enjoyed spending time together. We visited museums, went shopping, and had some lovely meals, just the two of us.

It was heaven, and I'd loved every minute of it.

I'd hated it when Sunday came around and he'd had to head back home. I hadn't wanted him to go, but he promised he would come back down the next weekend. As a parting gift, he'd bought me my very first mobile phone, so we could call and text each other as often as we wanted, which we did. All the time.

I'll always remember the disappointment I felt when Caleb didn't come to see me the following weekend as planned. He'd text me to say he had to work and couldn't get out of it. I had no reason to doubt him, but of course, my young and irrational self chose to believe a multitude of other reasons why he wasn't coming to see me.

When his absence extended to the following five weekends, too, and his texts and calls got fewer and fewer, my paranoia took hold and I convinced myself he didn't want me and my initial reservations about going to college had been right.

His arrival in Birmingham six weeks after he'd brought me down resulted in one of our deepest conversations. One, even to this day, I struggle to forget.

CHAPTER 14

Crissie

November 2006
Birmingham, England

*H*e's on his way.

Caleb is finally coming to see me. He's just text me to say he'll be here in thirty minutes. I've no idea what to say to him. It's been over a month since I last saw him. I've missed him, desperately. Missed seeing him, missed his touch, his words. I've missed everything about him. But I can't stop thinking that he's hiding something from me.

Six weeks.

It's been six weeks since he brought me down to Birmingham, so I could start college. Even though he promised he would visit me every weekend, this is the first time he has come down to see me. He's told me he's been working, but before I moved, he never worked a weekend.

Ever.

The only thing that's changed is that I'm here and he's there, and without his work, there's no excuse for him not to come and visit me. I can't shake the feeling there's something he's not telling me; that work isn't the real reason he's hasn't come down to Birmingham.

I knew coming here for college was a mistake, but I let him talk me into it with sweet words and promises that nothing would change between us. I let him convince me he wasn't going anywhere, and he loved me and would stick by me. I chose to believe him, but deep down, there was always a part of me that knew things wouldn't go to plan.

I'm just not that lucky.

Grabbing my phone off the bed when it chirps, I see the text from Caleb telling me he is now only fifteen minutes away. The message also has a smiley face and several kisses. At any other time, the sight of those little x's would make me smile from ear to ear, but not at the moment.

Elise has made herself scarce, obviously thinking that after almost six weeks, Caleb and I would want some time alone, and normally, she'd be right. Part of me wants nothing more than to grab Caleb as soon as he walks through the door and spend the entire weekend with him locked away in my room. Unfortunately, there's a bigger part of me that just wants to know what's been going on. Why hasn't he come to see me?

Glancing at the clock, I see the time and know Caleb will be here any minute. I grab my phone and stuff it in the pocket of my hoodie and leave my room. As I descend the stairs, I see his car pull onto the driveway, and I freeze.

What's wrong with me? I should be so excited to see him, my boyfriend, after six weeks apart, but I've no idea what to say to him.

I watch through the glass panels in the front door as he climbs out the car and grabs a small black case from the backseat. Within a few seconds, he's stood at the door, and I see him raise his hand and rap his knuckles against the wood.

Taking a deep breath, I descend the remaining stairs and see him grin when his eyes meet mine. I smile back, but I know it's not as excited as his. As I open the door, he bursts through, drops his case, and wraps his arms around me tightly.

God, he smells good—just as good as I remember. It's a mixture of his body wash, aftershave, and something that's uniquely him. It takes a moment, but I wrap my arms around his waist and hold him. I've missed him so much, but I'm so confused. I'm struggling to reconcile the man standing before me now, holding me in his arms, with the same man who has cancelled on me week after week for six weeks.

As if he can sense something isn't right, Caleb pulls away and looks down at me. His confusion is clear on his handsome face, and it takes everything in me not to break down in front of him. I love this man, more than I ever thought I would love anyone, and suddenly, the thought of him not feeling the same way slices through me like a knife.

"Cris, what's wrong? Has something happened?"

Removing my arms from around his waist, I move them to his chest and push. He stares as he releases me, his expression clearly showing what he's thinking. I've never pushed him away from me before. I'm usually the one pulling him toward me, but right now, I can't let him get too close. I need answers.

Wrapping my arms around myself, I walk through to the living room and sit on the sofa, seeing him still standing in the same position I left him.

He opens his mouth to say something, then closes it again before following me into the living room, sitting on the sofa opposite. As I look at him, I realise I've no idea what to say to him. I told him I trusted him before I left. I'm basically going to be calling him a liar if I come out and ask him what he's really been doing for the last six weeks.

"Cris? Please, you're scaring me."

Here goes nothing.

"Six weeks, Cal. It's been six weeks since I saw you last. I've missed you."

Caleb gets up from his seat opposite and comes around the coffee table to sit next to me. He reaches out to take my hand, but I pull it away, causing him to frown at my reaction. "I know. I've missed you, too, but I had to work. I told you."

"You never had to work weekends before I left." I can barely look at him as I say the words. I don't need to see his face to know what he's thinking. His audible gasp is enough to tell me that.

"You don't believe me?" he asks, and I can't answer him. "What exactly do you think I've been doing, Crissie?"

What *do* I think he's been doing? Now that he's asked me, I don't have an answer. All I know is he promised to come and see me every weekend, and he hasn't.

"You said you'd come and see me, but you've not been down once since I got here. We saw each other every weekend when I was home. You never worked a weekend in the whole time we've been seeing each other, and then I move away and suddenly you're working every weekend? As much as I want to believe you, Cal, I don't believe in coincidences." I watch him as he leans back against the cushions and lets out a long sigh. His eyes are watching me intently, and I have no idea what he's going to say or do next.

"You're right. I haven't been working every weekend."

I knew it. I knew I wasn't being paranoid.

"But it's not what you're thinking, Cris." He shifts forward and takes my hand, holding it tightly so I can't pull it away. "The first three weeks you were here, I did have to work. My boss got a new contract. You remember I told you about it?" I nod as I recall the brief conversation we had halfway through my first week here. "Well, we had almost two dozen cars that needed to be worked on. I was practically living at the garage. We all were. We even had to take on a new mechanic to keep up with everything. I didn't see anyone other than my boss and the pizza delivery guy for almost two weeks."

That makes sense, I guess. I do remember him telling me about a new contract his boss had signed, but he never mentioned anything about how much work would be involved, even when we spoke several times during the week. I'd commented about how tired he sounded, but he always brushed it off, saying he wasn't sleeping well because I wasn't there. I thought the answer was sweet so hadn't pushed it. "And the other three weeks?"

"Those three weeks I wasn't working." I try and pull my hand away, but his grip remains firm. "But it's not what you're thinking. You have to know how much I love you, Cris. I would never do anything to jeopardise what we have."

"You told me you were working, Caleb, and now you've just told me you weren't. You lied to me. That's putting what we have in jeopardy." I can feel the tears filling my eyes, and I know that pretty soon they'll be slipping down my cheeks. I was right. He was lying to me. I knew something was going on. To me, it looks like he spent three weekends without me and realised his feelings for me weren't as strong as he thought. Sure, he's just told me he loves me, but that's just because I'm here in front of him. As soon as he returns home, those feelings will diminish again.

"Yes, I lied to you, but I had a very good reason for it."

"What possible reason could you have for lying to me? If you didn't want to see me, you only had to say. At least then I would know where I stand."

"You've got it wrong, Cris. There hasn't been a single moment in the last six weeks when I haven't thought about you. Everything I see, smell, and touch reminds me of you. My bed has been so empty without you there to share it with me that I've slept on the sofa. I've hardly slept because I've not had you there by my side. I've missed you more than I ever thought possible, and honestly, that scares me, but not as much as seeing those tears in your eyes. It's killing me knowing they're there because of me."

I close my eyes when his free hand comes up to stroke my cheek. God, I love this man. I never thought I'd meet anyone who could invoke this much of a reaction in me. Have I really got it all wrong? My heart is screaming at me to believe him, but my head doesn't want to listen.

"Cris, what date is it?"

I open my eyes, confused by his question. "November eighteenth. Why?"

"And what date was our first official date?"

May eighteenth, I think to myself. That's not a date I'm ever likely to forget. It was the day the man in front of me asked me out. The day my life changed forever—not that I knew it back then. What does our first date have to... Oh my god!

"Today is our six-month anniversary." I see him smile as I confirm what today is, and suddenly feel bad because I didn't remember it.

"Exactly. I've arranged all this stuff for us to do over the weekend, and I knew if I saw you, I wouldn't be able to keep it to myself and it would ruin the surprise. I realise now that was a stupid idea. It's made you doubt me and my feelings for you."

Tears spring to my eyes again, but this time it's for an entirely different reason. This handsome, sweet man—the same man I was having doubts about less than an hour ago—wanted to surprise me for our anniversary. How could I have been swayed so easily? "I'm so sorry, Cal. I feel like an idiot."

"Hey, don't do that. I shouldn't have lied to you, even if it was for a good reason."

I smile at him through teary eyes and shift closer, wrapping my arms around his waist as I rest my head against his shoulder. When his arms go around me, I feel a wave of emotion sweep through me, and I can't hold back the tears any longer as they slide down my cheeks, soaking into Cal's t-shirt.

"I thought you'd had enough of me. That you not coming to see me was your way of saying it was over." I sniffle and will the tears to stop as his arms tighten around me. God, I feel so stupid. How could I have doubted him?

"Never, Cris. I'll never get enough of you. You're all I think about. You're all I want—no, all I *need* to make me happy. There will never be another girl for me, Cris. You're it for me."

I lift my head to look at him, seeing the sincerity in his eyes. He really means it. I've spent the last few weeks thinking the worst of him, of us, and I was way off base. He really does love me.

"I'm sorry I doubted you, Cal. I promise it won't happen again."

His hand goes up to tangle in my hair, tugging gently so I have to look up at him.

"And I promise not to keep you in the dark about stuff, especially if it means I'm not able to come and see you." Leaning down, he drops a kiss against my nose, making me smile. "So, do you want to know what I've got planned for us this weekend?"

I grin up at him, my hand moving from his waist and coming round to his front, tugging at the material of his shirt until my fingers find the bare flesh of his stomach. I see his eyes darken immediately, and the grip he has on my hair tightens, sending a shot of pleasure right through me.

"It's been six weeks, Cal. A girl has needs. What do you think I want right now?"

And just like that, all my doubts are erased as his lips claim mine.

CHAPTER 15

Crissie

Christmas Eve 2006
Chester, England

I am so excited I could pee my pants.

Well, not really, but you know what I mean. Tomorrow is the first Christmas for Cal and me, and I can't wait!

We've agreed to spend Christmas Eve with his parents and sister, then we're going back to his flat for the evening, then going round to my mum and dad's to spend Christmas Day with them. It's weird having to split my time between two families. It's the first time I've had to do it, and it's something I know I can get used to.

Right now, Caleb is in the shower as I try and decide what to wear. I've decided on my favourite dark blue jeans that I know Caleb loves. He can't stop staring at my backside when I wear them, and it's strangely empowering knowing I can affect him in that way.

We've been together almost eight months now and that feeling never gets old. Every now and then I'll catch him watching me for no reason other than he wants to. He tells me he thinks I'm beautiful all the time, and when he's staring at me like that, he's wondering how he got so lucky. Every time I tell him it's the same for me. Yeah, we can get quite sappy when we get going.

Flinging open the door to Caleb's wardrobe, I look through the few items of clothing I have hanging in there. At the moment, my clothes are split between home, Caleb's flat, and the house I'm sharing with his cousin, Elise, when I'm at college. I'm just hoping I have something here I can wear.

Caleb told me his family don't really 'dress up' for Christmas, but he has always made the effort to look presentable, so I feel the need to do the same. Not that I'd go round looking a mess. I know his parents like me, so I don't want to give them any reason to change their minds.

Reaching out, I grab one of the hangers and pull out the black, slash neck top Caleb got me for my birthday. Its long sleeves come down to my wrists and the soft fabric is loose, apart from the bottom that tightens around my hips. Due to the slash neck, the material falls off one shoulder, creating a casual yet elegant look. I loved the top when he gave it to me and have only worn it once before.

Deciding the top is perfect, I close the wardrobe and hang it on the front, before I turn, stopping dead in my tracks when I see Caleb stood in front of me wearing nothing but a towel around his slim hips. His dark hair is damp from the shower and sticking up at all angles due to the towel he's rubbing though it.

Water droplets are present on his chest, almost screaming at me to come and lick them from his skin. I swallow hard and look up at him, seeing the smirk on his face, and my cheeks flame red. I've every right to ogle him —he's mine, after all—but I still feel embarrassed when he catches me doing it.

Suddenly aware I'm only wearing my jeans and a bra, I instinctively cover myself, an action which only gets a snort from Caleb as he walks over and gently tugs at my arms until they're back by my sides.

"If you can ogle me, then I'm damn sure I can return the favour," Caleb says with a grin as his free hand comes up, his fingers lightly running across the swell of my breasts, following the black lace of my bra.

I suck in a breath, my body reacting the way it always does when he's near me. He drops the towel he has in his other hand and it then comes up to join the other, his palms scraping over my sensitive nipples. My eyes connect with his, and I see what I always see when we're together; desire and passion. He reaches round me and unclasps my bra, the lacy material falling to the floor.

Reaching out, I tug at the towel around his waist and it comes away easily, joining the other in a soggy heap. Looking down, I see his reaction to me jutting out from his body. Tentatively, I close my hand around him and stroke gently, hearing his breathing change almost immediately.

"God, Cris. That feels so good." His hands close over my breasts and squeeze, causing me to close my eyes briefly as I let the sensations wash over me. I open them to see Caleb's head thrown back, his eyes tightly shut as I continue to stroke him. His hips are moving with my hand, setting a steady rhythm that matches the beating of my heart.

I've not touched him this way before. I've always been too nervous about doing it wrong but seeing how he's reacting to my touch makes me wish I'd plucked up the courage to do this sooner. If he reacts like this to my hand, I wonder...

"Son of a bitch!" Caleb shouts out as my lips close around him. I look up his body to see him gazing down at me, his hands now pressed against the wardrobe doors to keep himself upright. His breathing is ragged, and his body is tense as my hands rest on his firm thighs. I can feel the muscles bunch up tightly as I swirl my tongue around the head of his penis.

Empowered doesn't even come close to how I feel right

now. Being able to bring my man this much pleasure, whilst at the same time feeling strong and in control, is a powerful combination.

I open my mouth wider and slide down his length, and I hear the rumble in his chest as he struggles to remain still. Part of me wants him to lose it. He's always so gentle with me that, just once, I'd like him to give up a bit of that control and lose himself. His eyes are closed again, and when I graze my teeth lightly across the sensitive skin, they open immediately and look down at me. I release him briefly.

"Let go, Cal. I won't let you fall. I've got you. Always." I see a look cross his face as I close my lips around him once again, and this time he does what I ask. He let's go as he starts pumping his hips, his penis tunnelling in and out of my mouth. All I can do is hold onto his thighs and match his rhythm as I take him.

"God, Cris, I can't hold on."

As I look up at him, I shake my head, and I see the moment he understands as his whole body tightens, and in one powerful thrust, he empties himself down my throat. I swallow repeatedly until he stops, a strange sense of female satisfaction washing over me as he pulls out of my mouth and collapses on the floor next to me.

He's breathing quickly, and his eyes are closed. I'm unable to stop the grin that spreads across my face when he eventually sits up and looks at me. "I don't know how the hell you knew how to do that, Cris, but that was amazing."

I can't wipe the smile off my face at the fact that I've given him pleasure in the most intimate of ways. "Merry Christmas, Cal."

When he bursts out laughing, I join him, and we just sit there, me topless and him naked, right in the middle of his bedroom floor.

~

"*T*hat was lovely, Mrs Roberts. Thank you."

"You're very welcome, Crissie."

I smile at Caleb's mum as we all sit around the dining table after enjoying a full roast dinner of chicken with stuffing, roasted potatoes, mashed potatoes, and various vegetables all topped with a thick, rich gravy. I'm so full I'm pretty sure I won't be able to move for the next hour, at least.

Caleb it sat to my right, his hand now resting on my knee as he pushes his plate away and takes a sip of wine from the glass in front of him. Lizzie is to my left, and clearly still unsure about me dating her brother as she's hardly spoken to me since I arrived.

"I hope you've got room for pudding, Crissie," Mr Roberts asks. "Elaine's Christmas pudding is renowned in these parts."

"I'm sure I've got room for a small piece, Mr Roberts."

"Crissie, how many times do we have to ask that you call us Elaine and Peter?"

I smile at her and feel Caleb squeeze my knee. As I turn to him, he smiles and picks up his wine glass before standing.

"I know we usually do this tomorrow," Caleb says as he looks around the table before settling his eyes on me, "but seeing as we'll be spending tomorrow with Crissie's parents, I wanted to do this now. Crissie, it's a tradition in this house that on Christmas Day, we each take turns in telling everyone what we're thankful for, kind of like Thanksgiving in America. Well, this year, for me, is a no-brainer. I'm thankful for you, Crissie. I'm thankful that you agreed to go out with me eight months ago. I'm thankful you're the strong, wonderful woman you are, and most of all, I'm thankful you've made me a better man. I can't imagine my life without you in it, Crissie, so thank you. Thank you for being mine."

I can't help it; the tears come thick and fast as he speaks, and in front of his family too. Standing, I take his wine glass from his hand and put in on the table before I wrap my arms around him and hold him. I'm so lucky to have him in my life.

As I hold him, I feel a hand on my shoulder and pull away, turning to see Lizzie looking at me. "I'm sorry I've been such a bitch, Cris. You don't deserve the way I've treated you. I guess I was just jealous that my brother has someone. I admit I thought you were just another fling for him, but I realise now I was wrong. I've never seen my brother like this before, over anyone. You're good for him, and it's clear you love him, and he loves you. Will you forgive me?"

"There's nothing to forgive, Lizzie. You were just looking out for your brother. But you're right, I do love him, with everything I am."

"I see that now. Friends?"

"We were always friends."

Releasing Caleb, I lean in and hug Lizzie quickly. When we're all seated again, I notice Mrs Roberts dabbing her eyes with a tissue as her husband rests his hand on her shoulder.

"Allergies, Mum?" Caleb asks with a soft smile as his mum sniffles and nods. "Thought so. So, where's that Christmas pudding?

~

It's almost midnight before Caleb and I walk through his front door after a lovely day and evening with his family. Lizzie and I are back on track, and I finally started calling his parents by their first names, earning me a hug from Elaine and a shoulder squeeze from Peter.

I drop my handbag by the sofa and fall down into the cushions, quickly followed by Caleb. It's been a long day, and I am ready to climb into bed with Caleb cuddled up behind me and sleep until we have to get up to go to my parents' house tomorrow.

I stifle a yawn as Caleb slumps to the side, his head now resting in my lap. He grumbles when he lifts his legs from the floor and tucks them in behind him on the sofa. I shake my head and grin at him as I lift my hand, threading the silky strands of his hair through my fingers. I hear a soft moan escape past his lips as his body relaxes.

I know he loves it when I run my fingers through his hair like this. He's been wearing it longer recently, which I wasn't sure of at first, but now, knowing how much he likes it when I do this, I'm happy with his decision.

"I love it when you do that," Caleb says as he sighs deeply. "It feels so nice."

"I'm so tired. I think your mum has put me in a food coma." I hear him chuckle as he shifts onto his back, his legs stretched out and hanging over the arm of the sofa and looks up at me.

"Yeah, she has a habit of doing that," Caleb says with a grin as he reaches out, takes my hand, and places a soft kiss against the knuckles. "I'm happy you were with me this year. It wouldn't have been the same without you there."

Smiling, I continue stroking his hair, and his eyes close briefly before they open again to peer at me.

"I wouldn't have been anywhere else," I say quietly, just at the clock on the mantelpiece gently chimes. "It's midnight. Merry Christmas, Cal."

He smiles up at me before launching himself off the sofa and vanishing behind the bedroom door. He returns a few moments later with a small box in his hands. As he sits next to me, he hands it to me, and I smile at the wrapping paper. It's not Christmas paper, as you would expect at this time of year. Instead, it is covered in lots of little kittens playing with balls of wool. It's so cute and so me, and the fact he knows that makes me smile even more.

"What's this?"

"It's a present," Caleb says, without cracking a smile, causing me to narrow my eyes at him.

"I know that, genius. I mean why are you giving it to me now?"

"Because I want you to open this one, just the two of us."

I look at him as I turn the small box over in my hands and begin to open it. We agreed to wait to open our presents until we arrive at my parents' house. My family have always opened presents together and wanted that tradition to continue, something Cal was happy to do.

Looking down at the present I hold in my hands, I'm torn between tearing into the paper in my eagerness to find out what he's bought me or taking my time to preserve the pretty paper and the cute kittens. I can see the amusement on Caleb's face as I choose the latter, carefully pulling at the tape holding the paper together.

When I have the paper removed and folded neatly on the sofa next to me, I'm left with a square, black, velvet box in my hands. I know its jewellery; this is just the right kind of box. Unless it's a pen? No, Cal wouldn't buy me a pen, would he?

Taking a small breath, I open the box, unable to stop my gasp as I take in the contents. The simple gold chain is stunning in and of itself, but it's what hangs from it that I can't take my eyes off. Nestled into white satin sits my name in a beautiful sweeping script font, with one diamond and one peridot dotting the "I's." The design is gorgeous in its simplicity, and I instantly love it.

"Oh, Cal, it's beautiful." I can feel the tears forming in my eyes as he takes the box from my hands and removes the delicate chain from the satin interior. As he works to undo the clasp, I give him my back and sweep my hair off my neck, smiling when I see him pass the chain around my neck and fasten it.

Dropping my hair so it falls around my shoulders, I turn back to Caleb and look down, seeing my name resting against my skin. I peer up at him after several moments to see him smiling at me.

"The stones are our birthstones. A Diamond for me, and a peridot for you."

"I love it, Cal," I say as I throw my arms around his neck. "Thank you."

We separate after several minutes, and I look down again, lifting the chain so I can see my name more clearly.

"You deserve pretty things, Crissie."

"I don't know what I did to deserve you, Cal, but I

thank God every day that you asked me out all those months ago." I hug him again, but this time I press my lips to his. I feel my body react almost as soon as our lips meet. Within seconds, I'm tugging at his shirt as his fingers work on the button and zipper to my jeans, and I know we're not going to make it to the bedroom.

CHAPTER 16

Crissie

Present Day

*O*ur first Christmas holds many happy memories.

We spent Christmas Day with my family. I knew my mum already loved Cal. She had practically from our first date, but my dad had always been unsure. Then again, even before Cal came into my life, I'd known for a while that no guy would ever be good enough for me. I'm his baby girl, his only daughter, but on Christmas Day, my dad actually went up to Cal, shook his hand and actually thanked him for making his little girl so happy.

For the second time in two days, I'd been in floods of tears as I hugged my dad tight and he told me how proud he was of me and that I had a good man in Cal. Of course, I already knew this, but the fact my dad now saw it too, meant so much to me.

We'd exchanged presents, eaten another enormous Christmas dinner followed by sweet apple crumble and piping hot custard. When everything had been tidied away, we'd spent the afternoon playing board games. Cal had laughed as I lost at every game, calling me cute as I'd pouted like a child.

It was the early hours when we'd fallen into bed and, unlike the night before, we just slept soundly in each other's arms.

I have so many happy memories of all the Christmases we have shared, and I smile into the mirror as my eyes shift to the delicate gold necklace that bears my name.

There really was no other choice when it came to what jewellery I would wear today. When my mum asked me what I would wear around my neck, I'd just looked at her and rolled my eyes. The answer to that question was the definition of a no-brainer.

Caleb has given me many pieces of jewellery throughout our years together, and each piece has a special meaning attached to it. But none mean as much to me as what I'm wearing right now.

The necklace you already know about, but you don't know about my bracelet, earrings, and the most beautiful engagement ring Cal could have chosen for me. There's a story behind each item of jewellery I'm wearing today, including the little diamond bar I wear in my belly button, but you only want to know about my engagement ring, right?

Well, it was on my eighteenth birthday...

CHAPTER 17

Crissie

August 2007

*W*oohoo!

I'm officially an adult, so the law says anyway. I can't believe I've finally reached the so-called "age of consent," when it comes to drinking anyway. It's not like I've never had a drink before, but it's only ever been when I've been at home or with family. Tonight, I can go out with Cal and my friends and have a drink in a bar, and they can't stop me!

God, I never thought I'd be this excited to actually be able to have a drink outside of home. Tonight, I'm going out for a nice meal with Cal to celebrate my birthday. He refuses to tell me where we're going, despite my incessant pleas, then we're meeting my friends in town for a few drinks and maybe some dancing.

I've already been out most of the day with my parents. They treated me to lunch at my favourite pizza place, then Dad left Mum and me to go shopping for my outfit for tonight, which was no easy feat. I wanted to look classy for the meal with Cal, but not too over the top for drinks with my friends afterwards.

After much window shopping and several outfit changes, we finally decided on a baby pink, chiffon dress that is fun and flirty and will easily fit both venues. The hem stops a few inches above my knee and is shorter than I'm used to, but Cal has often said I have killer legs, so I threw caution to the wind and decided to show them off.

Two tiny buttons behind my neck fasten the dress, and the high neckline hides any hint of cleavage from view. After much consideration, I also splurged on a pair of silver high-heeled sandals and a matching clutch bag, something Mum says completes the outfit. I hope Cal likes it.

~

Caleb

I can't believe my girl is finally eighteen. Even more so, I can't believe that we've been together for over a year.

I'll admit, when I first asked her out, I had hoped we would go the distance, but as my history with women isn't great, I daren't actually believe Crissie and I would go anywhere. How wrong was I?

I learnt pretty early on that Cris was unlike the other girls I'd dated. She challenges me. She isn't afraid to call me out when I'm in the wrong or I say or do something stupid. I know I can be difficult and moody at times, but instead of just throwing a fit or just huffing at me, Cris recognises when I need to be left alone and she does just that. It's just one of the many reasons why I love that girl more than life itself.

Tonight, I'm taking her out for a meal, just the two of us, to a new French place that opened up in town. I've no idea if she likes French food—hell, I've no idea if I like French food—but this place is classy and sophisticated, just like her, and she deserves only the best.

I actually made this reservation not long after my birthday back in April, before the place had even opened. I've known for a while that I wanted to do something special for her eighteenth birthday; make it a day she would never forget. I've even gone and bought a suit for the occasion. The deep charcoal grey jacket and trousers look the part and paired with a plain white shirt and my favourite black loafers, I think I scrub up pretty well.

As I grab my wallet and keys from the side table, I glance at the clock above the fireplace, seeing I have twenty minutes to get from my flat to Crissie's parents' house. I know she's spent the day with her parents, something I was happy for her to do as I knew I would be with her all evening and into the night.

I can't wait to see what she's wearing. Wondering about what a woman is wearing for a date has never bothered me before, mainly because I knew she wouldn't be wearing it for long. Crissie has changed me in so many ways, and all of them for the better. I no longer look at women as objects, which I have to admit, I was guilty of doing before now.

Blame it on teenage hormones if you will, but now I have Crissie in my life, I see women in a whole different way. Yes, I still look at them, and I can appreciate an attractive woman when I see one, but none of them have the affect on me that she does.

No one else makes my pulse race just by walking into a room. No one else makes my heart skip a beat when they smile at me. She's everything I could ever want in a partner, and I can't imagine being with anyone else.

Locking my front door, I make my way down to my car and jump in. As soon as the engine kicks into gear, I pull out of my parking space and head towards the woman who holds my heart.

Crissie

*T*his place is just...wow!

I know I must look like a goldfish as I sit at our beautifully dressed table and wait for our desserts to be brought out.

We've been here for almost two hours, and I still can't believe how great this place is. It's a lot bigger than what I expected with at least three dozen tables able to sit two, four and in some cases, eight people, and they're all spread out over a massive dark, hardwood floor that's so shiny you can see your face in it. It took all my concentration not to look like Bambi on ice as I walked across it in my four-inch heels.

The walls are decorated in artwork and, while I know next to nothing about art, every piece looks like it could cost a small fortune. There are four huge crystal chandeliers hanging from a high ceiling that is accentuated by the thick black beams that you see in so many buildings in Chester.

The tablecloths are brilliant white with a large cream-coloured church candle sat dead centre. All the glassware and silverware is polished to within an inch of its life. Our table is in a secluded alcove that gives us a small amount of privacy, but still gives the illusion of being part of the main eating crowd.

The overall effect is breath-taking, and the fact Cal has brought me here confirms to me how much he cares. This place hasn't come cheap, that much I know. The thing that gives it away is there are no prices on the menus, something I noticed straightaway and something Cal quickly told me not to worry about.

"Are you happy, Cris?"

I switch my gaze from the beauty of the building we're sat in and look at the beauty that is the man who holds my heart, wondering where that question came from.

"Of course. Why wouldn't I be?"

"No reason. I like to see you happy. You deserve to be happy. Have I ever told you how much my life has changed since you agreed to go out with me? How happy you make me?" I shake my head and smile shyly at him. "Before I knew you, I was just going though the motions. Getting up, going to work, coming home. Occasionally, I'd go out with some friends, but it was pretty much work, sleep, and work again. I didn't really have much in my life other than that, and then I met you. You brought a light into my life, Cris. You gave me a purpose; a reason to get up in the morning other than motor grease and car engines." He smiles as he says the words, and I try and calm my erratic pulse. "I've never met a girl like you before, Cris, and I don't think anyone I may meet in the future will ever come close to meaning as much to me as you do. So..."

Oh my god. Oh my god. Oh my god.

I watch as Caleb smoothly slides from his seat and lowers himself to the floor, down onto one knee.

"Crissie Elizabeth Walker, there will never be another woman for me. You're my sun, my moon, and all the stars in the heavens. I love you with everything I am. I know we're young, and there are probably hundreds of reasons why I shouldn't ask you this, but they all pale in comparison to the fact that I want you to be mine, always, as my wife. Cris, will you marry me?"

I look into Caleb's face as everything around us fades away. Right now, there is only the two of us. In this moment, as I feel tears spring to my eyes, I know there is only one answer I can give this man.

"Yes, Caleb. A thousand times yes!"

Within seconds, I am in his arms and my lips are pressed to his. I can hear the cheers and applause from the other diners sat around us, but none of that matters as we break apart and Cal slips the diamond and emerald ring on my finger. The tears come thick and fast now as I look at my ring finger and realise Cal remembered my perfect ring. A princess cut emerald set in a platinum band encrusted with diamonds.

It couldn't be more perfect from the man I love and will love for the rest of my life.

CHAPTER 18

Crissie

Present Day

I dab at my eyes with a tissue, knowing my friends will kill me if my mascara runs. It took them hours to get my eyes right. They won't be impressed if they have to do it all again because I got weepy over the memory of our engagement.

Then again, I find it impossible not to think of that moment and get sentimental. I don't know a girl who doesn't get a bit teary-eyed when they think of the moment their man proposed to them.

I remember thinking how handsome Cal looked in his suit when he picked me up. It was the first time I'd seen him all dressed up like that, and I had made him promise to do it more often. When he had realised just how much I liked it, something I had shown him that night when we got back to his flat—three times—whenever we went out for a meal, out came the suit.

Ah, the memories that suit helped to create.

I throw the tissue in a nearby bin and glance down at my ring again. I bet you're all wondering why it's taken so long for us to get here? After all, I was eighteen when Cal proposed and I'm twenty-eight now. I could tell you we were too young to marry, so we decided on a long engagement, but that would be a lie.

The truth is, we've been through a lot over the last ten years. Our relationship and dedication to each other has been tested more than once, in some of the worst ways possible. The first three years after our engagement were some of our happiest times.

I stayed at college in Birmingham and got the grades I needed on my A-Levels to get into the University of Chester to complete my degree in Criminology and Forensic Biology, completing the three-year course with a 2:1 outcome.

While I got the degree I had dreamed about, finding work in that area proved harder than I had thought, so I started working as an admin assistant for a local recruitment firm. The people were nice, the hours were flexible, and, for what I did each day, the pay wasn't too bad either.

As for Cal, when the owner of the garage he worked at

suffered a near fatal heart attack, he decided to retire. Even though he had two sons, one who worked with him at the garage, he had no interest in taking over the company from his father, so he handed over the reins to Cal, trusting him to run the business in his absence.

Shortly after I came back to Chester, I moved in with Cal, deciding I couldn't be in the same city as him and not live with him. I passed my driving test on the first attempt, which was a shock to all of us, and as a surprise for my twenty-first birthday, Cal got me a cherry red Mini, and it quickly became my pride and joy.

I had never understood Cal's obsession with his car, until I had one of my own. I wouldn't let anyone drive her but me, and I affectionately called her Ethel, after my grandmother.

Things were going well for us, but six months after my twenty-first birthday, not long after we'd received some of the best news ever, everything came crashing down.

CHAPTER 19

Crissie

October 2010

Nope, definitely nothing showing yet.

I look at my reflection in the mirror and smooth my top down over my belly. It's been four weeks since Cal and I found out we are expecting our first child, and, according to the doctor, I can start showing at any time after twelve weeks. Well, if his calculations were correct, I'm sixteen weeks now, and there's still no sign of Little Bean.

Yeah, I know it's a silly nickname, but as we've opted not to know whether it's going to be a boy or a girl, and it looks like a kidney bean on the twelve-week scan, the name just stuck. We decided to wait a while before telling our families; wanting to have some time with it being just our secret. However, that's all about to change this Sunday.

We've been invited round to Cal's parent's house for Sunday dinner. Lizzie will be there with her new boyfriend, and Elaine even said my parents could come too, an invitation they accepted without hesitation. We're lucky our families get along really well, and we decided that, seeing as we would have them all together, Sunday would be when we make the big baby announcement.

I know exactly how my parents will react. Mum will be in floods of tears as soon as she realises she's going to be a grandma. My dad will be a little more restrained, but I know he will be just as emotional as Mum will be. It's going to be a huge tear-fest, of that I have no doubt.

Even though I have no bump yet, I am seeing other signs that my body is changing. I've had to spend a small fortune on new underwear. I swear, my boobs have doubled in size over the last few weeks, and Cal definitely isn't complaining about that. Turning my back to the mirror, I frown as I see my arse is also getting bigger, if the tightness of my jeans is anything to go by. I am most certainly not happy about that.

I've upped my exercise, something the doctor has encouraged, as it will only help me stay healthy during the pregnancy. Hopefully, if I stay relatively fit, the size of my arse won't get out of hand. The last thing I want is to have to replace all my jeans.

"I hope you make an appearance soon, Little Bean," I

say as I rest my hands over my still flat belly. "We're eager to see you start growing."

As I take one last look at my appearance, I hear the front door open and turn to see Cal walking through into the living room. He's wearing his usual work clothes of a tatty white t-shirt that's been washed dozens of times but still has grease and grime marks all over it, and an old pair of light blue jeans. He looks a mess, but at the same time, hot as hell.

In my pregnant state, my hormones are all over the place, and I seem to want sex all the time. Every time I see Cal, no matter what the time of day, what he's wearing or where we are, my libido kicks into overdrive.

He's always had a strong effect on me, but right now, I've only got to sense his presence and I can't wait to get my hands on him, and, judging by the look on his face right now, he knows exactly what I'm thinking as he grins at me.

"I'm going to go grab a shower before I get this grease all over the place." He takes a few steps closer until he is standing directly in front of me. "Care to join me?"

Hell yes! I think as I take his hand and drag him towards the bathroom, the sound of his laughter bouncing off the walls.

Caleb

*I*f I'd known Cris getting pregnant would have had this effect on my sex life, I'd have mentioned having kids a lot sooner. Her sex drive has gone through the roof. The woman is insatiable; she can't get enough of me. Every time we're alone, she gets this look in her eye, the same one she got when I walked through the door last night; and when I was in the shower this morning. Don't get me wrong, I love all the sex, but a guy needs a rest too.

I toss the grease-covered rag I've used to wipe my hands on the growing pile of rags by the engine I've been working on all afternoon. I still can't figure out why the damn thing won't start and it's frustrating me no end. I've come close to kicking the hunk of metal several times in the last hour. Doing so might make me feel better but wouldn't do the engine much good.

After checking my watch, I realise I've only thirty minutes before I have to go and meet Cris. We're checking out three potential venues this afternoon for our wedding reception, and she'll kill me if I'm late.

Thankfully, one of the first things I did when I took over the garage was have a small shower room installed. I often work late and sometimes it's just easier for me to shower here, especially if I'm going somewhere else other than straight home.

As it's a Saturday and I'm the only one working, I make sure the front gate is secured before I head past my office and into the shower. Stripping out of my dirty clothes, I make quick work of cleaning off before drying myself on a nearby towel. After pulling on my jeans and a clean t-shirt, I grab my car keys and I'm on the road to meet Cris less than ten minutes later.

We're going to see three very different venues this afternoon, all of which have told us they have the capacity to hold the almost 130 guests we want to invite to the party. Finding the reception venue has been the hardest part so far. We've had the venue for the actual wedding secured for some time now.

Crissie told me it has always been her dream to get married in the same place her parents tied the knot almost twenty-five years ago, so, after doing a bit of digging, I made some enquiries and boom, the place was booked less than two weeks after I proposed.

I must admit, I was surprised they were willing to take the booking, considering the wedding is still more than two years away, but they were more than happy to accommodate us, saying it wasn't unusual now for people to have long engagements, and their venue gets booked up pretty quickly. Surprisingly, they had bookings further into the future than ours.

The stately home, whilst large, can only accommodate thirty-five people in the room it uses for wedding services, so we've had to be brutal with our guest list. We know a few people are going to be pissed they're not invited, but it's our day, and if they don't like it, well that's just tough shit.

When I broke the news to Cris, she'd jumped around the place like a kid on Christmas morning. Seeing the look of happiness on her face had made all my hard work securing the venue worthwhile, and I'd realised I would do everything in my power to give her the perfect wedding, even if it sent me bankrupt in the process.

Making a left at the traffic lights, I see our first venue in the distance, and Crissie is sat on a bench, her face stuck in the baby book that was recommended by her doctor. Since she got the book a week ago, it's all she's been reading, absorbing all the tips to becoming a perfect mum and what to do and not to do when pregnant. I swear most of the things are old wives' tales, but if it makes her feel better, I'm happy to go along for the ride.

I pull up behind Crissie's Mini and turn off the engine. She looks up when she sees me and smiles, putting the book in her bag as she stands. God, she looks beautiful, and she's carrying my baby. I never used to believe it when I heard people talking about how a pregnant woman glows, but now I've seen it for myself, I know it to be true.

Collecting my scattered thoughts, I jump out the car and join her on the pavement. Taking her hand, I bend slightly to brush my lips across hers, inhaling her scent before breaking away.

"How was work?"

I know today is the day she was going to tell her boss that she is pregnant. As she hasn't been there that long, she was really nervous about how they would take the news.

"Work was great. I told Amanda when I got in this morning and she was really happy for me and so supportive. She sent me an email with all the information I need to know about maternity leave and what I needed to do to inform HR. I really don't know what I was worried about."

"That's great, Cris," I say as I kiss her again, before looking up at the building behind her. "Shall we go in and see this place, then?"

Cris nods and turns, and we climb the few steps to the main entrance of what could be our reception venue.

~

Crissie

I fall into the cushions on the sofa and kick off my shoes. Three venues visited, and three venues discounted. Not one of them is right for our wedding reception. They each had their good points, but none of them screamed 'pick me.' Caleb thought the same thing, so before we head around his parents' house tomorrow, we're going to do a little bit more research to see what other venues we can find.

I close my eyes briefly and sigh, opening them again

when I feel the weight of the sofa shift as Cal joins me. I watch as he takes hold of my legs, bringing them onto his lap, where he proceeds to rub my feet and ankles.

One side effect of being pregnant is that my ankles tend to swell if I spend too long on my feet. I can't stop the groan that spills over my lips as Cal presses his thumbs into my instep, my head falling back as my eyes close again. I hear him chuckle as he continues.

"That feels good, I take it?"

"You have no idea," I reply with as a small smile plays across my lips.

We remain silent for the next fifteen minutes as Cal works his way from my feet to my ankles and then up my calves. By the time he's finished, my legs feel like jelly and I'm more than a little bit turned on. Yeah, I know it sounds weird, but having Cal's hands on me, even doing something as non-sexual as rubbing my aching feet, brings my body to life.

I blame the pregnancy hormones. When I open my eyes to look at him, how I'm feeling must be evident.

"Oh no, woman. No sex for you. We need to eat, and maybe after that I'll let you have your way with me."

I try my hardest to pout but fail miserably. I know my sexual demands on him, whilst welcomed most of the time, are tiring him out. Especially when I wake up in the middle of the night, horny as hell and wanting nothing more than for him to press me into the mattress and take me hard and fast.

He's been getting up most mornings and heading to work like a zombie. Part of me feels bad that me being pregnant is affecting him this way, but then I think back to how being with Cal makes me feel; how my body comes alive when our bodies become one, and any bad feelings I have evaporate.

"What are we having to eat, then?" I ask as he stops rubbing my calves and rests his hands on my legs.

"How about pizza?" Just thinking about melted cheese, pepperoni and mushrooms causes my stomach to growl and Cal to laugh out loud. "Pizza is it, then."

As Caleb lifts my legs so he can slide off the sofa, I grab my phone and send a quick text to my mum to check we're still okay for dinner the next day. She quickly replies saying both her and my dad are looking forward to seeing Cal's family again.

Seeing my battery is almost flat, I move to cross the room to get my charger, stopping suddenly as a pain shoots through my lower back. Moving my hand, I rub the offending spot and slowly straighten, releasing the breath I had sucked in when the pain hit.

The doctor had warned me there would be aches and pains throughout the pregnancy, but that had come out of nowhere. Bending slightly, I move again when I'm sure the pain is gone, but only make it two steps before the pain comes back tenfold, this time lancing through my belly so strongly I double over and cry out. Within seconds, Caleb is by my side, his arm around my waist.

"Cris, honey. What is it? What's wrong?"

"Oh god, Cal, it hurts so bad." I force my eyes to open as I look at him, my arms wrapped around my middle. "Please say it's not the baby. It can't be the baby."

As another pain shoots through my belly, I fall to my knees, tears streaming down my face as I hear Cal screaming into his phone for an ambulance. Moments later, he's back by my side, holding me in his arms as he whispers everything will be okay, and for the first time in my life, I pray to God that he's right.

CHAPTER 20

Crissie

*M*y head hurts.

Why is everything so fuzzy?

Whose voice is that?

Why can't I move?

What's happening?

What's wrong with me?

"Hey, Cris. Crissie, you're okay. You're safe. Calm down, baby, I'm here."

"Caleb? What's going on? What's happening? Where am I?" I try and sit up as my vision begins to clear, and I see Caleb looking down at me. He's smiling, but I can tell something isn't right. His eyes are red and puffy, like he's been crying. Jesus, what's happened?

"You're in the hospital, Cris. Can you remember how you got here?"

Hospital? What am I doing in the... Oh god. My stomach. The pains. Cal called an ambulance. The baby.

"The baby? Is the baby okay? Cal, please tell me the baby is okay?"

I don't need him to verbalise the answer. I can see it written all over his handsome face. He averts his eyes for a moment and swallows, before turning back to me, his eyes glistening with unshed tears.

"I'm so sorry, Cris. The baby is gone. You had a miscarriage, sweetie."

A miscarriage? No, he must be wrong. That only happens to women who don't look after themselves during pregnancy. He must be wrong.

"But I did everything right. The doctor told me what to do, and I did everything right. You're wrong, Cal. You have to be wrong."

"I'm sorry, baby. You did everything right, everything you should have done, but this can sometimes just happen."

"Caleb is right, Crissie." I hear the unfamiliar voice and watch as Caleb steps to the side and a woman in a white lab coat steps forward. She looks at me with kind eyes hidden behind pink-rimmed glasses. Her blonde hair is pulled back into a high ponytail. She sits on the edge of the bed and looks at Caleb before turning back to me.

"Sometimes this just happens, Crissie. With all the

medical advances that have been made, sometimes there is just no way of telling what causes a miscarriage. From what your young man has told me, you did everything right. We'll probably never know what caused it, and while you probably don't want to think about this now, there's no reason why you can't go on to have a normal pregnancy and healthy babies in the future."

I hear what she's saying, but the words don't penetrate my brain. She says I did nothing wrong, but how can she know? How can anyone know? I just lie there, staring at the ceiling as both the doctor and Caleb look at me.

I don't know what to say to him right now. What can I say to the man whose baby I've somehow killed? I need time to think, time to digest what's happened.

"I'm tired," I say on a sigh, turning away from Cal and the doctor. I move onto my side so I'm looking towards the wall.

I feel Caleb stroke my hair and squeeze my eyes shut as he places a soft kiss on my head. "I'll be right outside when you need me, baby. Sleep now. I love you, Cris."

A few moments later, the light is turned off and I hear the door close quietly. I wait a few more minutes before I turn over on to my back, seeing I'm alone in the room; alone with the thoughts of my lost baby and everything I could have done to deny me one of the greatest gifts a woman can receive.

Caleb

The doctor told me she might blame herself. She told me it's common for a woman who loses a baby to think up things they did wrong and somehow use them as a reason for the loss. She also said most of the time, especially if the woman is in perfect health, as Crissie is, there is no medical reason for it. As much as it's horrible to say, sometimes miscarriages just happen for no reason at all.

The ambulance had arrived at the flat within five minutes of me calling them. By that time, Crissie was in tears with the pain, and, while I didn't tell her, I could see she was bleeding. My heart had broken on that ride to the hospital. The paramedics had given her something for the pain, which had calmed her, but I knew, as did they, what had happened.

When the paramedic looked over at me, I could see by the look on her face that my worst fears had come true. Cris had lost our baby, something that was confirmed by the doctors when they examined her. They'd given her a mild sedative to help her rest, and the doctor had explained she would need to stay in for a few days.

Due to the fact she was almost seventeen weeks, the doctor explained that Cris would need to give birth to the baby. I hadn't told her that yet. Telling her our baby had died had been hard enough. When I had to tell her she would still have to give birth to a baby we would never be able to take home with us, I knew it would break my heart more than it already had been.

"Mr Roberts?" I hear the doctor say my name and turn as she walks over. "Miss Walker's parents are on their way up. Do you want me to tell them what's happened?"

God, I'd almost forgotten I'd called them. It seems like hours since we got here, but it's only been ninety minutes. How do I tell them their baby girl has lost her own baby? A baby that, up until a short while ago, they didn't even know existed. Pushing my hand through my hair, I hear the lift doors slide open and then hurried footsteps coming towards me.

"I'll do it, doctor. Thank you."

She nods as she returns to the nurse's station, just as Matthew and Diane Walker come to a stop by my side. Diane grabs my hands and holds on tightly. "Caleb, what's wrong? How's Crissie? Was there an accident? Is it the baby?"

I look between my future in-laws, all words failing me. I open my mouth several times, but nothing comes out. After a few moments of just looking at them, I feel the tears returning to my eyes. It's then I feel a gentle hand on my arm and see the doctor is back.

"Caleb, Crissie is asking for you. You go, I'll speak with Mr and Mrs Walker."

I give her a small nod and then turn towards Crissie's room. When I go in, I see her lying on her back staring up at the ceiling. She turns her head to look at me as I enter, her eyes locking with mine. I see the moment she breaks, her breath stuttering as she tries to speak.

"We've lost our baby, Cal. Our Little Bean is gone."

I cross the room in seconds and gather her into my arms as the barriers finally break and she sobs into my chest. Her hands clutch at my t-shirt as her whole body shakes in my arms. I let myself grieve with her as I hear a female cry from outside the room, knowing it must be Crissie's mother.

Without releasing my hold on her, I manoeuvre myself on the bed next to Crissie and lie down, taking her with me. She curls in against my body and clings to me, her sobs coming thick and fast. As I lie there with her by my side, I have never felt more useless. All I can do is hold on and let her cry for the baby we will never know but will always love.

CHAPTER 21

"*E*asy, honey. Take it slow. There you go. Do you need anything?"

"I'm good, Mum. Thank you."

I love my mum, really, I do, but for the last four days she's been driving me crazy. I know she's only trying to be useful, and she cares for me, but I'm close to pulling my hair out with all the fussing she's doing.

Ever since the day I had to give birth to my daughter, she's been by my side, making sure I don't have to do anything. Part of me has welcomed it, knowing that after the emotional and physical trauma of everything that happened, I needed someone to lighten the load.

Cal and I decided to call our daughter Aria Natasha Roberts. She was so tiny she fit into the palm of my hand. Little Aria had all her limbs, and even though we would never see her grow up, to us, she was perfect.

We held a service for her in the hospital chapel as I was unable to leave the hospital for several more days, and she will have a headstone in the children's cemetery at our local church. She might have never taken a breath, but she will always be loved and remembered.

As I sit down, my mum reaches down and takes off my shoes, lifts my legs, and places them on the sofa so I'm stretched out. She then grabs the throw off the back of the sofa and lays it out over me.

"Can I get you a drink? Something to eat?"

"No, Mum. Really, I'm fine." I see Cal come in after parking the car and grabbing my bags. He smiles as he sees my mum tucking the throw in around my legs, and I roll my eyes at him over my mum's shoulder.

"Really, Diane, we'll be fine. Thank you for being here for Crissie, for me too. We really appreciate it."

"Nothing to thank me for, Caleb. Crissie is my baby girl. There is nowhere else I'd have been." She sits on the sofa next to me and continues to mess with the throw, until I reach out and stop her.

"Please, Mum, I'm okay. Stop fussing."

"I'm sorry, darling. I'm just worried."

"I get that, Mum, but it's over now. I'm home and I have Cal here to look after me."

"Actually, I need to pop to the garage, just to check in. I shouldn't be longer than an hour. Diane, are you okay to stay until I get back?"

"Of course, Cal. I'll look after our girl."

I inwardly groan at the thought of spending another hour with my mum fretting over everything, but I know Cal has been away from the garage for almost five days, so he needs to make sure things are running smoothly in his absence.

He comes over and kisses me gently on the lips before vanishing through the front door. I watch him leave and feel my mum's hand on my arm. When I turn to her, I see concern on her face. "What's the matter, honey? If you wanted him to stay, you should have told him."

"No, it's not that, Mum. It's just... Cal has been great. He's held me when I've cried and listened to me when I've needed to talk."

"But..."

"But what will happen when he finally realises I killed his baby? What will happen when he realises it's all my fault and he goes and finds a girl who can give him a family?" I feel the tears filling my eyes for what must be the hundredth time since Saturday. I'm amazed there are any tears left for me to cry.

"Now you stop thinking like that. You hear me? Caleb loves you and he knows this is in no way your fault."

"Then who's fault is it, Mum?" I almost shout in her face. "I was the one carrying the baby. I was the one eating for two and exercising. Maybe I ate the wrong food or did the wrong exercise. Either way, the baby died whilst inside my body, so I really don't see who else could be to blame. If you know, then please tell me, because this is killing me." I'm sobbing now, but it's more through anger than being upset. This has been coming ever since I woke up in the hospital, so it was only a matter of time before it all came out. I've tried so hard to believe what everyone has been telling me; that I did nothing wrong, that sometimes these things just happen. But no matter how hard I try, I can't convince myself it's the truth.

My mum stays quiet for several minutes, waiting for me to calm down, if I had to guess. When I've stopped shaking and the tears have subsided, she speaks. "I know what you're going through, Cris."

"Sorry, Mum, but you can't possibly know what I'm going through." I push the throw off my legs and stand, walking to the kitchen. When I've poured a glass of water, I down it in three gulps before turning to see my mum standing in the doorway.

"I know exactly what you're going through, honey, because I had a miscarriage too."

All I can do is stand and stare at my mum as she crosses her arms and heads back into the living room. I place my empty glass in the sink and follow her, sitting back in my original position on the sofa next to my mum. I have no idea what to say to her.

"You were sixteen months old when I found out I was pregnant again. Your father and I were over the moon. We always wanted at least two children. I was six weeks or thereabouts when we found out. We both knew of all the so-called bad omens related to pregnancies, so we agreed not to tell anyone until we'd had the twelve week scan. For the next few weeks I was on cloud nine. I couldn't stop smiling, and I'd even started buying little outfits. Every time I went shopping, I'd come back with something new for the baby. It drove your dad mad."

My mum smiled a little at the memory, but that smile soon faded as she looked at me.

"We went for my twelve-week scan full of excitement. We couldn't wait to see that little heartbeat on the screen and to meet our little baby for the first time." She paused again before taking a deep breath. "When the doctor put the scanner on my belly, she looked around for two minutes before we realised something wasn't right. It only took them a few seconds to find you on the scan. She called in another doctor to have a look, but when he couldn't find a heartbeat either, they broke the news that I'd miscarried. They told me that because I was in the early stages, it would just feel like I was having a heavy period, and I might have some discomfort in my belly. We were like zombies when we left the doctors, and it was several days before I started bleeding."

"God, Mum, I'm so sorry. I didn't know."

"No one knew, honey, just me and your dad. We hadn't told anyone about the pregnancy so decided no one needed to know about the miscarriage. The reason I'm telling you this now is because I went through exactly the same as what you're going through. I had all the same thoughts and all the same feelings. I was convinced that, even though we had you, your dad would end up blaming me for the loss of the baby and would leave me for someone else. It took me a while to realise I was being crazy, and it was just one of those things. I did everything right and it still happened. You're not to blame, Crissie. You and Cal love one another and can have more children. Don't let this affect your relationship, honey. You'll both grieve, together and separately, and then you'll go on and have a wonderful wedding and a beautiful family."

I nod at my mum's words and swipe at the tears that were silently slipping down my cheeks as my mum relayed what had to be one of the most painful times in her life.

"Didn't you and Dad want to try again for another baby?"

"We did, more than anything, but I got an infection after the miscarriage that meant I wouldn't be able to conceive naturally. We were devastated at first, but then realised that we had you, and you were already so precious to us, we didn't need another baby to make us a family. We already had the perfect family."

I reach out and take my mum's hands, seeing the tears in her eyes. "I love you, mum."

"Oh, I love you too, baby girl."

I move in and wrap my arms around my mum, and we both just sit there, crying softly for the children we would never see again, but would always love.

∽

Caleb

I lean my head against the front door, fighting the tears as I listen to the conversation Cris is having with her mother. I got back from the garage five minutes ago and was about to open the door when I heard their conversation.

Not wanting to disturb them, I decided to stay outside. I know I should have gone back to the car and waited for them to finish, but something compelled me to stay, and I'm so glad I did.

How could I not know Crissie felt the way she did? Part of me is hurt she ever thought I could blame her for the loss of Aria, but the other part of me understands, in a way.

While I know what her parents went through all those years ago was probably the most painful thing they'd ever been through, I'm glad Diane understands what Cris is feeling and can help her put it into perspective. Leaving Cris isn't something I would ever contemplate, and I can only hope she finally believes that after speaking with her mum.

When everything goes quiet in the flat, I take a breath and push my key in the lock. Turning the lock, I open the door to find both women on the sofa, their hands clasped between them. I can see they've both been crying, but I decide not to mention it. If Cris wants to tell me what they discussed, she will. She doesn't need to know I heard their conversation.

"Hey. How're you feeling?"

"I'm good. Mum and I had a good talk." I watch as Crissie smiles at her mum, who just lifts their hands and kisses her knuckles.

"I should get going and leave you two alone to get some rest."

I watch as Diane stands and grabs her jacket off the back of one of the dining chairs. After she's slipped it on, she comes over and gives me a hug, whispering that I should give Crissie time, and that she loves me. When she pulls back, all I can do is nod at her, while I swallow the lump in my throat.

"I'll see you out, Mum." Cris uncurls her legs from underneath her and follows her mum to the front door. I watch as they hug again before her mum vanishes out of sight and Cris turns back to me. She just stands there, her hands wrapped around herself, and looks at me, as if unsure about what to do or say, so I do the only thing I can think of. I open my arms to her, and she's wrapped in my embrace within seconds.

I close my eyes and just hold her, knowing she needs this as much as I do. We've been through a hell of a lot the last few days, and right now, we just need to know the other is still there, something I feel the need to convey to her in words.

"I love you, Cris. I'm not going anywhere."

She doesn't respond, but I hear her exhale as she fully relaxes against me, her hold around my waist tightening. Without releasing her, I move slowly towards the sofa and sit us down, tucking her against my side. We sit there in silence for what feels like hours, before she lifts her head and looks up at me.

"You heard us talking, didn't you?"

Damn it, I knew I should have just kept my mouth shut.

"I'm sorry, Cris. I know it was a private conversation between you and your mum, but I was right outside the door."

"It's okay. In a way, I'm glad you heard it. It saves me having to say it all again to you."

All I can do is nod at her, understanding what she means. Although, I can't help but wonder whether she would have ever mentioned her doubts if I hadn't heard the conversation. Part of me is struggling to come to terms with the knowledge that she really believed I would blame her for the loss of Aria and eventually leave her because of it. Would one conversation with her mum really change her mind?

"You have to know I would never blame you for any of this, Cris. I have to admit, it hurts to think that after more than four years together, you really believed I would leave you because of what happened. I love you, baby."

Cris puts her hand on my thigh and pushes herself into a sitting position, turning her body so she's facing me directly. "I don't think I ever actually believed it, Cal. I just couldn't understand why this happened when I did everything the doctor told me to do. I mean, how can something like this just happen for no reason? My mum helped me to understand that sometimes these things are outside of our control, and that you blaming me won't happen as I didn't do anything wrong."

I see the tears building in her eyes again, and I reach out to pull her against me. "No, you didn't, Cris. It just wasn't meant to be, this time, but that doesn't mean we won't be able to try again, when you're ready."

I feel the movement of her head as she nods against my chest. The doctors have said it could be a few weeks before we're able to be together again physically. It's going to be a tough time for both of us, especially seeing as just looking at her is usually enough to make me want to drag her off to the bedroom. We're both going to have to restrain ourselves until she gets the all clear from her doctor.

The room is silent, apart from the steady ticking of the wall clock. I trail my fingers along her arm as hers rest lightly on my thigh. Her breathing is even, and I think she's asleep, until I hear the growl of her stomach and the chuckle that passes her lips.

"I think someone is hungry," I state as she sits up next to me.

"Yeah, I could eat," she says as her stomach growls again.

"Shall I cook something, or would you rather have takeout?"

"Takeout. It's been a long day, and I just want to sit here with you and stuff my face with pizza." The laughter I hear from her is a welcome sound after the last few days, and I'd forgotten how much I loved to hear her laugh. "I'll go grab us a drink. You order the food?"

"Yes, ma'am."

She laughs again as I salute her and grab my phone to do as she asked, my eyes never leaving her as she heads into the kitchen, my doubts gone as and I finally believe that we will be alright.

CHAPTER 22

Crissie

*I*t's about bloody time!

Five weeks it's been since Cal and I were last together, and I can't tell you how much I've missed being with him. I mean, we've done other stuff, but we've always had to put on the brakes before things have gone too far. Now, finally, the doctor has given me the green light to be intimate with my fiancé again.

I jump in my Mini and start the ignition, pulling away into traffic as I head into town. I've got tonight all planned out in my head. I'm going to light a few scented candles, cook Cal a nice meal, open a bottle of wine and then seduce the hell out of him. He's not going to know what hit him.

It only takes me ten minutes to get to town, and,

when I've found a parking space and paid for parking for up to six hours, I walk towards the centre, almost squealing like a baby when I see Pippa coming towards me.

I break into a run and we collide, hugging each other and jumping around like idiots. It's been almost two years since I last saw her. As most of us did, we all went away to college. I went off to Birmingham and Pippa went up to Manchester. Tasha and Missy both went down to the south coast and loved it so much they've decided to stay down there.

We talk every now and again, but we aren't as close as we once were. Pippa and I, on the other hand, talked almost every day when we were in college. Like I did, Pip moved back to Chester when she graduated. She's still living with her mum and stepdad but is in a steady relationship with a great guy she met on a night out several months ago.

She's completely smitten and it's nice to see. Pip was always cautious around guys, mainly due to trust issues she developed when her father upped and left when she was just seven years old. Lance has managed to push through those issues, and I'm pleased she finally has someone in her life other than her family and friends. She deserves to be happy.

"It's great to see you, Pip. How's Lance?"

I grin as she blushes at the mere mention of his name. If I had to guess, I'd say she's come here straight from leaving him, if the slightly ruffled hair and swollen lips are anything to go by.

"He's good, great actually. He's asked if it's okay if he meets us for lunch? I said I'd check with you before confirming."

"That's fine with me. It will be nice to see him again."

Pip gives me another quick hug before pulling out her phone and sending her guy a quick text confirming today's lunch date. When he responds with a smiley face and several kisses, she links her arm with mine and we start walking.

"So, what do you want to do today?"

As I explain my plan to her, she smiles, laughs, and nods enthusiastically, indicating she's fully on board with my idea. I'm happy she's not mentioned anything about what Cal and I have been through recently. Pip knows everything about what happened, but she also knows I'm getting pissed with everyone asking me how I am every time they see me.

My friend knows me well, and she won't bring it up unless I do first, which I have no intention of doing. I don't want what happened to put downer on our day. It's been too long since I last saw her, and I just want to enjoy today and have some fun.

We stop in front of a shop Pip has loved since we were teenagers and didn't yet know what was fashionable.

"So, where do you want to go first?"

"Not here, that's for sure," I say with a small laugh

when she pouts. "Come on, Pip, the clothes in this place aren't really what I'm going for, not for tonight."

I see her mulling it over as she turns to look at the shop and then back to me. "You're right, something a little more sophisticated I think."

She links her arm with mine again and we set off down the street. She's a woman on a mission, and I don't know whether I should be pleased or scared.

~

Tucking my shopping bags underneath the table, I slide into the booth as Pippa does the same thing across from me. We've spent a small fortune in the last three hours. If I weren't driving, I'd be having a large glass of wine right about now.

Pippa grabs the menu and gives it a quick once over before passing it across to me. I don't know why she bothers looking; she always has the same thing whenever we come here.

"Cheeseburger and Cajun chips again, Pip?" I ask as she grins at me.

"What? Their burgers are the best in Chester. You should try one. And don't get me started on those chips."

I pull a face at her and look back to the menu, glancing up to see Pip looking at something, or rather someone, over my shoulder. If the look on her face is anything to go by, I know Lance has just arrived. Pip stands up as he gets to our table, and I roll my eyes as she locks lips with him, not caring who sees them.

"Get a room you two." I grin up at them as they part, Pip giving me a beaming smile while Lance looks a little embarrassed. Looking up at him, I can see what initially attracted Pip to him. He has dirty blond, curly hair, which he wears just long enough to still be considered short. He has a square jaw and bright green eyes that light up when he smiles, especially when he smiles at Pip. I'm glad my friend has found someone who clearly adores her, even after only a few months together.

The lovebird's slide into the booth opposite me and within moments, a waitress comes up to our table. Pip and Lance both order a cheeseburger and chips, with a side order of onion rings, and, despite the fact I don't usually eat burgers, I order the same, which earns me a smile from my friend. We also ask for a round of lemonades and the waitress walks away to put our order through the till.

"So, Lance, how's work going?"

"Same as ever. It's just a stop gap until I've finished my degree to be honest."

I nod, knowing what he means, my job as an admin assistant is just temporary, at least that's the plan anyway. I still want to work in criminology and forensics, but if only I'd known how tough it was to get into. I've sent out my CV to various companies, but nothing good has come back yet.

Having said that, staying where I am at the moment

wouldn't be completely terrible. My boss has been great since I lost the baby, telling me to take as much time as I need. I only had two weeks off, as sitting around in the flat was starting to make me go stir crazy.

Going back to work was easier than I thought it would be. Only my boss knew what had happened, something I was grateful for. I didn't think I could stand all the sorrowful looks from people wondering what to say to me.

We all thank the waitress when she returns with our lemonades and informs us our food will be out shortly. The conversation between the three of us is easy and covers a whole host of topics, from mundane subjects like what was on TV to deeper topics such as what we planned to do with our lives.

Pretty soon, it is time to pay the bill as Lance has to get back to work. The soppy goodbye between the two of them makes me want to gag and grin at the same time. Were Cal and I ever like that? Yeah, we probably were. During our first few months together, it was all we could do to keep our hands off each other. We drove our friends mad with all our touchy-feely antics, and I have a feeling Pip is exaggerating her goodbye with Lance purely for my benefit.

When Lance has left, Pip and I grab our bags, and after thanking the waitress with a nice tip, we leave the restaurant and enter the chilly autumn air. Linking arms, we set off down the street, stopping in front of a shop I hadn't planned on visiting today. Pip sees my face and frowns.

"Oh, come on, Cris, you can't get a whole new outfit and not get anything for the bedroom," she says as she waggles her eyebrows at me.

I don't have the heart to tell her I hadn't planned on wearing anything under my outfit tonight, but Pip loves pretty lingerie—hell, she loves all kinds of lingerie. She has a small chest of drawers in her bedroom full of the stuff, in every colour, style and material you can think of. I've a feeling she wants to go into this shop more for her than for me.

"Fine. Let's go see what we can find." Pippa practically squeals as I agree, and she all but drags me into the shop where we are greeted by a perky blonde sales assistant who smiles and offers her assistance if we should need it. Pip tells her to stay close as she leads me through all the 'safe' colours towards the 'sexy' colours.

What makes a colour sexy, I've no idea, but Pippa does, and before I know it, I'm being pushed into a changing room with both arms full of lace and satin in every colour imaginable.

Over and hour later, I'm walking out of the lingerie shop with two new bras and matching knickers, one black and one a deep purple, plus a lacy black bodysuit, which Pip says I have to wear tonight, along with a suspender belt and black seamed stockings.

I've never worn stockings, ever, but Pippa says men

love them and Caleb will be no exception. I'll probably never wear them, not even for Cal, but I guess having them, just in case, can't hurt.

I check my watch, seeing it's almost three p.m. Doing a rough calculation in my head, I have approximately three and a half hours to get home, prepare dinner and get myself ready for when Cal gets back. He promised he wouldn't be late tonight, saying they didn't have much on at the garage at the moment and anything that was left at half five could be done the following day.

"I should be heading back, Pip. Can I give you a lift?"

"No, I'm good, thanks, Cris. I'm going to spend a little bit more money before I head back. Lance will come get me when I'm finished."

I smile as we move in for a hug. I hold my friend tightly, so grateful I have someone like her in my life. I realise that I don't think I've ever told her that. Without releasing her, I speak. "Thanks for everything, Pip. You've been a real strength over the last few weeks. I don't say it enough, but I'm so happy we're friends."

"Don't you dare make me cry, woman," Pippa says with a small laugh. "You know how mushy I can get. Seriously though, I'm always here for you. Anytime."

After holding on for several more moments, we eventually part, and Pip averts her eyes briefly and swipes at her cheeks before turning back and smiling. "You should get home and get ready to wow that man of yours.

What I wouldn't give to be a fly on the wall when he sees you tonight."

"Pervert," I say without any heat, and she just laughs.

"You know what I mean. His jaw is going to drop through the floor when he gets a load of you in that outfit. Maybe you should warn the neighbours."

"That's the idea. It's been way too long, Pip."

"Now who's being the pervert?"

Narrowing my eyes, I flip her the middle finger and we both laugh, hugging one more time before she heads back to the shops and I cross the street, rounding the corner towards the car park.

~

*H*alf an hour later, I'm walking through the front door, dumping my purchases on a nearby chair as I kick the front door shut with my foot. I shrug out of my jacket and hang it up before grabbing two of my bags and moving through to the bedroom. After emptying my purchases onto the bed, I put the stuff away I don't need for tonight, leaving the slinky black dress and lacy bodysuit on the bed.

I head over to the wardrobe, open the doors, and pull out Cal's white linen, button down shirt. It's my favourite of all his shirts, and I always feel proud to be on his arm when he wears it when we go out.

I mean, he looks hot no matter what he wears, but

there's something about him in that white shirt with his dark hair and facial hair that just does it for me every time.

I hang it on the front of the wardrobe and then place his favourite Levi jeans on the bed. I know when he comes back, he'll head straight to the shower, as is his usual routine, and this is what I want him to wear when he comes out.

I close my eyes and imagine him in the outfit and my body instantly warms at the images my mind conjures up. Opening them quickly, I shake my head and move to the kitchen, double-checking I have everything I need to make tonight perfect. The wine is chilling in the fridge and the steaks are marinating on a plate, smelling good enough to eat already.

Going back to the living room, I pick up the third of my bags and remove the three candles I purchased in town, and place one in the middle of the small dining table and the other two on the mantelpiece above the fireplace.

Satisfied I have everything I need, I practically skip through to the bathroom to begin getting ready for tonight. My hair will take at least an hour to get just right and my makeup another half hour. I need to get moving if I'm to be ready in time.

I strip off my clothes and jump under the warm spray of the shower. I make quick work of scrubbing and shaving before bundling myself into my fluffy bathrobe and wrapping a towel around my hair. As I stand in front of the mirror, I sort through my makeup bag and decide on a simple lip with smoky eyes, something I've only recently perfected with the help of Pippa.

After taking out the items I need, I unwrap the towel from my hair and begin the long, drawn out process of getting it perfect for tonight.

CHAPTER 23

Caleb

*W*hat a fucking day.

I've been on my feet since the moment I got up this morning to the moment I sat in my car to come home. When I left the garage last night, we only had two jobs scheduled for today, which we should have been able to handle easily, but then, for some reason, we had a flurry of MOT requests come through, which meant working non-stop all day to get them all done.

If it hadn't been for the fact I promised Cris I'd be home on time tonight, I'd probably still be there now rather than hunting in my pocket for the front door key.

When I find the key, I open the door and step inside, immediately wondering why it's so dark in here and why I can smell vanilla and cherries. Stepping into the living room, my jaw nearly hits the floor when I see Cris waiting for me, wearing the sexiest little black dress I've ever seen.

It's sexy to me in that it doesn't reveal everything. It's tight enough to show off her curves, but not too short or low cut that it flashes everything she has to offer. Her hair is styled in waves round her shoulders, and whatever she's done to her eyes makes them look darker than usual. She looks absolutely stunning, and I realise I've not moved since I set foot in living room.

"Wow, Cris, you look... wow!"

She smiles at my inability to put together a coherent sentence and walks over, quite confidently, in four-inch stiletto heels. She stands in front of me and turns me around. I angle my head, so I can still see her.

"Cal, I love you, but you stink," she says with a small laugh. "Go shower. I've laid out some clothes for you for when you're done." With a gentle push, she shoves me towards the bathroom and vanishes into the kitchen, my eyes on the gentle sway of her hips in that sexy as hell black dress.

"Eyes off the arse, Roberts," I hear her shout from the kitchen, and I grin as I head towards the bathroom, seeing my favourite jeans and Crissie's favourite shirt lying out on our bed.

She's up to something, this much I know, and I can't wait to find out what it is.

~

Crissie

I hear the shower switch off and know Cal will be back out soon. It doesn't take him long to get ready after a shower, so I reach into the fridge and grab the wine. Heading to the table, I pour two glasses before placing the wine in a cooler next to the dining table.

Less than five minutes later, Cal walks into the living room in the outfit I laid out for him, and, as if it were the first time we met, I feel the butterflies take flight in my stomach. The fact he can still elicit this strong a reaction in me after over four years together says so much about our relationship.

After so long, he can still make me feel like that teenage girl I was when we first started dating. To this day, there are still times I can't quite believe he's mine.

Pulling myself together as he walks over, I hand him one of the wine glasses and lean in to place a kiss to his lips. I inhale the scent of him, a mixture of body wash and aftershave, a combination I will forever associate with him. It's a heady mix, and I feel my head spin before I've even touched the wine.

Moving back, I take a sip of my wine, the cool liquid a refreshing contrast to my heated skin.

"Take a seat, handsome, dinner will be ready soon." I place my glass on the dining table and he does the same, before grabbing me round the waist and pulling me against him. My hands automatically go up to rest on his biceps, ignoring the immediate thought that he's been working out.

"I don't know what all of this is for, but I want you to know that you look stunning, and I can't wait to eat whatever it is you've prepared. It smells delicious." He kisses me on the tip of my nose before turning me towards the kitchen and swatting my arse. "Now go get me food, woman."

I glare at him over my shoulder and am met with his signature grin, the one that makes me forgive him anything. Smiling as I shake my head and he sits, I flick on the hob and drizzle some oil into a griddle pan. When it starts to sizzle, I place the marinated steaks into the pan and scatter some mushrooms and asparagus around the sides, knowing they don't take long to cook.

After a few minutes, I turn the steaks and gently shake the pan to stop the vegetables from sticking before taking the new potatoes off the hob, draining them, and adding six small potatoes to each plate. When the steaks are cooked, I take them off the heat and let them rest for a couple of minutes whilst the asparagus and mushrooms finish off.

When everything is done, I pick up the plates and take them in to the living room, receiving a huge smile from Cal as I place his meal in front of him.

"Tonight, sir will be eating a medium-rare, peppered sirloin steak with mushrooms, new potatoes and asparagus."

"This looks wonderful, Cris," he says as I put my own plate down and sit opposite him. "You didn't need to do all this."

"I know," I say with a smile. "I wanted to."

We eat in silence for the next ten minutes, each of us making sly glances at the other while we enjoy our food. I must admit, I've surpassed myself with this meal. While it's a simple dish, I have a habit of either burning something or undercooking it, no matter how easy it should be to cook. Hell, I could screw up boiling an egg, I'm that bad.

Cal finishes first and sits back in his chair, picking up his wine and taking a few gulps before I finish my food few moments later. Both plates are now clean and the glasses almost empty as I reach out to take the wine bottle and refill our glasses.

"That was wonderful, Cris. What's for dessert?"

Smiling at him, I put the wine bottle back in the cooler and stand, steadying myself in the heels I'm beginning to regret buying. They look sexy but kill the feet. Oh, the things women do to look good.

"Dessert?" I ask as I reach behind me and start to pull down the zip on my dress, seeing Cal's eyes widen. "How about me?"

Releasing the zip, I push the dress off both shoulders and it falls to my waist. With a little shimmy of my hips, the dress slithers to the floor with a hiss, and I kick it away, revealing my lace clad body to the man I love.

His eyes are like saucers now, and his reaction to me is clear as I glance at the crotch of his jeans. Cal's breathing is laboured as he stares at me, his expression a mixture of lust and confusion.

I take a few steps closer to him and position myself so I can straddle his lap easily, linking my hands behind his neck. My fingers playing with the hair at the nape, causing his eyes to close briefly as I feel him twitch beneath my thighs. Leaning forward, I kiss his neck gently, eliciting a groan from his lips before I whisper in his ear, "We're good to go, Cal, and I want you so badly right now."

Leaning back, I look at his face to see the confusion has gone. All I see now is lust and desire; it's a powerful combination as I rock my hips, feeling him harden behind the confines of the denim.

"Fuck," I hear him mutter as his arms band around my back and he crushes me to him, his lips coming down on mine almost painfully as he plunders my mouth.

I have to wrap my legs around him as he stands and moves, but we don't go far. I feel the soft cushions of the sofa against my legs as I unwrap them from his waist and settle myself over him.

God, I've missed this; missed him. I can't get close enough as I shift forward, the friction from his jeans rubbing me in just the right spot as I rock my hips against him. He tugs at my bottom lip with his teeth as I reach down and flick open the button on his jeans. I have to move back slightly so I can lower the zipper, but as soon as I have, I take him in my hand, and find him hard as iron.

I don't wait—I can't wait—and I pull open the fastening on my bodysuit and sink down onto him. It's been so long since I felt him inside me that I close my eyes, savouring the feeling as he stretches me, filling me completely.

The rumble I feel in chest tells me he feels the same as I do as he lifts my head and kisses me again, just as hard and full of passion as before. I haven't moved yet; I'm just savouring the feel of him inside me again. His hands are working their magic on my breasts through the lace of the bodysuit.

The roughness of the lace against my already sensitive nipples and the sensations created by his kisses is almost too much for me, and I feel the familiar warmth in the pit of my stomach.

Before I know what's happened, Cal has shifted so he's on his back and I'm sitting astride him. He grabs my waist and lifts me, before he begins pumping his hips upwards, pounding into me. All I can do is throw my head back and hold on to the back of the sofa as the takes me hard, just the way he knows I love it.

"Oh, Cal, yes. I'm so close."

I hear a string of expletives cross his lips as he flips us so I'm now on my back. He leans forward, pressing my knees into the cushions. I'm completely open to him now, and when our eyes lock, he picks up the pace. It takes everything in me not to close my eyes again. I want to see him. I need this connection when we come. I can tell he's close, as his breathing turns ragged, and when he begins circling my clit with is thumb, I scream as I come apart beneath him.

He follows me over the cliff several moments later before collapsing on top of me, his weight pressing me into the cushions. I relish his weight on me as I gently stroke up and down his back, giggling when I realise he's practically fully dressed. He looks up curiously and grins when he realises why I'm giggling.

"How was dessert?" I ask as I pull his head down and kiss him.

"Dessert? That was just the starter."

Cal eases out of me and stands up. Holding out a hand, I accept it and squeal when he pulls me up and throws me over his shoulder as he strides towards the bedroom, my laughter filling the air.

CHAPTER 24

Crissie

<u>Present Day</u>

*O*ur sex life had always been creative, and sometimes explosive, but nothing could beat that night. We hadn't been together in almost six weeks, so that night was definitely making up for lost time. I lost count at the number or orgasms I had when I reached five.

Cal had made it his mission to make me come as many times as he possibly could that night. We tried so many new positions that the following morning, muscles ached that I didn't even know I had.

I have to admit, whenever I think back on that time in our life together, I realise that was a time that could have broken us, and I almost let it. It was speaking with my mum, and Caleb's encouragement and sweet words that made me realise I wasn't to blame for the loss of baby Aria. It just wasn't meant to be at that time in our lives.

After the miscarriage, we both decided that while we both still wanted children, we were too young to try right away, so I went back onto the pill. We both hated condoms, so it was an easy decision to make.

Our sex life got back on track pretty quickly after I was given the all clear from the doctor, and I would be forever grateful to Pippa for making me buy all that lingerie on our shopping trip. She'd been right when she said guys loved stockings and suspenders, something I found out two months later when Cal accompanied me to my work's Christmas party.

Even though I worked for a relatively small company, with only fifty staff in total, they always went all out for Christmas. That year, it was a masquerade ball, giving Pippa and I another excuse to go shopping. I had nothing formal enough for such an occasion, and while it wasn't black tie, Cal insisted on wearing a tux.

I'll never forget how my heart almost stopped beating when I saw him in it for the first time. The man could rock a suit like no one I know, so seeing him in a tux almost made me come on the spot.

He looked so damn handsome I couldn't stop staring at him, and that went for all the women I work with too. Even those who had husbands and partners with them stopped and stared as he walked past. I had never felt so happy and proud to say he was my man.

Oh yeah, I forgot, back to the stockings and suspenders. Cal really liked them, loved them actually, something he didn't want to wait until we got home to show me.

CHAPTER 25

Crissie

18th December 2010

Eight. Nine. Ten. Eleven.

I grin to myself as I take a mental count of how any women are staring at Cal as we enter the room reserved for my work's Christmas party, although, I can't say I blame them. My man looks hot with a capital 'H' tonight, and what's the best thing about it? He is completely oblivious to the attention he's receiving from my female colleagues.

The funny thing is, they've all seen him before, in pictures at least, so they know what he looks like. Then again, I see in him the flesh every day, and the sight of him in a tux almost knocked me for six too, so I can understand their reaction to him.

While he wasn't the only guy here wearing the formal outfit, he was by far the best looking. With his dark hair, trimmed beard and dark eyes, the only thing I can say is 'move over Pierce Brosnan, there's a new Bond in town'.

Cal accepts two glasses of champagne from one of the waiters walking around with drinks and offers one to me, noticing, for the first time, that people, male and female alike, are watching us.

"I think that dress is drawing some attention, Cris."

I'm so surprised by his words that I almost choke on my champagne. Seriously, he thinks it's the dress creating the attention?

"Really? You think it's me?"

"Well who else could it be?" Cal says as he takes a sip of the fizzy drink.

"Have you seen you?" I say, keeping my voice quiet. "You look like you just stepped off the cover of GQ magazine in that tux. Every woman in the room has had their eyes on you since we walked in."

Cal looks at me and then glances around the room, seeing dozens of female eyes look away as he does, and for the first time since we got together, he actually blushes. Reaching up, he tugs on the collar of his shirt and clears his throat.

"Well, don't I feel a little self-conscious," he says as he turns back to me.

"Just be your usual charming self and you'll be fine. I know one thing though: I'm going to be the envy of every woman in the office when I go back to work on Monday." I see Cal roll his eyes at my comment when I feel a hand on my shoulder. Turning, I see Amanda, my boss, smiling at me. Her sleek blond hair is fixed in an intricate up do. Her blue eyes are showcased by a dark grey shadow with sparkly silver lashes, and her lips are painted ruby red to match the floor-length dress she's wearing.

"Amanda, you look great. This place looks amazing."

"Crissie, thank you so much. I'm so glad you could make it," she says as she gives me a quick hug before turning to Cal. "And you must be Caleb. Crissie has told me all about you."

I watch Caleb as he extends his hand to my boss, who accepts it in a quick shake. I was half expecting her to pull him in for a hug. I know Amanda is single and, whilst I don't think she would try anything with Cal, I know she has a weakness for guys who look after themselves. Even though Cal is fully clothed, anyone can see he's a guy who works out.

In fact, I didn't realise how much he works out now until a few weeks ago. He'd pulled me in for a hug, like he does every so often, and my hands were on his biceps, and I remember thinking, like I have done so many times but never mentioned, how there was more definition there.

When I asked him about it, he confessed that throughout the time we'd been unable to have sex, he'd visited a local gym on his lunch break to help him burn off the excess energy. When I told him I approved, he'd started going more frequently, and I was definitely the one benefiting from it.

There's something to be said for having a strong man in the bedroom. Not that we had a problem in that area before, but with Cal bulking up like he had, any issues we may have had were completely banished. The man could fling me around like a rag doll, not that I ever complained.

Complaining was always the farthest thing from my mind when he picked me up, pinned me against the wall and pounded into me until I came apart in his arms. Coming back to reality, I see that Amanda had moved on and Cal has a smirk on his face as he looks at me.

"What's that smirk for?" I ask him.

"I know where your mind was just then," he says as he takes a step closer. "You were pulling your 'I want sex' face."

"I do not have a face like that," I exclaim, pretending to be offended.

"Oh, baby, you do, and it's so fucking hot." He moves closer to me and pulls me to him, so close I can feel he's getting hard behind his tailored tuxedo trousers. My eyes widen as I look up at him, my body beginning to react as he strokes his fingers across the bare skin at the small of my back.

"This dress was a great choice," he says, before leaning down to whisper in my ear, "Easy access to what's mine is always a good thing." His fingers dip below the material of my dress, and I hear him suck in a breath, knowing the reason why. "Fuck, Cris, you're not wearing knickers?"

I chew on my bottom lip and give him a slight shake of my head. I'm not sure why I chose to forgo my knickers tonight. I had no choice but to lose the bra, what with the glittery silver dress being practically backless, but the knickers had been an afterthought. We'd practically been out the door when I decided to remove them, and judging by Cal's reaction, he approved.

Because of the way we are standing, no one can see that Cal's hand is now caressing my bare backside, or that his trousers are now a bit snug in the crotch area. Quickly, Cal removes his hand and grabs mine, and we weave our way through the growing crowd.

I wave at a few people as I hurry behind Cal, which is no mean feat in my four-inch heels. We leave the hall hosting the party and head down a hallway. We stop every now and then as Cal tries a few doors, each one locked. I smile when I realise what he's doing, my smile only widening when I remember what I'm wearing under the dress.

After a few more tries, one of the doors swings open. Without preamble, Cal pulls me inside and closes the door, before he pushes me against it and starts kissing me hard on the mouth. I match his urgency as he fists his one hand in my hair, tugging my head back as he drags his mouth down my throat, nipping and licking as he goes.

With his other hand, he tugs the neckline of my dress down, pushing my breasts up to his eager mouth. I let out a whimper as he latches on to my nipple and bites gently before swirling his tongue around the tip. When he bites again, the stab of pain shoots straight to my clit, and I feel it begin to throb, needing his attention.

Cal slides his hand down my body and hooks it under my knee, lifting my leg up to his side. He strokes my thigh, stopping suddenly as he releases my breast and looks down, pushing the skirt of my dress up past my hips.

"Fuck, that's hot."

I know Cal is referring to the stockings and suspender belt I'm wearing, and a wave of female pride washes over me as I look down at him. He drops my dress and pulls me over to a nearby table. He spins me around and pushes me forward, so my hands are flat on the wooden surface.

Glancing over my shoulder, I see him throw my dress up, so my arse is revealed to him, and he gently strokes it before giving it a gentle slap. Okay, that was strange. He's never done that before, and I actually liked it. I hear the buckle of his belt, followed by the zipper on his trousers, and within seconds, he is pushing inside me.

We both groan at the sensation as he fills me before withdrawing slowly. When he slams back, I fall forward onto the table, my chest pressed into the wood, my head facing the door as he continues to hammer into me. His fingers dig into my hips as he pulls me back onto him, going deeper with every thrust. Anyone could walk in on us right now, and that thought alone is enough to work my body up, and I feel my muscles begin to tighten.

"You're so hot, Cris. I fucking love being inside you." His thrusts pick up pace, and soon enough we're both panting and groaning every time he slams into me, and it's not long before we're both crying out as we come together.

"Holy shit." I sigh as Cal slips out of me, using a few of the tissues off the desk to clean me up before he straightens my dress and helps me stand. "Where the hell did that come from?" I say as I fix my hair, hoping I don't have the so-called just fucked look.

After Cal cleans up and tucks himself away, he grins at me. "You're wearing no knickers with stockings and suspenders. You're lucky I didn't take you as soon as I realised about the knickers."

The look he gives me is full of heat, and if I weren't already flushed, the colour would be filling my cheeks at his words. I check my dress, making sure I'm not flashing anything before Cal takes my hand and kisses me gently on the lips.

"We should head back before people realise we're missing."

"I think that ship sailed as soon as you walked out the room." When Cal shoots me a look, I continue, "Everyone woman would have seen when you left the room, and those who didn't would have realised you'd gone within seconds."

Cal opens the door and peers into the hallway, making

sure it's clear before leading me out and back towards the party.

"You know, the same could be said for you. There wasn't a man in that room who didn't fantasise about seeing what you look like out of that dress."

"Well, they can fantasise all they like, only you get to see what's underneath," I say as we round the corner.

"I should damn well think so," Cal says with a grin as he kisses my nose before we head back in to the party.

CHAPTER 26

Crissie

<u>April 2011</u>

I think that's everything.

Standing with my hands on my hips, I stare at everything I've got laid out on the bed. Tomorrow is Cal's twenty-third birthday, and, as a surprise, I'm taking him for a short break in Spain. It took me forever to decide what to get him, and it was actually Lizzie's suggestion to go away for a few days.

She was able to get his passport for me, which only had twelve months left on it, so I lucked out there. I had spoken with his boss, who assured me his son would be able to manage for the few days Cal would be away, and

Amanda was more than happy to let me have a few days off.

When I had all the information, I managed to book flights leaving from Manchester airport tomorrow morning, returning to the UK the following Tuesday. We would be staying in a lovely four-star hotel situated right on the beach. We'd have four days and nights of sun, sea and sand with no work and no interruptions.

It was going to be heavenly.

When I was sure I had everything, I grabbed my suitcase from on top of the wardrobe and started packing everything we needed for our weekend away.

After being together for almost five years, this would be our first overseas holiday together. We'd been away in the UK a few times, staying in caravans or chalets, usually on the south coast, but neither of us had ever thought about going abroad. When Lizzie made the suggestion, I decided to run with the idea.

I can't wait to see Cal's reaction when I tell him what the plans are for the weekend. He thinks we're just going out for a meal on Saturday, the day of his birthday, which technically is correct. I just haven't told him the meal will be in Spain.

My dad has agreed to take us to the airport in the morning and will be picking us up at four-thirty a.m. He has told me it shouldn't take any longer than forty-five minutes to get to the airport at that time of day and seeing as our flight is at seven-thirty a.m., it gives us plenty of time to get checked in and browse through the duty free before boarding the plane.

When I've put the last of the items in the case, I zip it up and secure it with a padlock before sliding it underneath the bed. I don't want Cal to see it until I have told him where we are going.

Checking the time, I see it's almost six. Cal will be home any minute. Hurrying through to the living room, I flop down onto the sofa and use the remote to turn on the TV. By the time Cal walks through the door five minutes later, I'm watching a repeat of The Simpsons.

"Hey, baby. How's your day been?"

"Same as usual. When you've seen one engine, you've seen them all. How about yours? Did you manage to get rid of your headache?"

In order to get out of going to work today, I told Cal I wasn't feeling well this morning. Truth was, Amanda had let me take today off so I could get everything sorted for our trip, but Cal didn't have to know that. Not yet anyway.

"Yeah, I feel loads better now. Sleep and a dark room helped."

"That's good to hear, Cris. I'm going to go jump in the shower. Can you order our usual Chinese? I shouldn't be too long."

I nod and smile at him as he heads into the bedroom, hoping he doesn't notice the missing suitcase from on top of the wardrobe. I hold my breath until I hear the shower turn on, then release it. Safe. For now, anyway.

Getting up from the sofa, I grab the Chinese takeaway menu from the drawer in the TV unit and call them, placing our usual order of chicken curry, beef with black bean sauce, two portions of egg fried rice and a portion of chips. The lady tells me it should be with us within half an hour, and I thank her before ending the call.

I head into the kitchen and open the fridge, hearing the shower turn off as I grab a beer for Cal and pour a glass of wine for me. As I walk back through to the living room, Cal enters, and I stop in my tracks. I try my hardest not to stare at him but fail miserably.

His hair is damp and dishevelled from the towel he usually rubs through it. His chest is bare and he's barefoot in just a pair of jogging bottoms that sit low on his hips. How he makes a simple pair of bottoms look so sexy, I have no idea, but seeing him like this, especially since he has been going to the gym more often, has done wonders for my libido. Not that I had any issues before, but now, seeing the changes to his body, it makes my blood sing as it rushes through my veins.

Averting my eyes when I glance up and see his knowing smirk, I hand him his beer as we sit on the sofa.

"I've been thinking about getting a tattoo."

I put my wine down and turn to him, surprise evident on my face. "Where's that come from? You've never mentioned getting one before."

"You don't like the idea?"

"No. I mean, yes, I do. I think a tattoo on you would be sexy as hell. I just wondered where the idea came from?"

"Nowhere in particular. One of the guys at the gym was showing off his new one the other day and it got me thinking. I think I could pull off a tat, don't you think?"

I smile and burst out laughing when he begins flexing his biceps, pulling all sorts of poses from his place on the sofa, stopping when the doorbell chimes. Cal jumps up from the sofa and heads to the door, opening it quickly. I'm unable to stifle my giggles at the face of the delivery girl when met with a shirtless Cal.

He'd never carried much weight before the gym, but now that he goes at least three times a week, the definition in his chest and the six pack that is now his mission to maintain are all on show, and the poor girl doesn't know where to look.

"Umm, hi, here's your food. That'll be £16.25 please."

Cal accepts the bag containing our food, then realises he has no money on him as he turns to me. I grab the money from my purse and walk over. He's still standing there in all his bare-chested glory as the delivery girl tries her hardest not to stare at him. I almost feel sorry for her.

"Go sort the food out and leave the poor girl alone." Cal looks at me, confused by my statement before turning towards the kitchen. I hand over a twenty to the girl and shake my head. "Sorry about him. He has no idea of the effect he can have on women."

The girl smiles and hands me my change.

"How do you get anything done with him walking around like that?" she asks curiously as I glance over at him getting the food ready, the muscles in his back twisting and stretching as he moves.

"It's a hardship I have to bear, so others don't have to." Turning back to the girl, we both burst out laughing just as Cal walks through to the living room and deposits the food, plates and cutlery on the table. The girl wishes us a good evening before I close the door and join Cal at the table.

"What was all that about?" he asks as he empties one of the rice containers onto his plate and takes a few handfuls of chips.

"Oh, just girl talk. Nothing for you to worry about."

"If you say so." Cal spoons his beef over the rice and chips, leaving me the other portion of rice, the remainder of the chips and my favourite: Chinese chicken curry. We take our loaded plates back over to the sofa and settle in for the evening.

Twenty minutes later, my stomach feels like its full ten times over and I'm struggling to move as I sit forward, stand, and take my plate into the kitchen. Cal follows a few minutes later, his plate now clear. He grabs another beer from the fridge and leans against the counter as I fill the sink, so I can get the washing up done and out of the way.

"So, this tattoo? What were you thinking of getting, and where?"

"I've not decided on the 'what' yet, but I was thinking

about across my left shoulder and down my arm to my elbow." He shows me with his other hand where he imagines the tattoo will go, and I decide that I one hundred percent approve. I love his biceps, so they will only look even better when they're inked. I nod my approval as I continue washing the plates and cutlery from our dinner.

I haven't told him about our weekend away yet, and I know I need to soon as we will need to be up early tomorrow to make sure we're ready for when my dad comes to pick us up. When the washing up is done, I dry my hands on a nearby towel and go back to the living room, followed by Cal.

"So, it's almost your birthday. What would you like to do?" I ask him, trying to sound as casual as I can.

"I've not thought about it really. It's not like it's a big birthday or anything. To be honest, I'd be happy with just spending a weekend with my best girl and having a meal out on the Saturday night."

I smile at him as he takes my hand in his and kisses my knuckles. I lift my legs and tuck them under me as I turn to face him. "Well, what if I were to tell you that tomorrow morning, my dad is coming round to take us to the airport so we can fly over to Spain for a few days to celebrate your birthday?"

Cal looks at me, trying to figure out if I'm being serious, before he shakes his head. "That sounds great, Cris, but I have work to get done and—"

"Work is all sorted, Cal. You don't need to worry about that. We fly out from Manchester tomorrow and come back on Tuesday."

"You're serious?"

I nod, hoping he's happy about this because, right now, his facial expression isn't telling me one way or the other. The silence is almost deafening as we sit there, and I wish he would say something. This was not the reaction I was expecting. I continue to watch him when his mouth makes an, 'O' shape, as if a light bulb has just gone on in his brain, and he smiles. "So that's why the suitcase was missing. I wondered what had happened to it."

He turns to me, his face now beaming, and I release the breath I didn't know I'd been holding.

"So, you're happy with this?" I ask him, still a little unsure.

"Happy? Why wouldn't I be happy? I get to spend four days with a beautiful woman lounging around a pool in nothing more than a bikini, sipping cocktails. What's not to be happy about?" He leans in and kisses me before pulling back, a serious expression on his face. "Although, I am going to have to check what you've packed, because if there's anything in there for you, other than bikini's, especially that sexy green one, it's got to go."

When he waggles his eyebrows at me, and his eyes grow dark, I know we won't be getting much sleep tonight and tomorrow is going to be a long day.

CHAPTER 27

Crissie

*T*his is the life.

I could seriously get used to this. Lying here, in the sun, cocktail in hand and my man lounging next to me. This is something we should have done a long time ago.

After a chaotic journey to the airport yesterday, we just about made our flight with minutes to spare. Sometimes, even the best planner can't account for someone deciding to cause trouble by driving the wrong way on the motorway.

Two lanes were closed, so it was single file traffic for a good two miles, which meant we only just made check-in before it closed and then had to go straight to the gate.

Thankfully, the flight was delayed by ten minutes, or

they wouldn't have let us board. The flight itself was uneventful, as was getting through customs in Alicante. Surprisingly, our luggage was amongst the first ones to come along the conveyor, which never happens to me, so we grabbed them and headed straight to the coach that would take us to our hotel.

As an extra bonus, when the hotel staff realised it was Cal's birthday the next day, being today, they had upgraded our standard double room to a suite, meaning we now have a corner suite with an extended balcony, a free mini bar and spectacular views over the pools and beach.

Within ten minutes of us getting to our room, the management had sent up a bottle of champagne, two glasses and a basket of fruit. So far, this break was turning out to be the best we had ever had.

"Señor, señorita. Would you like another drink?"

I look up at the waiter, who's smiling down at me, and across to Cal, who's giving him a look that could kill. I grin before requesting another Cosmopolitan for myself and a beer for Cal. The waiter nods and walks off to take other orders. I sit up and lean on my elbows as I look at Cal again, whose eyes are still fixed on the back of the waiter.

"Cal, you can't glare at every guy who looks at me," I say with a small laugh. "Besides, you're getting way more attention than I am."

I lie back down on my lounger and shake my head when he looks as oblivious as ever. Part of me likes this possessive side of him, but the other part is getting a bit pissed at the constant looks he's giving every guy who even dares a glance in my direction.

What I said was true. I'm practically covered in my one piece, yellow, zip front swimsuit. Cal, on the other hand, is just wearing a pair of short swim shorts. When you add in the tan he's already begun to develop, the slicked back wet hair from the pool, and the six pack abs he's flashing, I'm surprised more women haven't passed out, and it wouldn't be because of the heat.

The waiter returns after a few minutes with our drinks, and I thank him as he places them on the small table between us.

"Gracias," I say with a smile.

"De nada, señorita." He flashes me a wide smile, highlighting perfectly straight, white teeth as he walks off to deliver more drinks. I don't look at Cal, knowing what I'm going to see. After another few minutes, I'm surprised when Cal swings his legs round onto the floor, downs his drink in a couple of gulps, and starts putting our stuff in my beach bag.

"What are you doing?" I say as he slips his feet into his flip-flops and stands with my bag in his hands. "Seriously? You're that pissed that guys are looking at me that you want to go back to the room?" I hiss at him.

Cal removes his sunglasses, and I see his eyes are dark, but not because he's pissed. Shit, he's turned on.

"I wouldn't call this pissed," Cal says as he shifts

position and removes the bag from in front of him. I glance down his body, seeing the erection starting to tent his swim shorts. "Unless I do something about this damn quick, it's going to be embarrassing for both of us."

Downing my cocktail, I grab my book and put on my flip-flops. Once I've slipped on my cover-up, I accept Cal's outstretched hand. He's definitely a man on a mission as he all but drags me across the pool area and into the hotel. We whizz past people in the lobby and over to the lifts. He punches the call button several times before the door slides open and we enter.

Before an older couple behind us enters, Cal stabs at the close button and the doors slide shut. Then our stuff is all over the floor and I'm being pressed against the mirrored wall, his mouth on me.

"Fuck, Cris, I need you. Right now."

Alarm bells are ringing in my head as I know the lift could stop at anytime for someone else to get in, but all negative thoughts escape as he drags down the zipper on my swimsuit and takes my nipple in his teeth. He bites down hard and a sharp stab of pleasure goes straight to my clit as I cry out, my hands raking through his hair as I fight to stay upright.

I feel him tug my swimsuit to the side as he fumbles with his shorts, and then he thrusts upward into me. I almost scream at the intrusion, my fingernails digging into his shoulders.

"This is going to be quick, Cris, and it's going to be

hard. I can't hold back." He doesn't give me any chance to answer. Instead, he begins thrusting into me, hard and fast. His grunts and my quick breaths are the only things that fill the silence as my body begins to tighten after only a minute.

Cal lifts my legs and wraps them round him, altering the position so he can slide even deeper into me. My head falls back against the wall, and I see our reflection in the mirrors. Cal's eyes are shut tightly, the muscles of his arms and legs bunching with the exertion each time he pummels into me.

All I can do is hold onto him as he continues, and, only moments later, when he leans in and bites my nipple again, do I scream out his name as my body convulses around him. After two more strokes, Cal empties himself into me, my name on his lips as his body shakes.

I hold on tight until he lifts his head and smiles, and it's only then I realise the lift has reached our floor and hasn't moved. I look around, then at Cal, before I burst out laughing. Our bodies are still connected, and I feel him twitch inside me as he begins to grow hard again. My eyes widen when I realise, and he just grins.

"As hot as that was, I don't want to push my luck," he says as he slips out of me and tucks himself back in his shorts. I zip up my swimsuit, my nipples still sensitive as they rub against the fabric.

Cal pushes a button and the door opens. Once we've gathered our stuff that's now scattered all over the floor, we leave the lift and make our way to our room. I've a feeling we won't be leaving the room again until dinner tonight.

No complaints here.

～

I lean my head against the window as we begin our descent into Manchester airport. It's been a wonderful few days, especially after Cal fucked his jealousy and possessiveness out of his system. That is one day I shall never forget, and a memorable birthday for Cal. It was as if other men looking at me made him want to stake a claim on me, and by taking me in the way he had, he was branding me. Not that I was complaining.

That was some of the hottest sex we've ever had, including the last night where we threw caution to the wind and made use of the table and chairs on the balcony, not caring if anyone saw, or heard, us.

"Back to reality, eh?"

I turn my head to see Cal looking at me. He looks as depressed as I feel.

"Yeah. Do we have to go back to work tomorrow?" I say with a pout as Cal gets rid of our empties as the flight attendant walks down the aisle with a rubbish bag.

I hate this part of a holiday. Gone is all the excitement of going away and it's replaced with disappointment at having to come back to the real world and carry on with life.

"You know," Cal says quietly, "There is one more thing we can do to make this holiday memorable."

I don't need to ask him what he's referring to when he glances over his shoulder towards the back of the plane. My heart rate kicks up a notch or two as I imagine what it would be like to join the mile-high club, and I have to admit, it's a very appealing thought.

Just as I'm about the give him the green light, the seatbelt sign lights up, and at Cal's audible groan, I let out a giggle.

"Oh well, maybe next time," I say as I fasten my seatbelt and squeeze his thigh as we descend into a cold and wet Manchester.

~

Caleb

By the time we clear customs, get our baggage, and make it home, it's almost two in the morning. I'm running on empty, and all I want to do is dump our stuff and crawl into bed. Cris is the same, if not worse than me. She dozed off in the car on the way back from the airport, and she's walked up here on autopilot.

Leaving our case in the living room, I take her hand and lead her towards the bedroom. After I've pulled back the covers, I sit her down, take off her shoes and tug off her jeans. Deciding to leave her in the vest top she's wearing, I gently push her back into the pillows. When her eyes flutter closed, she sighs and tucks her legs in. I cover her with the duvet and she's fast asleep within seconds.

After kicking off my shoes, I strip off my t-shirt and go back through to check the front door is locked. Bending, I grab the few envelopes on the floor from the post that was delivered while we've been away. I flick through them as I walk over to the coffee table to leave them there until the next morning, when the return address on one envelope catches my eye.

Canada? Who is writing to Crissie from Canada?

I glance back towards the bedroom, seeing Cris is still fast asleep. I put the other letters on the table and look again at the letter in my hand. She's never mentioned Canada to me, other than to say it would be her dream holiday spot. After taking a breath, I drop the letter onto the pile and head back towards the bedroom. I'm sure Crissie will tell me about it tomorrow.

As I unbuckle my belt and unfasten my jeans, I push them down my legs, keeping my eyes on Crissie's sleeping form in our bed. It can't be anything major or she would have told me about it before now. Kicking my jeans to the side, I pull back the duvet and climb into bed. As if by instinct, Crissie turns over and snuggles into my side, a position she always adopts when we first get into bed.

Closing my eyes, I will myself to sleep without thoughts of Canada running through my head.

~

*S*he opened the letter over breakfast, her expression revealing nothing to me as she read it before folding it up and putting it in her handbag. She hasn't mentioned it to me or said anything about what it might have contained.

I've not been able to concentrate all day. I might as well have just stayed in bed for all the work I got done. I know it's probably something really stupid and unimportant and I'm stressing over nothing, but somehow, I don't think that's the case.

My instincts have always been something I rely on, and in this case, my instincts are telling me Cris is hiding something from me. I think back to the time when she hid the fact she'd been offered a place at a college in Birmingham. She didn't tell me about that until her mum accidentally mentioned it, believing I already knew. If Diane hadn't said anything, I've a feeling Cris would have never gone to college and I'd have still been in the dark to this day.

I don't think she would have ever told me about the college offer if she hadn't been forced to. Could this be something similar? I can't leave it up to her to tell me. I need to ask her about it and gauge her response. If it's one thing I'm good at, it's telling when Cris is lying. After almost five years together, there isn't much I don't know about her.

For the first time in, well, ever, I'm home from work before Crissie. The garage had run so smoothly in my absence that we only had three jobs to do, and we'd done them by three p.m., so with no new jobs due in until tomorrow, I'd decided to shut up shop early.

Now, I am trying my hardest not to pace the floor as I wait for Cris to come home. I've no idea how I'm going to ask her about the letter. Shall I just come out and ask her about it? I'm still debating it when I hear the front door open and she walks in, a smile on her face when she sees me.

"Hey, you're home early. How's your day been?" she asks me as she crosses the room and kisses me on the cheek before stripping off her coat and hanging it up.

"Quite quiet really. The guys did a great job while we were away. How about yours?"

"Emails followed by more emails and then, just for something different, a few more emails."

I force a smile, hoping she believes it, but I can tell instantly that she doesn't when her expression changes. "Hey, you okay?"

"Not really. There's something I need to ask you, Cris."

"Okay. Sounds serious."

"I hope it's not and it's just me being paranoid." I take a breath and look at her as she stands in front of me. "When

I picked up the post yesterday, I noticed you had a letter from Canada. You opened it this morning and put it straight in your bag, not on the letter rack or in the recycle bin like you usually do." I pause for a moment as Crissie just looks at me, her expression not changing, but her eyes do widen slightly. "I'm probably being silly, but I was just wondering why you did that?"

Crissie stays silent for several moments before she goes to her bag and takes out the letter, bringing it over and placing it on the counter between us. "I was going to speak with you about it over dinner tonight. Before you read it, I need you to know that I ordered this before we lost her. It wasn't cheap, probably more than we can afford, but I figured she was worth it. I didn't want to cause you any more pain by showing it to you, so I was just going to send them an email from work today to cancel and then get rid of the letter. Work was so busy that I didn't get chance to contact them."

I hear Crissie's voice break as tears fill her eyes, and I begin to feel like a bastard for making her feel that way, and I've not even read the letter. Reaching out, I pick it up and scan the contents, now understanding why Cris has reacted the way she has. I feel my eyes fill with tears, and I don't try and stop them when a couple slip down my cheeks.

Crissie had seen a crib online from a manufacturer in Canada and had ordered it two weeks before we lost Aria. The letter was an apology saying that, due to popular demand, they had yet to ship the item and they were offering us a discount because of the delay.

Dropping the letter on the counter, I brace my arms on the edge and let my head drop forward. I don't realise the tears are coming thick and fast until I feel Cris squeeze in between me and the counter and wrap her arms around me, holding me tightly as I bury my face in her hair.

There hasn't been a day since we lost her that I haven't thought about Aria, but this is the first time in several months that I've cried like this, and the first time ever that I've cried in front of Cris.

I release the counter and wind my arms around her back, pulling her close as we both cry for our lost daughter.

CHAPTER 28

Crissie

Present Time

*A*fter I received that letter, Cal and I realised that even though we'd both been through the loss of losing Aria, we hadn't actually talked about it, not together anyway. I'd spoken with my mum several times and had tried to speak with Cal, but he repeatedly told me he was okay.

In hindsight, I should have known he was putting on a brave face; not wanting to discuss it because it hurt too much, or he didn't want to upset me. At the time, I was too busy trying to forget to consider what Cal was going through. It was only when I received that letter and I was faced with having to tell him, that I actually considered how it would make him feel.

We were in a good place in our relationship after everything that had happened, and I didn't want to rock the boat in any way. I should have known it would somehow backfire on me, and it did, but in the best way possible.

It got us talking about Aria, about how we had felt when we lost her and how it had changed us. One thing we agreed on, though, was that we both still wanted children and we would try again when the time was right, which we decided would be after the wedding.

Talking of the wedding, we did eventually find a location for our ceremony, and it couldn't have been more perfect. I had always had my heart set on a specific venue for my wedding, and Cal, being the perfect guy he is, had managed to arrange it.

The reception had proved to be a bit harder. We hadn't been able to find a venue we could both agree on, and when we did, we decided it was just too far away from the wedding venue for it to be feasible. We had all but given up hope, when out of the blue, we received a phone call that would make our wedding day even more perfect.

CHAPTER 29

Crissie

<u>January 2012</u>

"*D*oes it hurt?"

"Yes and no. It's a weird feeling. I can't explain it."

I sit and watch Cal as the tattoo artist works on the tattoo Cal had mentioned to me months ago. He had asked around for the best place and this guy had been recommended, but he had a waitlist as long as your arm.

When Cal contacted him and explained what he wanted, the guy had told him it would take several hours, but he could do it in one sitting. Cal had agreed, booked, and paid a deposit to secure it.

Due to the length of time it was going to take to

complete the design Cal wanted, January was the earliest the guy could fit him in. So here we are, almost twelve months after Cal suggested it, getting his tattoo.

I'll admit, when I walked into the studio, I was pleasantly surprised. The place wasn't what I expected. Call it a cliché but I thought we'd be walking into a dirty, dark place where everyone would look as rough as houses. Instead a light, bright space with every wall decorated with tattoo designs to suit everyone's taste, greeted us.

There were four rooms near the back, one for each tattoo artist, which were just as bright and airy as the main space. We had been greeted by a young girl, with full sleeves on both arms and an intricate rose design going around her neck and vanishing behind her top and down between her breasts. I'll admit, I hadn't been a fan of tattoos, but hers looked beautiful.

We were three hours in and Cal had just made the decision to keep the design black and white rather than add any colour. The artist, who himself was covered in many striking and detailed images of his own design, had said keeping it black and white would be more effective when it was completed, and I had to admit, I was excited to see the finished product.

I know we've at least two hours left here, so I take my phone out my pocket and open up a new game that everyone's talking about. I downloaded Candy Crush on the way here so haven't tried it yet, but apparently, it's very addictive.

Before I know it, Cal is standing and receiving instructions from the artist on how to care for his new tattoo while it's healing. I glance at the clock and see that I've been playing the game for almost two hours. I'm on level thirty-six and it feels like only ten minutes since I loaded up the game and started playing.

After paying and collecting the cream to care for his tattoo, we are outside and walking to the car. Cal's arm and shoulder are covered in what looks like cling film, obscuring the design from my eyes, but I can see the redness on Cal's skin. I wince as I imagine how it must feel and decide that I'm a massive coward as I would never, knowingly, let someone that close to me with a needle gun.

Never going to happen.

"It wasn't that bad, Cris," Cal says, as if reading my mind. "It stung more than it hurt, kind of like when you have a blood test."

"Yeah, I don't like having a blood test either, so that doesn't really make me want to run in there and get one for myself."

"I wouldn't want you to get one anyway," Cal says before looking at me. "Don't get me wrong, it's your body and all, so if you want to get one, it's your decision, but I love your body the way it is."

"Thanks, I think. You've nothing to worry about though. I didn't see anything in there that would make me want to go back."

Cal laughs as he takes my hand and leads me over to the car, stopping when his phone starts ringing. He tosses me the car keys, and I unlock the car and climb inside. Cal follows as he takes his phone from his pocket, and I see his brow furrow before he answers.

~

Caleb

hy would they be calling me? God, I hope nothing is wrong.

"Hello."

"Mr Roberts? This is Cheryl from Nunsmere Hall. Are you free to talk at the moment?"

"Yes, Cheryl, how can I help you?" I see Cris looking at me with an odd expression on her face. She's just as curious about the call as I am.

"I have some news for you, Mr Roberts, that I hope you and your fiancée will like. We've recently undergone quite an extensive refurbishment, and as a result, we now have the space to accommodate an evening reception for you and Miss Walker. Would that be something you'd be interested in?"

I listen as Cheryl gives me a bit more information and find myself wanting to scream a massive 'yes' down the phone. I know Crissie will feel the same way, but when

Cheryl explains the pricing structure, the colour almost drains from my face.

"That sounds great, Cheryl. Could I ask that you email over all the information, please. I'll discuss it with Crissie and let you know in a couple of days?"

"I'll get that arranged for you, Mr Roberts. I feel I should mention, though, we can only hold the space for you for a few days. We've already had several enquiries since we updated the information on our website, and at least one of them has been for your date."

"Okay, thank you, Cheryl. We'll get back you to as soon as we can." I hang up the phone and turn to Crissie, who's still watching me.

"What was that about?"

"The wedding. We may have a venue for our reception."

Her face lights up at my words as I take the keys from her and start the engine, filling her in on the conversation I just had with Cheryl as we drive home.

Crissie

See! This is why I never went into finance. I hate figures and budgets. Especially when it's my own money, or lack of as the case may be.

Ever since Cal told me about the call from Nunsmere

Hall, I've be trying to figure out if it's financially viable for us to have our wedding reception there. We've struggled to find anywhere suitable that fits our budget and requirements, and Nunsmere would be perfect. Keeping everything under the same roof, so to speak, would be the perfect solution, if only it wasn't so damned expensive.

We've already factored the actual wedding and wedding breakfast into our budget, so know we can do it, but having the reception there, with the number of people we want to invite, will stretch our budget to the max, and may mean we have to take out a small loan to cover the cost.

I've always had an idea in my head about what my perfect wedding would be, but one thing I always wanted to do was pay for it myself. The last thing I want to do is for us to go into debt to afford it.

After going through the figures, I can only come up with two ways for us to have our wedding at the same place; either we cut the number of guests coming to the reception by half, or we push back the wedding by at least twelve months to give us enough time to get the money together so we can have everyone there. Neither option is appealing, but if I had to choose, I know which one I would go for.

"It's up to you, Cris. I'll marry you wherever, whenever, and in front of whomever you want. As long as you're there, everything else is just window dressing."

I smile at his sweet words, and I know he's being

sincere. He'd marry me on the street with our neighbours watching from their windows if it was all we could afford. Thankfully, we don't have to go down that route, but I'm still unsure which option is the best for us.

Do I want a wedding next year where half of the people I love can't attend or do I want a wedding where everyone can attend, but not until two years time?

I chew on my bottom lip as I look at the figures in front of me. There really is no way we can do next year and have everyone there without going into debt to get it, and to me, that just isn't an option.

"Cal, call them up. Ask if they can give us the same weekend in 2014. If they can, we'll take the whole package."

"You sure?"

"Yes," I say quickly, before I change my mind.

Cal grabs his phone from the coffee table and redials the number Cheryl called on earlier. I can hear the phone ringing, before it stops and a voice answers.

"Hi, Cheryl, it's Caleb Roberts. We spoke earlier today about the possibility of holding our wedding reception at your venue. I've discussed everything with my fiancée and we were wondering whether you could offer us the same weekend, but in 2014 instead? Sure, no problem."

I hear music coming from Cal's phone, so I'm guessing she's put him on hold while she checks the date is available. It stops after a few seconds and the voice comes back. The huge smile and thumbs up that Caleb gives me tells me she's come back with good news.

"That's great, Cheryl. Yes, the whole package. Are you able to transfer over what we've paid so far to the new date? That's brilliant. Thanks for your help, Cheryl. I'll await your email." Cal hangs up and turns to me. "It's all done."

I stand up from my seat at the dining table to jump into Cal's arms, planting a firm kiss on his lips. "I love you, Caleb Roberts."

And I proceed to show him exactly how much I love him.

CHAPTER 30

Crissie

Present Day

The venue was so beautiful.

We went to see it two weeks later and Cheryl was more than happy to show us around where the ceremony, wedding breakfast and evening reception would be held. What we hadn't realised at the time was that, included in the package, was a two-night stay in the honeymoon suite, which we were thrilled about.

They were willing to accommodate any colour scheme we preferred and would dress the tables and chairs accordingly. They could also block out a number of rooms at a preferential rate for any of our friends and family who wanted to stay over. All in all, despite me initially second guessing myself, we were very happy with our decision to push back the wedding, if it meant our day would be as we imagined.

On a completely different note, Cal's tattoo healed really well, and when I finally got to see it, I cried. He had originally told me it was going to be a tribal design weaving across his shoulder and down his arm, but what he'd actually had done was an angel, with Aria's name woven into the design. It was beautiful in its simplicity, and I loved it, and loved him more than I ever felt possible.

The next few weeks and months that passed by were uneventful, until the time came for me to hunt for my wedding dress. I'd looked at dozens of magazines and websites to try and find my perfect dress, but none of them called to me.

I'd always been told that when you find the dress, you just know, kind of like when you find the man you're meant to be with, but it was proving more difficult than I ever imagined it would do.

CHAPTER 31

Crissie

22 June 2013.

*T*oday should have been mine and Cal's wedding day. Well, it would have been had we not chosen to put it back twelve months. So, instead of marrying the man of my dreams, I'm out with my bridal party hunting for the perfect wedding dress.

I'd made an appointment at a bridal boutique in Chester over two weeks ago, and now I was here, bright and early, with Pippa, who was my maid of honour, Lizzie, my mum and Cal's mum. We had four hours to try and find my perfect dress. The consultant, Wendy, had explained that brides rarely find their dress on the first visit and that it usually took two or three before the right dress was found.

That scared me. Just looking at the rails and rails of dresses scares me. God, I am really getting married. Even though Cal and I have been engaged for some time—hell, we even have everything booked—it's only now sinking in that I am actually going to be wearing the big white dress and pledging to spend the rest of my life with him.

As if Wendy can sense how I feel, she puts a reassuring hand on my shoulder and smiles.

"Don't worry, sweetie. We'll take this at your pace. Do you have an idea of what you're looking for?" When I shoot her a blank expression, she just smiles. "That's not a problem. I'll go and pick out a few different styles I think will suit your figure and we'll go from there. You're a size ten, I'm guessing?"

I nod and smile at her as she walks towards one of the rails. Wendy pulls out three dresses and hands them to one of her assistants before moving to another rail and pulling out two more. All I can see is a mass of white and ivory material as the assistant takes them over to the large changing area and hangs each one up.

"Do you want one of your party to come in and help you, sweetie, or are you okay with me? Some of these dresses you need to be laced into, so someone needs to help."

Laced into? The expression on my face must show my fear as the consultant laughs and takes my hand. "Come on, honey, we'll start with a zip and work our way up to the laces."

All I can do is nod and follow her towards the changing area, leaving my family sitting in their chairs, sipping their complimentary glass of champagne as they wait for me to, hopefully, find the wedding dress of my dreams.

❧

*T*hree hours in and still no dress. I've tried on ten so far, I think, and whilst they've all been beautiful, and had my mum in tears more than once, none of them have felt right.

Even though I've not found the right dress yet, at least I know what I'm looking for now. I don't want a big merengue style dress. I don't want something that's covered in sparkles and sequins. What I want is something simple and classy; something that shows off just enough skin to be deemed sexy, but not so much that it looks trashy.

I've explained all of this to Wendy, and she beamed at me, saying she had the perfect dress. Her smile is infectious, and I found myself smiling with her as she hurried out to find the so-called perfect dress.

Now, I'm standing here in my undies, wrapped in a bathrobe while I wait for her to come back in. I find myself thinking about Cal and everything we've been through over the last seven years. Jesus, we've actually been together seven years.

I think back to the day he asked me out. Never in a million years did I think we'd last this long. I couldn't have possibly imagined that I'd be shopping for my wedding dress and preparing to marry him in twelve months' time. It's been a long road and we've been through a lot of ups and downs, but I couldn't imagine being with anyone else but him.

Cal is my rock. He's the one I go to when things get rough, the one I count on to get me through the tough times. I know he will support me in anything I choose to do with my life, and I love him more than anything for it. I can only hope he feels the same way about me.

I'm about to grab my phone from my bag to text him when the consultant comes back in with a huge smile on her face.

"I've been doing this for over twenty-five years, honey, and let me just say, I think this is your dress." She hangs the dress up and stands back next to me as we both look at it. "It's simple yet elegant. It has clean lines and the only bit of detailing is on the back and down the train. You're going to look beautiful, Crissie. Now, let's get you out of that robe and into this dress. I can't wait for your family to see you."

Fifteen minutes later, I'm in the dress, looking at my reflection, in floods of tears. Oh, they're happy tears. Wendy was right. The dress is perfect.

How such a simple dress can look so right is beyond me. The entire dress is ivory silk-satin, with a wide band of lace cinching in my waist. The front has a deep V-neck that's sexy but doesn't flash too much cleavage. The back mirrors the front and is fastened by a row of pearl buttons. The dress has a two-foot train that fans out behind me when I walk.

It's *the* dress.

"You ready to go out and show everyone?" Wendy asks as she fixes my train, so it falls correctly when I walk out.

I manage to stem the tears and nod, unable to speak because of the lump in my throat. I take a few deep breaths before Wendy opens the door to the main area and I'm greeted with gasps as my family see me for the first time. This time, it's not just my mum who cries.

Wendy's assistant is busy handing out tissues as I turn to give everyone a full 360 of the dress, before I stop and look at myself in the mirror.

"You look beautiful, Crissie. I can't believe my baby girl is actually getting married."

I hear my mum's tearful words, but I don't respond. I can't. If I do, my voice is going to come out all garbled with the tears I'm trying so hard to suppress.

"That's the one, Cris," I hear Pippa say from behind me. "That's the dress."

Smiling, I turn to her and nod. I've been doing a lot of that since we walked into the boutique, first out of shock, then fear, and now happiness. My friend is right; everyone is right. Taking a deep breath, I force the words out, grateful my voice sounds relatively normal. "This is the dress."

~

*F*our hours after leaving the bridal boutique, I'm walking in my front door. Everyone was in agreement that I found my wedding dress today. The fit was perfect, and Wendy had said that, barring me losing or gaining weight before the ceremony, no alterations would need to be made.

My mum and Elaine headed home after we left the boutique, but Pippa, Lizzie and I had gone to lunch and discussed their dresses for the wedding. Luckily for me, both girls were happy with my idea of a floor-length, Grecian style dress with one shoulder and embellishments around the waistline. The colour I'd chosen—a light ice blue—also went down well.

I hadn't expected them to agree so readily, which made my life a whole lot easier, so we had agreed a time to meet up in a couple of weeks to start the hunt for their dresses, not to mention accessories for all three of us.

I've decided against having a veil, that much I know for certain. I have plenty of time to decide how I want to do my hair and make-up, which Pippa has already agreed to do for me. Things are starting to come together, and I hope Cal and the men in the wedding party have had just as much luck as I have today.

While I went looking for my dress, Cal, my dad, his dad, his best friend and also his best man, Gary, had gone hunting for their suits. We'd agreed on a standard three-piece suit, agreeing that a full morning suit wasn't for us. The rest, I was leaving up to Cal. I knew I could trust him to pick something that would look good on all the men.

I check my watch and see that it's a little after five p.m. I've been out most of the day and my feet are screaming at me. I kick off my shoes just as my phone starts to ring. I smile when I see Cal's face on my screen and answer.

"Hey, baby, did you find the dress?"

"I think I might have done. How are you guys doing?"

"All sorted. Just got to wait for them to be ordered in. They said it should take no longer than six weeks."

"That's great, looks like we both had a productive day." I sit down on the sofa and curl my legs underneath me, waiting as I hear Cal's muffled voice as he talks to someone who's with him. He comes back on the line a few seconds later.

"Your dad and mine have gone home, but Gary and I were thinking of grabbing some food and then a few drinks. Do you want to join us?"

Do I want to join them? Normally, I'd say yes. I've not spent much time with Gary, so it would be good to get to know him a bit better before the wedding, but my feet are telling me to have a nice hot bath and a quiet night in.

211

"Thanks for the offer, but I think I'm just going to have a bath and then crash. It's been a long day."

"Okay, baby, if you're sure. I shouldn't be too late. I'll drop you a text when I'm on my way back. Love you."

"I love you too. Have a good night." We end the call and I plug my phone in to charge before heading into the bathroom. Turning on the water, I pour in a generous amount of my jasmine bath oil and go and grab a couple of towels before stripping off my clothes and climbing in to the warm water.

I sigh loudly as I sink down up to my shoulders, closing my eyes as I lean my head back and just let myself relax. My mind wanders as I lie there, and I find myself thinking about the last few years and how much my life has changed since I got together with Cal.

I never thought this would be my life. This was the life others had, not me, a normal girl from Chester. What have I done to deserve being this happy? Sure, we've had our ups and downs—what couple doesn't—but we've come through them stronger than before. We're a team, a unit. You want one of us, you get both of us. I can't imagine what my life would have been like without Cal, and I don't want to. He's my future husband, and just thinking that puts a ridiculous grin on my face.

Sighing again, I close my eyes and let the warmth of the water envelop me.

$\sim$

I wake with a start, seeing the room is in darkness. Realising I must have fallen asleep on the sofa, I push myself into a sitting position and check the time on my phone, seeing it is almost two a.m. Swinging my legs round so they're planted on the floor, I unlock the screen and see a text from Cal, sent at 11:23p.m., saying he was on his way home.

I smile and get up from the sofa and walk through to the bedroom. He must have come in, seen me asleep and didn't want to disturb me. The room is lit by the streetlight outside, and I can see Cal isn't in our bed. He sent that text almost three hours ago, so where is he.

Returning to the living room, I snatch up my phone and call him. When I receive his cheery voice telling me to leave a message, I furrow my brow. Scrolling through my phonebook, I groan when I realise I don't have Gary's number.

My rational brain is telling me he probably just stayed out for a few more drinks and his battery died, but it's my irrational brain that's screaming louder, telling me something's wrong. This isn't like Cal. If he had decided to stay out longer, he would have let me know. He hates it when I worry, and he knows that telling me he was coming home and then not arriving would worry me.

Taking a breath, I try my hardest not to panic as an idea comes to me. I practically run through to the bedroom and grab Cal's tablet, praying that it has power.

When I touch the screen, I smile when it comes to life and I scroll through the apps to locate the one to help find his phone.

I don't know if his phone battery has died or if he's just switched it off, but I'm hoping the app will be able to give me an idea where Cal's phone was before it lost signal.

I wait impatiently while the app starts up before asking it to find Cal's phone. My heart sinks when I see the last known location, and I grab my bag and slip my feet into my ballet flats as I race out of the flat.

CHAPTER 32

Crissie

*I*t's almost three a.m. by the time I make to the Countess of Chester hospital. I park my car and rush through the double doors that lead to the accident and emergency department. I don't know if Cal's even here. Part of me is hoping his phone lost signal as he was walking past on his way home, but deep down I know that's a ridiculously long shot.

I stop in the reception area and see about two dozen people all waiting to be seen by a doctor. I scan the crowd, seeing no sign of Cal or Gary, before I walk over to reception.

"Can I help you, miss?"

I look up when I see the girl behind the counter

looking up at me. She seems tired, and I briefly wonder how long she's been here today. "Um, yes. I'm looking for Caleb Roberts. Can you check to see if he's been brought in tonight, please?"

"Are you family?"

"Yes, I'm Crissie Walker. I'm his fiancée."

"One moment, Miss Walker. I'll check for you."

I wait by the desk as her fingers fly over the keyboard. I see nurses coming through and calling the names of people who are waiting to be seen and wonder how long they've been there already. I turn when I feel a hand on my arm. "If you'd like to take a seat, Miss Walker, a nurse will be out to see you shortly."

All I can do is nod as I walk over to an empty seat, realising the app was right and Cal is here. Part of me had been hoping—no, praying—that my theory on him just walking past when his phone died was true. What is he doing here? What happened?

The number of questions running through my mind is never ending, and I jump up when I see a nurse walk over to the reception and speak to the girl who points over to me with a small smile.

"Miss Walker?" the nurse asks as she comes over. "Please come with me and I'll take you to Mr Roberts."

"What happened to him? Why's he here?"

"From what his friend has said, they were attacked as they were waiting for a taxi to take them home earlier tonight. He hasn't stopped asking for you since he got here, even refused to let the doctors treat him until they got you here. They had to give him a sedative to calm him down."

"Attacked? Oh god." I stop walking as my vision blurs and my head begins to spin. Before I can fall, I feel hands take my arms and lead me over to a chair. I sit and hear a soft voice telling me to take deep breaths as a glass of water is placed into my hands.

After several minutes, I begin to feel normal again and see the nurse crouching next to me, her hand on my arm.

"You feeling better now?" she asks softly, and I nod, a little embarrassed. "Want me to take you through you Mr Roberts? The nurse has just told me he's woken up. He's asking for you again."

I jump up from my seat, water sloshing over the rim of the glass and onto the floor. "Oh, I'm so sorry. Let me—"

"Don't worry about it. Someone will clean it up."

"He's awake? He's not—"

"No, Miss Walker, he's alive. I won't lie to you, his face is pretty bruised and swollen, but it looks a lot worse than it is. He has a couple of cracked ribs and several pretty nasty bruises on his back and legs, but considering what his friend has told us, he's a lucky man."

She takes my arm and leads me down the hallway. I see several bays, the contents shielded by a curtain. I hear moans and groans from the patients hidden from view, and I'm about to say something when I hear someone shout my name.

I look up and see Gary coming towards us, his left arm is in a sling, and he is limping as he moves. He has a split lip and the start of a black eye. When he reaches us, he wraps his free arm round me in a brief hug before pulling away.

"I'm so sorry, Cris. I tried, but they wouldn't stop. One of the guys held me back. I tried, Cris. I really tried to get away to help him, but they just kept kicking and punching him. I don't know why. They didn't say anything; they just came out of nowhere and jumped us. If someone hadn't seen everything and called the police, I don't know what would have happened."

I feel myself begin to shake at Gary's words, hearing the emotion in his voice as he tells me what happened. I've never been as grateful to a complete stranger in my life. Whoever rang the police will be getting one hell of a thank you present, if I ever find out who it was.

"I had no way of getting in touch with you. I don't have your number, and Cal's phone is dead. It must be damaged, as it won't charge. God, Cris, I'm so sorry."

I try to tell him it's not his fault, to make him feel better somehow, but all I want to do right now is see my man. I turn back to the nurse as she carries on forward, stopping when she reaches one of the bays. She puts her hand on the curtain before turning to me. "Now remember, it looks worse that it is. Provided all his tests come back okay, he should be able to go home tomorrow. Apart from his ribs, which will take a few weeks to heal properly, the rest of the injuries are superficial. As I said, he's very lucky."

I nod at her words and take a breath as she pulls the curtain across. When I see him, my heart falls and I fight to keep back the tears that have been threatening to fall since I found out he was here. I try and remember what the nurse said, but it's hard when I see how bruised his face is.

Like Gary, he has a split lip which is starting to swell, and both of his eyes are already swollen and red. A bed sheet covers him up to his waist, and I can see his chest is wrapped in bandages to support his ribs. He has bruises covering his arms. When he turns his head and smiles, I can't stop the tears from falling as I hurry over to him.

I want to hug him, but the thought of causing him more pain stops me, and I just grip his hand tightly.

"Oh God, Cal. I thought... I was so worried."

"Hey, don't cry, baby. I'm going to be fine."

"When I woke up and saw your text, but you weren't there, I knew something was wrong. I just had a feeling."

"How did you know I was here? Gary said he hasn't been able to contact you. Did the police get you?"

"No, I used your tablet and that app that helps find your phone. It told me your last location was here."

Cal nods and smiles, and I just look at him; my strong, handsome guy. A guy who would do anything for anyone, lying here because some scumbags decided they wanted to beat someone up for no apparent reason. I feel myself starting to get angry, just as the curtain is pulled back. I turn to see the nurse stood there, with two police officers behind her.

"Sorry to disturb you both, but the police would like to speak with Caleb, if that's okay?"

I glance at Caleb who nods at the nurse before turning back to me. "Will you stay?"

"Of course. I'm not going anywhere."

~

Three days later, the hospital released Cal, and he was able to come home. The doctors had recommended keeping him in for observation as they had some concerns about one of his brain scans. They had said the CT scan showed some slight swelling and they wanted to monitor him to ensure it didn't get worse.

When a repeat scan two days later had shown the swelling had gone, they were happy to release him. He was still in pain with his ribs, but the medication he'd been given helped. The bruising on his body had come out fully now, and he looked like he'd gone ten rounds with Mike Tyson.

The doctors had assured me that, once everything had healed, there would be no lasting effects from the attack, something that I, and Cal, were really happy about. Thankfully, we lived in a ground floor flat, so there were no stairs to climb, which made getting around a lot easier for Cal.

I was to be his chauffer until his ribs healed, which Cal hated. He was a terrible passenger, and I caught him using his right foot to press on the imaginary break more than once. I thought I was a good driver and, up until now, so had Cal. I've always known he hates losing control, so I've no doubt that as soon as the doctor says he can drive again, my chauffeuring days will be over.

My work has been great. When I called Amanda to explain what had happened, she told me to take as much time as I need, which took a lot of pressure off me and meant I could make sure Cal would be okay. I've spoken with his parents and they've agreed to keep and eye on him when I go back next week. He's going to hate it; I know he will, but I wouldn't be able to go back to work knowing he was here on his own.

The police made an arrest the following day. CCTV from the shop across the street had caught the attack, and the faces of all four people who had set about Cal and Gary. I couldn't believe it when the police told me they'd been kids, the oldest being only seventeen. To add insult to injury, it had turned out to be a case of mistaken identity.

Apparently, one of the kids had believed Cal was the guy who had stolen away his girlfriend, and he was out for revenge. They'd kept calling him Robbo during their interrogations, and because of Cal's last name, the police didn't pick up on it straightaway.

It wasn't until the ex-girlfriend came in to the police station to find out what they wanted to see her for that they put everything together. They'd all be charged with assault, and now we were just waiting for the court date to come through so Cal could go and testify.

It had been a long few days, and I was physically and emotionally drained. Cal hadn't done much more than sleep since he got home, mainly due to the medication he was taking for the pain, which had given me some time to rest also, and boy do I need it.

Finishing off my coffee, I walk into the kitchen and place the cup in the sink. Checking my watch, I see it is almost five p.m. and realise Cal has been asleep for most of the day. Clearly, he needs to rest, which, according to the doctor, can only be a good thing, especially when it comes to his ribs healing.

I put more water in the kettle and flick it on, then prepare a mug to make Cal his favourite hot chocolate. He never used to drink it much before the attack, but, apart from water, it's all he's drunk since he's been home.

I know he's going stir-crazy being limited to what he can do. He just wants to get back to work and has been making several calls a day to the garage to check up on certain jobs. He's driving the other mechanics nuts with his constant phone calls. They've told him more than once, in the nicest possible way, to leave them alone and to concentrate on getting better, even hanging up on him more than once.

When the kettle clicks, I pour the boiling water into the mug and stir until the drink is ready. I pick it up and go through to the bedroom, placing the mug on the bedside cabinet. I take a moment to just look at Cal's sleeping form. The swelling on his face has mostly gone now, and the bruises are turning that horrible yellowy colour.

I know in a few more days, they'll be gone, and all that will be left is the cut lip. The rest of his injuries can be covered with clothes. No one can see them unless Cal wants them to. Reaching out, I brush his hair off his face, smiling when he stirs and turns his head into my hand but doesn't wake.

I feel a lump form in my throat as I watch him, realising how close I came to losing him. I haven't seen the CCTV footage that helped the police catch the kids who did this, but from what the police had said, it was a completely unprovoked attack, and was really vicious.

I shiver as I think of Cal going through that; the pain he must have been through. While he was in the hospital, he told me that, when it was happening, all he could think about was me, and by concentrating on me, he was able to imagine he was in another place. He said he didn't actually feel any pain until he woke up in the hospital, and then they gave him painkillers to combat it.

I continue to look at him as his eyes flutter open and he gives me a small smile.

"Hey, you," I say quietly. "How are you feeling?"

"Better. A little sore, but better."

I sit on the bed and watch him wince as he pushes himself into a sitting position. The sheet falls away, and I can see the bandages that are still wrapped around his chest. The doctors said they needed to stay for at least another week, just to support the ribs, but they've said they're healing nicely so, as long as he's careful, he shouldn't need the extra support after the week is up.

"I brought you a hot chocolate," I tell him, indicating the mug on the bedside cabinet.

"Thanks, Cris," he says with a sigh as he leans his head back, briefly closing his eyes before opening them again. "How can I still feel so tired? I've been asleep all bloody day."

I can hear the humour in his voice, but also the frustration. It's hard for him to just lie around doing nothing. Usually, he's so active; either at work or at the gym. He knows he's got at least another week of taking it easy, and it's not going to get any less frustrating.

"The doctor said you'd feel like this for at least several days. He said something about your adrenaline spiking from the attack and this is the come down. The painkillers aren't helping either, I bet."

Cal nods and winces again as he shifts. It's only his ribs that are causing him the pain now. The bruises are healing well, but the ribs will take longer. The more rest he gets, the quicker they'll heal, and I know it's for that reason Cal is taking the doctor's advice to rest as much as possible.

It's not going to be easy—we both know that—but the sooner Cal is back on his feet and out of pain, the better. We just want things to get back to normal, so we can carry on with planning our wedding, move on with our lives and put this horrible episode behind us.

CHAPTER 33

Crissie

<u>Present Day</u>

*I*t took another three weeks before the doctor cleared Cal to go back to work. It was three weeks of whinging and moaning and generally feeling sorry for himself. If I didn't love him as much as I did, it might have been enough to drive me away. Luckily for him, I did love him more than anything, and for that reason, I was entitled to tell him the truth, which I did on more than one occasion.

I chuckle as I recall his expression when I called him a whining baby and that he needed to grow up and stop complaining. I hadn't planned on saying that to him, but after a tough day at work, I'd literally just walked through the door and he started moaning, so I just let rip.

From then on, he chose his words more carefully and I didn't have to say anything more to him. I'd glare at him occasionally when I heard him grumbling to himself about stupid doctors not knowing what they were doing, but other than that, things went back to normal pretty quickly.

Once Cal went back to work, we slowly slipped back into our normal routine and it was business as usual, at least for a few months anyway. Then fate dealt us another blow, only this time, it threatened to tear us apart.

CHAPTER 34

February 2014

*J*ust four months to go.

Four months before I become Mrs Crissie Roberts. It's come around so fast and feels like only yesterday that we were setting a date and deciding on locations and a guest list.

I had my final fitting for my dress at the weekend, and my bridesmaids finally agreed on a dress that, luckily, the bridal boutique could get in stock in both of their sizes. They've been driving me crazy over the last few months with their inability to agree on any dress I suggested to them. In the end, I gave them a deadline and told just told them to find a dress or they wouldn't be alive to attend the wedding.

With the threat of violence coming their way, they'd

chosen a weekend they were both free and spent the whole day visiting numerous dress shops before finally agreeing on their dress for my special day. Luckily for them, I loved their choice.

The last thing Cal and I had to do was find a caterer, which we found surprisingly easily. We eventually chose the basic food package, and various members of the family agreed to bring a platter of food to try and keep costs down as much as possible.

We were pretty much all set now. I'd gone down my check list several times to make sure I'd not forgotten anything, and so far, everything had a firm tick by the side. I'd even asked my mum to go through it too, just to make sure everything was in order.

Today was a Saturday, and Cal had needed to go into to work to complete a rush job that the client needed done by the end of the day. That had put the kibosh on our plans for the day, so I was stuck in the flat with nothing to do but watch crappy daytime TV or play games on my phone.

That's what I've been doing for the last hour and it's already getting old. I snatch up my phone from beside me and scroll through the phonebook. When I find the number I want, I send a quick text, not surprised when a response comes through within a few seconds, saying just two words.

Hell yes.

~

*A*n hour later, Pippa and I are in our favourite bar. We've ordered a platter of food to nibble on and Pippa is currently stood at the bar waiting for our second pitcher of the Pornstar Martini cocktail. Our favourite.

It's just after one p.m., so we don't feel bad about drinking. There are plenty of people who've been here longer than we have, some of whom are staggering all over the place when they try and walk. We're probably the most sober of anyone in here, but we've agreed that is something we plan on rectifying pretty soon.

We have both sent a text to our other halves to let them know where we are, and both said they would try and join us later if they got off work early enough. I know Cal will join us, regardless of the time. It's been a while since we've enjoyed a night out with friends, and he gets on well with Pippa and Lance. So much so that he's asked Lance to be one of his ushers on our wedding day.

I thank the server as he brings over our food platter; my mouth beginning to water as I look at the mixture of spicy chicken wings, breaded mushrooms, satay chicken, cheese topped garlic bread and fish goujons with a selection of dips. I'm deciding what to eat first when Pippa returns and begins to pour us two glasses of the bright orange drink.

I see her eyes light up when she spies the food on our table, and she doesn't wait as she reaches out and grabs one of the chicken wings before sitting in the booth and biting down on the wing.

"Thank god. I'm famished," Pippa says through a mouthful of chicken.

I laugh at her as I pick up one of the fish goujons and dip it in the barbeque dip before taking a bite. The food they serve here is partly why I love this place so much. The selection they offer is wide and varied, and it always comes out quickly and tastes delicious.

Their cocktail menu is one of the best in Chester, too, although we've yet to order anything other than the Pornstar Martini. Why break the habit of a lifetime?

"I can't tell you how relieved I am that you and Lizzie have finally agreed on a dress, Pip. You two were starting to get on my last nerve."

"Yeah, I kind of gathered that when you threatened us with bodily harm. Lizzie and I decided that, when we went out, we wouldn't come home until we found a dress. Just the thought of you going postal on us was enough to scare us into finding one." Pippa finishes off the chicken wing and wipes her fingers on a napkin as I smile at her words.

"Yeah, I guess I did lose it a little bit. It's just, there's only four months left, and you guys were dragging your heels and refusing to agree on anything I suggested. I thought a little kick up the backside was needed. Glad it worked."

"Oh, it did. You're scary when you're pissed, Cris." We both laugh again as we drink our cocktails and eat the food in front of us. In less than thirty minutes, the platter is clear, and I decide I could easily eat everything again. The food doesn't seem to have made a dent in my appetite, but I decide I should wait until Cal and Lance arrive before considering more food.

I know the guys will be hungry if they've been at work all day, and, while I can't speak for Lance, I know Cal won't have eaten today, so he will be ravenous by the time he gets here.

It's almost six by the time Lance and Cal walk through the doors. Pippa and I are on our fifth cocktail pitcher, and everything Pippa says seems to make me laugh. Yeah, I'm well on the way to being as drunk as a skunk, and judging by the look on Cal's face, he knows it.

"Someone looks like she's had a few to drink," Cal says as he leans down to kiss me, his arm sliding around my shoulder as he nudges me over, so he can sit next to me in the booth.

"Who me? I'll have you know that this," I say, indicting the pitcher, "is just orange juice. Isn't that right, Pip?" When Pippa doesn't respond, I turn to see her practically climbing Lance in an effort to get as close as possible. Her lips are fused to his, and she's almost straddling his lap. Pippa's one leg is thrown over Lance's, and her hands are tugging at his shirt.

I've never seen my friend like this before; so uninhibited. She's usually quite restrained, not liking public displays of affection. This is a completely different Pippa to the one I'm used to seeing.

I know I shouldn't be staring at them, but I can't look away as Pippa shifts and climbs over Lance, so her knees are bracketing his hips. His hands are gripping her waist tightly, and he is just as into this as she is. Another few minutes and they'll be going at it right here in the middle of the bar. I jump when I feel Cal's breath on my neck as he leans in closer.

"You're turned on, aren't you? Watching your friend practically fucking her boyfriend in full view of everyone who wants to look."

I feel my pulse quicken as I hear his words and continue to watch my friend and her boyfriend making out in front of us. Cal's fingers are threading through my hair as his breath fans across my cheek. I can't tear my eyes away, until Cal takes my hand and brings it over to rest on his crotch.

My head spins in his direction when I realise how hard he is behind his jeans. He is just as turned on as I am by our friends' erotic display. I feel a flood of desire run through me, pooling between my thighs.

I know it's a combination of the alcohol in my system and Pippa's actions, but I find that I've never wanted Cal so much, and I don't care where. I just need him to fuck me. Now. Leaning in, I flex my fingers, feeling Cal twitch against my palm as I whisper in his ear, "Bathroom. Now."

I see Cal's eyes darken as I continue to stroke him

through his jeans, and before I can say anything else, he's taken my hand, pulled up from the booth, and we're headed down the hallway towards the restrooms.

We go straight past the ladies' room and head towards the gents. We stop briefly as he opens the door and peers inside, dragging me in behind him a few seconds later. Cal opens the door to the nearest stall and pulls me in, locking the door as he pushes me against it and crushes his mouth against mine. At the same time, his hands are tugging my skirt up around my hips.

We're a mass of lips and hands as I fumble with his belt, needing to feel him in my hand. The growl that passes his lips when I free him from his boxers is so animalistic my whole body trembles. I know this is going to be hard and fast as he puts both hands under my thighs and lifts me up, pressing me against the door as he tugs my knickers to one side.

In one quick thrust, he's inside me, his mouth covering mine, smothering my scream. He doesn't give me chance to adjust to his intrusion as my hands grip his hair tightly and he continues to pound into me. All I can hear is the sound of our rapid breathing and the slap of his skin against mine.

Within seconds, I feel the familiar tightening inside my belly, and I know it'll wash over me any moment. Breaking the kiss, I tug Cal's head back and rest my forehead against his, needing to see him as I fall over the precipice, his name on my lips as my vision blurs and my body shakes in his arms.

It's a few minutes before I feel Cal slip out of me as he lowers me back to the floor, holding me in place until I'm sure my legs will hold my weight. I watch him tuck himself back inside his jeans, zip his fly and fasten his belt, before he cups the back of my head with his hand and brings my lips to his in a gentle kiss.

"You never cease to amaze me, Miss Walker. That. Was. Amazing." He punctuates each word with a kiss as I smile up at him. He'll hear no argument from me.

I grab some tissue to clean myself, ignoring the all too familiar red splotches on the tissue as I toss it away. Cal unlocks the door and sticks his head out, before opening the door fully. He grabs my hand and leads me from the bathroom, heading back towards our booth.

We're not surprised to find it empty, with a note written on a napkin. It's from Pippa. It's brief and to the point:

Holy Fuck. The bill is sorted. Have fun x

I hand the napkin to Cal to show him, and, when he looks up at me, we both burst out laughing as I grab my bag and we leave the bar.

CHAPTER 35

Crissie

Two days later, I'm woken up by a sharp pain in my stomach. I draw my knees up to my chest and take a few deep breaths to try and ease the pain. After a few minutes, it subsides, and I stretch my legs out.

My breathing is back to normal after a few moments, and I close my eyes. I know I should go to the doctor about these pains. They've been happening for the last few weeks, always after Cal and I have had sex. I've also noticed blood, like I did Saturday night at the bar.

At first, I thought it was just because our love life had become pretty energetic recently, but when the same thing happened after our gentler times, I disregarded that. Sex has also been painful a time or two which, again, I put down to us being unable to keep our hands off each other.

When another pain hits, I bite my lip to stop from crying out as I squeeze my eyes shut, exhaling when the pain goes away as quickly as it hit. I know I can't keep ignoring this. It's probably something really simple that the doctor will be able to give me something for. I've nothing to worry about. I know I haven't. So why am I terrified about making that call?

Climbing out the bed, I hear the TV in the living room. Knowing Cal is probably playing on one of his game consoles before he heads to the garage, I decide to leave him be and cross the room towards the bathroom. Flipping on the shower, I strip out of the old t-shirt I slept in and climb under the spray. I sigh deeply as the warmth envelops me, lifting my face up towards the spray.

I stand there for several minutes before I grab my shower gel and proceed to wash myself, freezing when I see the blood on my fingers from between my legs. I stare at it for what seems like hours, but it's only a few seconds before I finish washing myself and turn off the shower.

Making quick work of drying myself, I pull on my bathrobe and go into the bedroom. I pick up my phone and dial the doctor's surgery before I can talk myself out of it. Surprisingly, the call is answered after three rings.

"North Street Medical Centre, how may I help you?"

"Oh hi, good morning. I know it's a long shot, but I was wondering if there is any chance I could get in to see the doctor today?"

"I can check for you. May I ask what it's in relation to?"

"Actually, it's personal, so I'd rather not say."

"Okay, one moment, please."

I never understood why the receptionist always asks that question. I mean, why does she need to know what's wrong with me? It's not like she can tell me what's wrong over the phone.

I don't know why I'm making this call. The chances of me getting in to see the doctor today are slim to none. I don't think I've ever managed to get an appointment on the same day when I've called in the past. Why this time should be different I've no idea.

"You're in luck. We've just had a cancellation. Can you get here for 8:45?"

"Oh, that soon? Yes, I can make it."

"Okay, could I take your name and date of birth, please?"

"Yes, it's Crissie Walker, fifteenth of August 1989."

"Thank you, Miss Walker. We'll see you later."

The call ends and I glance at the clock, seeing it's already 8:05 a.m. I know I've not got enough time to dry my hair, so I just throw it up in a ponytail as I remember I need to let Amanda know I'm going to be late. Picking up my phone, I send her a quick text to let her know I'll work through my lunch to make up the time, and she replies confirming that's fine with her.

I dress quickly and head out into the living room, seeing Cal closing down his game console. He's dressed in his usual work attire of an old pair of jeans and a black t-shirt. I imagine stripping the material from his body but quickly banish the thoughts, knowing we don't have enough time for anything that may happen if I let my train of thought continue down that path.

"Hey, baby." Cal smiles when he looks up and sees me standing in the doorway between the living room and bedroom. "You okay?"

"Yeah, I'm just tired, that's all. I've a long day ahead of me and I didn't sleep too well last night." I force a smile as I lift my lips to his when he comes over. I know I probably should tell him about my visit to the doctors, but he'll only worry when I tell him the reason for the visit. The last thing I want to do is cause him to worry about something that will probably turn out to be nothing.

"Sorry to hear that, baby. How about I cook for us tonight? I should be able to leave work on time, so I can cook my lasagne that you love so much. How does that sound?"

"I'd like that." I smile at Cal and kiss him again before I grab my bag from off the sofa and head over to the door. For some reason, I turn back to look at him, seeing him watching me. There's concern etched on his handsome face, and I suddenly feel guilty for not telling him what's got me so distracted.

"I love you, Cal."

His expression softens, but the concern is still in his eyes as he returns my words, before I vanish from the flat.

oOo

The doctor's surgery is only a five-minute drive away from the flat, so I arrive with plenty of time to spare. It's almost nine before my name is said over the intercom, and I stand, walking down the hallway towards the room I've been directed to. Knocking, I breathe a sigh of relief when I hear a female voice invite me to enter.

I don't know why, but I hadn't considered the sex of the doctor when I booked the appointment. I know it will be easier for me to talk to another woman about why I'm here, so at least that will make being here a little easier.

Opening the door, I step inside and sit in the seat offered to me by the doctor. She's an older lady of about fifty with short brown hair styled in a choppy bob. She's dressed in black trousers and a pale pink blouse, and when she turns and smiles at me, I feel instantly at ease.

"What can I do for you, Crissie?"

I spend the next few minutes going through what's been happening over the last few weeks, and she listens intently, asking questions here and there to gather as much information as she can. She turns back to her computer and brings up my personal information. "You're twenty-four at the moment, is that right?"

"Yes. I'm twenty-five in August."

"I see you had a miscarriage a few years ago. I'm sorry to hear that."

"Thank you. It was a tough time for my fiancé and me.

Do you think what's happening now could be related to the miscarriage?"

"Considering how long ago it was, it's doubtful. Crissie, if it's okay with you I'd like to perform a smear test. We don't normally do them until a woman turns twenty-five, but seeing as you're almost there, I doubt a few months will make a difference. Is that okay with you?"

"Um, yeah, I guess so."

"If you'd like to go behind the curtain and remove your underwear, please. I'll get everything ready and be with you shortly." She smiles kindly at me and I stand, walking over to the bed at the opposite side of the room. I jump when I hear the curtain close behind me and do as I'm asked, removing my underwear and then climbing onto the bed.

The doctor is back after a few moments and she talks me through what she's going to do. I nod and lie back on the bed as she gently eases my knees apart. I feel some pressure as she inserts the speculum, and I fight my body's reaction to push out the foreign object.

"It's okay, Crissie, just relax for me. This will be over soon."

I take several deep breaths as I hear the doctor continue speaking to try and distract me from what she's doing. I feel a weird sensation inside me before she pulls out the speculum and closes my legs.

"That's it, all done. You can get dressed now." The doctor vanishes behind the curtain and I swing my legs round and slide off the bed. I pull my knickers up my legs, suddenly feeling the need to pee. Well, that wasn't as bad as I thought it was going to be. Sure, it was a bit uncomfortable and a lot embarrassing, but if it helps find out what's going on with my body, I'm glad I did it. After adjusting my skirt, I pull back the curtain and retake my seat by the doctor.

"We should have the results within two weeks. We'll be in touch when they come through. In the meantime, take paracetamol for the stomach pains, and I recommend you go easy on the intercourse until we know what's causing the bleeding. It's probably something and nothing, so please don't worry. I know that's easier said that done, but I always tell my patients not to worry until we know exactly what's going on. Are there any questions you'd like to ask me?"

"No, I don't think so."

"Well, if you think of anything, please give me a call." She smiles at me again as I pick up my bag from the floor and stand. I'm back in my car less than five minutes later and on my way to work. So I have two weeks to wait until I get the results from the smear test. Two weeks of wondering and theorising what's causing the pains in my stomach and the abnormal bleeding.

It's going to be two weeks of hell.

CHAPTER 36

Crissie

*I*t's been less than a week since I went to the doctors, and here I am, back here in the waiting room. I got the call last night to say the results were in and could I come in and see the doctor again.

I don't know whether to be scared that the results came in so soon or happy that I don't have another week of wondering what's wrong. I still haven't told Cal I've been here. I figure there's no point worrying him until there is something to worry about.

If all goes well, I'll never have to tell him, and the doctor will prescribe something to sort things out. Everything will be back to normal and we can just get on with living our life and looking forward to our wedding day in just under four months time.

"Crissie Walker, please go to room four."

I stand and head in the same direction as I did last time I was here, clutching my bag to my side. When I reach the door, I take a breath and knock, hearing the same voice as before call to me to come in. I open the door and walk in, giving the doctor a nervous smile as I sit down.

She's wearing grey trousers and a white blouse today, but still looks every bit the professional she is. Why I'm examining her dress sense I've no idea. Oh yeah, that's right, I'm nervous as hell at what she's going to tell me.

"Thank you for coming in, Crissie. As you know, I've received the results from the smear test I did five days ago, and the test detected some abnormalities. Now, there's nothing to worry about at this stage—abnormal cells are quite common—but because of the other symptoms you've had, I'd like to refer you to have a procedure we call a colposcopy." The doctor pauses, letting me absorb the information she's just given me. There's no way I can get away with not telling Cal now. This sounds like something he needs to know.

"The procedure is very similar to a smear test, but this time, I'm going to ask that they perform a biopsy also, which means they will take a small tissue sample from your cervix for further examination. Now, have you told your partner about what's going on?" I shake my head before she continues, "Well, I recommend you tell him, as once this procedure is complete, you'll have to forgo intercourse for at least four to six weeks while you heal."

All I can do is nod as I try and understand what she's telling me. Since I came here five days ago, I've used all the excuses I can think of to not have sex with Cal, which has been no easy feat as I want him all the time. If I've got to avoid sex with him for longer, the doctor is right. I need to tell him the real reason why.

"You should have an appointment come through the post sometime this week. They usually get you in quite quickly, and I've mentioned I want you to get it done within the next couple of weeks."

As if she can sense my nerves, she reaches out and pats my hand. "Crissie, really, this is more common than you think. I'm referring you purely as a precaution to rule out anything more sinister. Please, don't let your imagination run away with you. I've seen it happen before to other women and it can end up causing more harm than good. Just wait for the appointment, have the procedure, and we'll take it from there. Okay?"

"Okay. Thank you, doctor." I stand and leave her office. I'm on autopilot as I walk back to my car, my imagination doing exactly what she'd advised me not to do. She said I have to have a biopsy. That's what they do when they're testing for cancer. She said abnormal cervical cells are quite common. Well, not for me it isn't.

What if I have cancer?

I'm back home within ten minutes, and I see Cal's car

parked in his allocated spot. Pulling my car into a visitors spot next to his, I switch off the engine and just sit there. I know I need to tell Cal. I know he will want to be at the hospital with me when I have the procedure. He'll support me one hundred percent. I know he will.

It's just, with everything that's happened since we've been together, we're finally in a good place. Our jobs are both going well and we're less than four months away from getting married. Why does this have to happen now?

Grabbing my bag off the passenger seat, I get out and lock the car before heading up to the flat. When I open the door, I see Cal sat on the sofa, his phone in his hand. He looks up and smiles when I walk in, before standing and walking over.

"Hey, baby, you're later than usual. It's not very often I'm back before you."

I give him a weak smile as I drop my bag by the door and hang up my coat, something he picks up on immediately.

"What's up, Cris? You look pale. Are you feeling okay?"

I turn to face him, take his hand, and walk over to the sofa. When we are seated, I just look at him. How am I meant to tell him this?

"I need to tell you something, Cal. Last week, I went to the doctors as I'd been having pains in my stomach, and there was some bleeding after we had sex, more than once. I didn't think it was anything too serious, which is why I didn't tell you about it. The doctor did a test, and I had to wait for the results. That's why I'm back later than usual tonight."

"Okay. I can't say I'm not a little pissed you didn't tell me you were in pain. What did the results say?"

I take another breath before I continue. I can't say I'm surprised by his reaction. If the tables were turned and he had hidden this from me, I'd feel the exact same way. "The doctor said the test showed some abnormal cells in my cervix, so I need to go and have a procedure, so they can check them further and so a tissue sample can be taken for further analysis."

"A tissue sample? You mean a biopsy?"

I nod, seeing his expression change as the colour drains from his face before he breathes deeply and squeezes my hand. "Well, you'll have the procedure and we'll wait for the results to come through. No point worrying until we have something to worry about. Right?"

God, I wish I could be as optimistic as he is right now. The fact is, I'm scared to death. Just the word 'biopsy' is enough to put the fear of God into me. It's true what they say, it's the not knowing that's the worst part. "Okay. I'm just going to go and have a shower."

"Do you want me to do anything to eat?"

"No, thanks. I'm not hungry."

Cal releases my hand and leans in to kiss me, and for the first time since I met him, I turn my head away, stand, and walk off. I can't look at him as I leave the room, feeling horrible for doing that to him. I know it's not his fault this is happening to me—it's no one's fault—but I can't be close to him right now. If I let him kiss me, I'll want more, and that's not something I can handle right now.

I might have told him about the stomach pains and the bleeding, but I've not said anything about the pain and discomfort I feel when we have sex. I had planned on telling him, but when I saw his face when he found out about the stomach pains, I knew that him knowing about the other stuff would only hurt him.

Knowing my body was causing me pain was one thing, but knowing I was in pain when we were together was another. I don't want him thinking he is in any way responsible for the discomfort, and I know Cal. I know he'll find a way to blame himself, which couldn't be farthest from the truth.

I'm in the shower a few minutes later, and I just brace my hands on the tiled wall, letting the water sluice down over my head. Why can't things just be easy for us? There's always something going wrong. If I were a religious person, I'd be thinking we were being punished for something.

We've done nothing to deserve everything that's happened to us over the last few years. Guess it's just a hell of a lot of bad luck that's been thrown our way.

I'm not sure how long I stay in the shower, but the water is running cold by the time I come out. Drying off, I towel dry my hair and pull a comb through it before slipping on my bathrobe and walking through to the bedroom. I stop in the doorway when I see Cal sitting on the bed.

He stands when he sees me and walks over, taking my hands and leading me over to the bed. When he sits me down, he reaches for a cup of tea he's placed on the bedside cabinet.

"Tea? I never drink tea."

"Yeah, I know. I just thought it seemed like a 'tea' occasion."

"Me possibly having cancer seems like a 'tea occasion' to you?" The words come out harsher than I intended, and Cal puts the tea down and just looks at me, the expression on his face one that I can only describe as shock.

"That's not what I meant, and you know it."

"Do I?" All I can do is look at him. My breathing has sped up, and I can feel my pulse racing. I don't open my mouth, knowing that if I speak, we're going to argue, and I don't want that. I hate arguing with Cal, and right now, I'm just too tired. Truth be told, all I want to do it curl up into a ball under the duvet, close my eyes, and forget everything the doctor just told me.

Willing my breathing to slow, I turn away from Cal and stand. After pulling the duvet back, I climb in, bathrobe and all, and pull the covers up to my chin. "I just want to sleep."

I close my eyes and sigh deeply. I can feel Cal is still sat there, probably looking at me, wondering what the hell is going on. I tell him I've got to have a procedure to determine if I have cancer. I then walk out on him to take a shower, and, when he comes in with a cup of tea to try and talk, I bite his head off then climb into bed, effectively shutting him out.

I know Cal didn't mean anything by what he said. It was just a poor choice of words. For some reason, we British have a reputation for thinking tea solves all problems. Had some bad news? Have a cup of tea. Bad day at work? A cup of tea will make it all better. Why we do it, I've no idea, but I think we've all been guilty of it at some point.

I remain still as I lie there, and I feel it when Cal rests his hand on my hip through the covers. I expect him to say something, but instead he just sighs and walks over to the window, closing the curtains before leaving the room and closing the door as quietly as he can.

When I'm sure I'm alone, I stretch out my legs and roll onto my back. What am I doing? I'm pushing away the one person who has proven numerous times that he loves me and will support me no matter what. Even after I treated him like crap after we lost Aria, he was there for me, never leaving my side. I was a real bitch to him, but he didn't budge.

How many times can I treat him like crap before he realises I'm not worth it and walks away. It's not what I want, of course it's not, but part of me can't help but think he would be better off without me.

Turning back to my side, I lift my head and thump the

pillow a few times. I drop my head with a sigh and close my eyes again. I know that when I wake, my problems will still be there, but at least in sleep, I can forget.

~

Caleb

I close the bedroom door carefully, resisting the urge to slam it in my frustration. How the hell can she think that of me? We've been together for eight years. Doesn't she know me at all? Haven't I proved I'll always be there for her, for us?

God, I love her with everything I am. I'd never dream of abandoning her when she needs me, especially now. Why the hell didn't she tell me what was happening. I'm her partner, her fiancée, and the man she agreed to spend the rest of her life with. Why would she keep this from me?

To me, it looks like she only told me because she had no choice. I can't help but wonder if she didn't have to have this procedure, she would never have told me. I guess it explains why we haven't had sex for the last few days. Usually, I only need to look at her and she's on me, but since last week, she's used every excuse under the sun not to come near me.

I guess that should have been my first clue that something was wrong, but I just didn't put it together.

Now, she's lying in our bed, and all I want to do is go in there and tell her she's wrong and that I'm there for her, but I have a feeling she won't believe me right now.

Falling down onto the sofa, I snatch up my phone and bring up the search engine. If I'm going to help her through this, and if worst comes to the worst, I want to be prepared. I'm not going to let her push me away like she tried to do when we lost Aria. I proved to her then that I'm in this for the long haul, and I'll do the same thing now.

We might not have said the vows yet, but I will always be there for her, in sickness and in health. Now all I need to do is convince Crissie.

CHAPTER 37

Crissie

Present Day

It was four weeks of hell waiting for the results of the procedure to come through. Cal tried, but no matter what he did or said, I found some way to bite his head off. In the end, he stopped trying to help or talk to me and just got on with things.

We barely touched when we were in bed, and the sex between us stopped completely. I mean, I knew we couldn't be together after the procedure, as I needed time to heal, but beforehand, there was no reason we couldn't be intimate. I just didn't want to.

The pain I was in after the procedure was persistent and uncomfortable, and there wasn't a day that went by that I didn't experience it. As the doctor had warned, there was intermittent bleeding too, which meant I had to wear protection all the damn time as I didn't know when it would happen.

Cal and I were just going through the motions. Getting up, going to work, coming home, eating, then going to bed. It had almost become a routine. We didn't go out, at least not together, and we'd even stopped talking about the wedding, something we usually did all the time. Truth was, we didn't discuss it because neither of us knew what would happen if the results came back and they weren't in my favour.

"Crissie, are you ready, honey?"

"Almost ready, Dad."

I look at the reflection of the door in the mirror, knowing I need to go out there soon. Everyone will be waiting for me to make my grand entrance and the short journey down the aisle. I flick my eyes away from the door, back to my reflection.

It's taken us twelve years to get here, to this place with all our friends and family here to celebrate with us. It hasn't been easy, as you all know. We thought we'd had everything thrown at us, but on the day I got the results, we were shown how wrong we were.

CHAPTER 38

Crissie

March 2014

*G*od, I hate this waiting room. I've seen far too much of it over the last couple of months. I've read and reread the same posters warning people how to recognise the signs of various conditions. I can tell you all the initial symptoms of someone who may have Chronic Obstruction Pulmonary Disease, more commonly known as COPD, and which spots are Chicken Pox, and which could be Meningitis.

Hell, I've spent so much time here I could probably diagnose most of the other patients' conditions. Well, maybe not, but that's how it feels. The only thing different about this visit is that Cal is with me. He's sat by my side, my hand firmly ensconced within his.

I have to admit, having him here is strangely comforting. I hadn't wanted him to come with me, and I told him as much last night. He'd basically turned around and told me that I could be as bitchy and nasty to him as I wanted to, but he wasn't going anywhere. He was going to be here with me today, even if he had to super glue our hands together.

The look on his face had told me he was deadly serious, so I'd not argued any further. Trying to sneak out of the house this morning had failed also. I still didn't know why I was trying to do this without him. He'd done nothing to make me believe he'd be anything other than supportive, yet I was doing everything I could think of to try and do this on my own.

"Crissie Walker, room four please." The familiar voice of the doctor comes across the intercom, and I stand, taking a breath as I turn to Cal.

"Let's do this," I say with a nod as I head off down the hallway with Cal by my side. I knock on the now familiar door, waiting for the voice to tell me to enter.

I've a strong feeling of déjà vu as I walk into the room. Everything is in the same place as it's been on my previous visits and the doctor is wearing the same outfit she did the first time I came to see her. The only difference is that, this time, I won't be asking for her help. She will be telling me whether or not I have cancer. We sit down, and the doctor looks at me, smiling when she sees Cal by my side.

"Crissie, thank you for coming in. I'm glad you decided to take my advice," she says, and I know she's referring to Cal. "I have the results from the colposcopy and biopsy you had." She turns to her computer briefly and brings up some information I can't see clearly. "The biopsy has shown that the cells in your cervix are showing the early signs of being cancerous."

I hear that word, and everything stops. My vision blurs and my blood roars in my ears. My heart feels like it's going to beat out my chest as I struggle to catch my breath. God, I can't breathe. Why can't I breathe? I'm gasping for air when I hear Cal's voice next to me, his hand on my back, stroking gently. "It's okay, Cris. Take deep breaths, baby. That's it, just like that. In and out."

I do as he says and almost sigh in relief as I finally get air into my lungs. My breathing is still coming fast, but at least I don't feel like I'm going to pass out. When my vision clears, I look at the doctor, her face a picture of concern.

"I have cancer?"

"Yes, but it's in the very early stages. There are several treatment options that are available and, I have to tell you, the survival rate for this type of cancer caught at this stage is very high. There's no reason that, after treatment, you can't go back to a normal life."

"But I'll definitely need treatment? How long will it last?"

"That depends on the treatment. What I'm going to do is refer to you an oncologist, who will go over all the options with you and explain the pros and cons of everything, then you and Cal can make an informed decision about which route you want to take."

I nod as I listen, realising there's something I need to ask, even though I know what the answer will be.

"Doctor, we're meant to be getting married in June." The doctor sighs and just looks at me, her expression telling me all I need to know. "We're not going to be getting married in June, are we?"

"I'm sorry, Crissie. There's a good chance your treatment will be over by then, but that's no guarantee, and even if it is, it's going to take time for you to get your strength back. Cancer treatment can really take it out of you, so I recommend you postpone the wedding until you know more about your treatment options and how you could react to them."

I feel Cal take my hand and squeeze. I turn my head to him. "It's okay, Cris. People will understand."

"But all that money. We won't get it back at this late hour, and we can't afford to lose it. I won't be able to work, and I can't expect Amanda to keep my job open indefinitely."

"Hey, don't you worry about any of that. I'll sort everything out when we get home."

"Here's some information for you to take away," the doctor says as she hands me over a bunch of leaflets. "You should hear from the oncologist within a couple of days. In the meantime, if you have any questions, please don't hesitate to call me. You're strong, Crissie. There's no reason for you not to get through this."

I glance down at the leaflets as Cal stands, gently pulling me to my feet.

"Thank you, doctor," Cal says as we walk towards the door and head back to the car.

We drive home in silence. I'm clutching the leaflets in my hands, my brain whirring as all the possibilities and scenarios run through my head.

I have cancer. I'm only twenty-four years old. This doesn't happen to people my age. At least, that's what I always thought. Naïve and stupid, I know, but I've never known anyone my age to get it, until now.

The doctor said I should hear from the oncologist within a couple of days, and we can then go and discuss my treatment options. God, this feels so weird. I'm actually thinking about cancer treatment options. I only know of one option, which is chemotherapy, and that does not sound appealing.

Before I know it, Cal is parking outside the flat and turning off the engine. I climb out of the car and head towards the flat, hearing him call my name as he locks the car and jogs over to me just as I enter the building. He stays by my side as we enter the flat and I walk over to the sofa, dropping the leaflets on the coffee table before heading to the bedroom.

I pass Cal as I go, but I don't look at him. I can't. I need time to process everything that's happening, and I know that if Cal is his usual kind and gentle self, I'll burst into tears. I don't need to do that right now. I just need time to think about things and formulate what's going to happen in my own mind.

When I'm in the bedroom, I turn and take the door handle, glancing briefly at Cal as I start to close the door, hoping he understands that I need this time on my own right now. I don't want him to think I'm shutting him out again, not after finally letting him in.

He gives me a small smile and a nod as the door closes, and I breathe a sigh of relief that he understands. A few seconds later, I hear him on the phone. He's doing as he said he would, trying to sort out our wedding.

I feel the tears begin to form in my eyes as I realise we won't be getting married in three months time. I won't be wearing the white dress I fell in love with when I first tried it on, and I won't be saying my vows in front of friends and family.

Refusing to cry, I rush over and jump onto the bed, hugging my knees close to my chest. Everything is going to change now. Nothing is going to be the same again. The doctor said I had options, and once treatment had been completed, things could get back to normal, but how is that possible?

I know there is no cure for cancer. Once you get it, it never truly goes away. Sure, you have treatment, go into remission, but there is always a chance that it can come back to bite you in the arse once again. You never fully get rid of it, so even if I do come through treatment, my life will never be normal. How can it be with the threat of the cancer coming back at any time?

It's like I'll always be looking over my shoulder, knowing it can sneak up on me whenever it feels like it.

As I hug my knees closer, all I can do now is wait for the appointment with the oncologist and hope my cancer is as early as the doctor believes.

CHAPTER 39

Crissie

"Now, Crissie, I've reviewed the report from your GP and also the results from the biopsy you had the other week, and I concur with your doctors' diagnosis. You have early stage cervical cancer. The good news is that there is a lot we can do to eradicate it at this stage, and I'll go through those options with you today. The fact that you're young and healthy can only go in your favour and should speed up the healing process once the treatment has been completed. If all goes well, you should be cancer free and able to get back to your normal life within six months."

Cal and I sit in one of the oncology suites listening to the specialist who will help me through the treatment I'll receive for, as the doctor says, early stage cervical cancer.

It's been four days since my GP told me the diagnosis, and Cal and I have finally come to an understanding. He can be there to support me, provided he doesn't treat me any differently.

The last thing I want is him constantly asking if I'm okay or if I need anything. It'll drive me up the wall and will only make me snap at him, which is something I don't want to do. I've given him enough grief over the past few weeks, so as long as he doesn't try and coddle me, I've promised not to speak to him like a piece of dirt. I've also decided that I won't let this thing beat me.

"I like your optimism, doctor, and I hope you're right. I don't want this disease to take over my life. I'm only twenty-four. I have the rest of my life to live, and I'm not going to let it take over. So, what are my options?"

"That's the right attitude to have, Crissie. Too many people come in here all doom and gloom, only thinking about the worst-case scenario. The fact you want to beat this and you're willing to fight is nothing but a good thing. Now, I think the best option for you is surgery, followed by radiotherapy."

So not chemo, then? I think to myself, almost breathing a sigh of relief. I know the side effects of chemotherapy, and they aren't pleasant. I don't know enough about radiotherapy to have an opinion. I guess that's why we're here today.

"What kind of surgery?"

"Well, we have a couple of options. I'm assuming you

want to have children in the future?" I nod at his question. "Okay, then I think the best surgical option is a Trachelectomy. Basically, it's a keyhole surgery, so there won't be a lot of scarring, and we remove your cervix and the upper part of your vagina. We then reattach your womb to the lower section of your vagina. It means you'll still be able to have children, although they will need to be born through a caesarean section."

I nod, taking in the information he's giving me. I'm struggling to get my head around what the surgery entails, and I'm guessing the doctor sees that as he smiles and pats my hand. "Don't worry, Crissie. I know it's a lot to take in. I can give you some information to take away with you, but you can also research the procedure online if you want to. If you decide to do that, I would recommend sticking only to reliable sources, such as the NHS website. There are so many sites out there that I'm sure were just set up to scare people. Now, I'd like to start treatment sooner rather than later, but I'll give you a few days to take everything in, and I'll get my assistant to give you a call on Monday to schedule the surgery, if that's okay with you?"

Monday. So that gives me three days to read up on the doctor's proposed treatment plan and sort out any questions I may have. I'd be lying if I said the idea of surgery didn't scare the hell out of me, but if it means it gets rids of this cancer, and I can still have children in the future, then it can't be all that bad.

"Yes, doctor, that's fine. Thank you."

"Good." He reaches into one of his desk drawers and pulls out a folder, obviously something he put together before we arrived. "Here is the information on the surgery and the radiotherapy. It includes information on the side effects and the expected recovery times for both. If we can get you in for the surgery soon, there's no reason why you can't be living a normal life by Christmas, at the latest."

The doctor stands, and Cal and I follow suit. He shakes hands with the both of us and shows us from his office. Cal has remained quiet throughout the consultation, and I can't help but wonder what is going through his head. The only indication he gave me that he was affected by the doctors' words was when he told me I could still have children.

I know Cal still wants a family as much as I do, so the fact that even after everything, it will still be possible, is the silver lining we've been hoping for. It's about time we had some good news, such as it is. It makes what I have to go through somehow worthwhile.

Yeah, I know how weird that sounds, believe me I do. I'd assumed that, with the location of the cancer, having children wasn't going to be a possibility. Now that I know it is, I'm even more determined to fight it.

We're back in the car and on our way home when I suddenly realise I have no idea whether Cal has been able to do anything about postponing our wedding. It's strange that only a few weeks ago, the wedding was all I could think about, but after my GP broke the news about the cancer, it's not been a priority.

"I forgot to ask you, have you been able to sort out the wedding?"

"Actually, everyone was really understanding. We only lost the deposit on the venue, but they've said that, under the circumstances, they'll transfer the deposit over to a new booking, if we still want to have the wedding there. The only downside is with them now offering the full wedding and reception package, they're pretty much fully booked most weekends for the next two years at least, so we may have to wait. I know you have your heart set on that venue, so I'm prepared to wait until they have a date free if you are?"

Wow. I can't believe we only lost the deposit, and that's not really lost if they'll transfer it to a new booking. I thought for sure we'd lose most of the money we'd paid out, and with me not being able to work while I'm having treatment, lack of money was making me feel even worse than I already did. Knowing that we've got the majority of it back has lifted the proverbial weight from my shoulders.

"That's great news, and yes, I'm happy to wait until that venue becomes available, even if it's two or three years down the line."

"That's good, because I told them as much and they're just waiting on us to pick a date and confirm with them."

For the first time in what feels like a long time, I smile at Cal and reach out to take his hand, grateful he recently swapped his Ford Focus for an automatic. Personally, I hate automatic cars, but right now, I couldn't be happier for having one as it means I can hold Cal's hand without any hindrance.

"I've missed that," Cal says as he looks between the road and me. "Your smile. I've missed your smile."

"I've not had much to smile about recently, but knowing our wedding will still be wonderful, albeit a bit further down the road than originally planned, is definitely a smiling occasion." I smile again when Cal lifts our joined hands and kisses my knuckles before turning the car onto the street that houses our apartment. "Do you fancy going to lunch somewhere? We've not been out for a while. It'll be nice to get out."

"Sure, why not," Cal says as he turns the car and heads back onto the main road into town. "I know just the place."

~

Caleb

I can't tell you how happy I am that Cris and I are getting back to normal. To say the last few weeks have been rocky would be an understatement. At one point, I didn't think we'd make it. Her determination to push me away and go through it on her own was so strong, I almost gave up on her, on us.

It was only when I insisted on coming with her to get her results that we finally sat down and talked. She explained how scared she was and that she felt like she had been nothing but bad luck for me. I assured her she couldn't be more wrong, and the fact she had cancer only made me more sure about us.

As if I didn't already know, it only served to solidify how I felt. Crissie was going to need me over the next few months. As soon as the doctor told us she had cancer, I went online and found out all I could about the type of cancer she had, and also about what treatments are available to her.

I'm not naïve enough to believe it's going to be a walk in the park. She's got a long road ahead of her, and I'll be with her every step of the way.

Her suggestion that we go to lunch today had been a surprise. She hasn't really been very sociable since her first visit to the doctors, so when she asked about lunch, I knew the perfect place. When we'd parked outside the little Italian restaurant I took her to when I first asked her out, she'd smiled the smile I'd come to love, and had missed recently.

Both Cris and I love it there. We had a lovely meal and just talked about everything and nothing, including the wedding. While we'd both been gutted at having to postpone, there was no other option. Once I'd explained to everyone the reason why we were postponing, everyone was more than happy to give us a full refund.

We agreed to wait until Crissie's treatment was over and she was on the mend before setting a new date. The fact that the venue was prepared to transfer our deposit to another time had been a big relief for the both of us. The place was costing us a small fortune. The deposit alone was close to £2000, money we couldn't afford to lose. The realisation that we wouldn't was a huge relief.

I walk into the kitchen and open the fridge, pulling out a bottle of wine and grabbing two glasses from the rack. Right now, Crissie is up to her neck in bubbles and warm water as she relaxes in the bath. When we got back from lunch, I went in and lit a few candles before starting the hot water and pouring in her favourite jasmine scented bubble bath.

She is under orders to stay there for at least thirty minutes while I pick a movie and get the wine ready. We agreed we would spend the rest of the day just having some time for us, to reconnect.

We need this time, just the two of us, while things are still relatively normal. When she starts treatment, everything is going to change, so we need to take advantage of normality while we can.

I'm pouring the wine when I see movement out of the corner of my eye and turn my head, seeing Crissie standing in the doorway in her Little Mermaid pyjamas. With her damp hair tied back and her face free of make up, she looks younger than her twenty-four years.

We've been together for so long I sometimes forget

that we're still quite young in the grand scheme of things. That only made her diagnosis all the more shocking to us and has made her more determined to face it head on. Yes, she struggled at first, but now she's ready to take the bull by the horns and kick cancer's ass, and I couldn't be more proud of her.

She walks over and smiles as I hand her the wine, which she promptly puts on the coffee table. I look at her quizzically, and before I can say anything, her lips are on mine.

Every nerve in my body feels like it's on fire as her tongue pushes its way past my lips and her fingers tug at my t-shirt. It feels like forever since we were together last, but it's only been a few weeks; a few long, excruciating weeks. My body is screaming at me to pick her up and take her, but my brain is holding back.

Covering her hands with mine, I pull back from her kiss. When she looks at me, I search her eyes, seeing a mixture of desire and confusion swimming in their depths. "What's wrong, Cal? Don't you want me?"

"Of course I want you, Cris. I always want you, but...why now?"

"Why not now?" she says, her hands flexing on my waist. "It's been weeks, Cal. I've used every excuse I can think of to *not* be with you because I was terrified it would make whatever was wrong with me worse. Now that I know that won't happen, there's nothing holding us back. I want you, Cal, and I don't want this cancer to come between us anymore."

As if to punctuate her words, she releases my waist and strips out of her pyjamas, revealing her naked body to me. I've always been amazed at how easily she can keep the weight off. Her body is still as lean and trim as it was back when she was sixteen, but now she has more curves in all the places I love. I want nothing more than to grab hold of her and make love to her for the rest of the day, but something is stopping me, and it's not something I can ignore any longer.

"I don't want to hurt you, Cris."

Cris tilts her head to the side and smiles as she takes a step closer to me. Taking my hand, she lifts it up to her breast, and I automatically squeeze the soft mound of flesh before I pinch the rosy pink nipple. I watch as her eyes flutter closed, and a soft moan passes her lips.

It has been so long since I felt her soft skin against mine; the way her body grips me when she's in the throes of an orgasm. It's a feeling I'll never tire of, and one I've not experienced in what feels like eternity.

I lift my other hand to take her breast in mine, before I lean down and latch on to the puckered nipple with my mouth. Her reaction is instant as her hands grip my waist, whimpers and moans escaping her lips. I can feel her fingers working to unfasten my jeans, and suddenly the urgency to be inside her takes over as I release her and shove my jeans and boxers down and away from my body.

Taking her hand, I pull her down to the floor with me and move her so that she straddles my hips. Her eyes are bright, and her lips are slightly parted as her breath leaves her in short pants. Reaching down, I take myself in my hand and position myself so I can slide up into her, but she takes control as she drops down hard, crying out as I fill her.

It takes me a moment to catch my breath before I realise she's moving over me, her hands pressing into my chest as she rocks back and forth. I soon realise she's not after slow and steady as she picks up pace, her eyes closing as she throws her head back.

The only thing I can do is grab on to her hips and thrust up as she drops down. The delicious friction our bodies are creating causing the familiar heat to spread through my body. I know she's close to the edge as her thighs squeeze my hips and her rhythm falters.

I know this will all be over for me after a few more thrusts, and I find that I want us to fall over the cliff together. Reaching down, I begin to circle her clit with my thumb, her reaction instantaneous as her whole body bucks and she begins to tremble.

"Come with me, baby. Come for me." My words do the trick as she comes apart above me, my name on her lips as I empty myself into her before she collapses on my chest. I'm almost gasping for breath as I gently stroke my fingers along her spine.

"God, I've missed that so much." I chuckle at her words

as my heart rate returns to normal. She shifts and rests her hands on my chest and looks up at me. "We'll get through this. Won't we?"

I can hear the vulnerability in her voice, and I wrap my arms around her back, moving us so we're lying on our sides facing each other, our bodies still intimately connected.

"You bet we will. We do this together, Cris. We're a team, and we're not going to let a silly little thing like cancer beat us down. You hear me?"

"Yeah, I hear you." She smiles up at me, and I feel myself begin to harden again, something I can tell she feels too as she flexes her hips towards mine, her one leg lifting over my hip as I slide deeper.

"Oh, you want to go again, Miss Walker?"

"Making up for lost time, Mr Roberts."

With her hands gripping my biceps and mine on her hip, I proceed to show her just how much fun making up for lost time can be.

CHAPTER 40

Crissie

*T*oday's the day.

In a few hours' time, it will all be over, and then I'll begin the recovery process. But first, I actually need to have the surgery to remove the cancerous cells from my cervix. The nurse has told me they'll be here to take me down to the operating room shortly, so all I can do until then is wait.

Cal and I spent the weekend in the flat, only going out when absolutely necessary. The times that we weren't making love, we spent discussing the recommendations presented by the oncologist and the other options available to me. In the end, we decided to take the specialists' advice, which we confirmed when his assistant called us on Monday.

Now, it's Friday, and I am sat in a scratchy hospital gown, in one of the most uncomfortable beds I've ever slept in. Cal is somewhere in the hospital with my parents, trying to keep them distracted.

I told my parents about my diagnosis over dinner Saturday night. Mum cried, as I knew she would, and my dad just looked at me before proclaiming I was his little girl and he didn't raise a wimp, so I was going to get out there and beat the shit out of this thing. That had earned him a slap on the arm from my mum, but a huge smile and a hug from me.

Even with his bravado, I knew my dad was scared. We all are. We just have different ways of hiding it. Cal and I were pretty similar, in that we just got on with things. Up until today, I was still working. Amanda knew about what was going on; there was no way I could have the treatment and not tell her.

She had practically screamed at me to go home when I arrived for work on Monday, and it wasn't until I explained to her that I needed to be there to keep myself sane that she started to understand.

Cal had gone back to the garage. He, too, hadn't been too happy when I'd told him I would be going to work until I physically couldn't. He seemed to believe I needed to rest as much as I could, as if resting was going to get rid of this thing that was growing inside me. I put my foot down and told him I'd be resting all the time during treatment, so he needed to back off, which he did, albeit reluctantly.

"Crissie, we're here to take you up to theatre now. Are you ready?" I look up when I see the nurse who tended to me earlier standing in the doorway with two orderlies by her side. I told Cal not to be long, and now they're here to take me up and he's not here.

"Could we wait just a few minutes? I want my fiancé to be here when I go up." I watch as the nurse checks the watch attached to her uniform before looking back at me.

"We can wait a couple of minutes, but then we have to get going." She gives me an understanding smile before turning and closing the door. Mere seconds later, Cal walks into the room and the apprehension I had felt only a moment ago dissipates almost immediately.

"I take it they're here to take you to theatre?" he asks, obviously having seen the nurse outside the room.

"Yeah."

"Hey, you'll be okay. It'll just be like you're going to sleep for a few hours, and I'll be right here waiting for you when you wake up."

I nod at him and force a smile. I'm not going to insult him by saying I'm okay, because I'm not. At only twenty-four, I'm about to have surgery for cervical cancer. Now there's a sentence I never thought I'd have to think, let alone say. All the doctors have told me it's a pretty routine surgery and they're confident everything should go smoothly. The nurses have bigged-up the doctors, saying they're the best at what they do, and everything will be fine.

I just wish I could believe them.

"I'm scared, Cal."

I see Cal's expression change before he envelops me in a hug. I hold on to him tightly, willing myself not to cry as he whispers that everything will be okay. I have no choice but to believe him.

"Sorry, Crissie, we really need to get going."

I pull apart from Cal when I hear the nurse's voice from the doorway, just as Cal places a gentle kiss to my lips. "Remember, I'll be right here when you wake up. I love you, baby."

"I love you too, Cal. Always." I smile at him as the orderlies enter the room, remove the brake from my bed, and begin wheeling me out. I see my parents stood in the hallway, and I reach out my hands to them. I can see tears welling in my mum's eyes, and my dad's face looks grim.

"Stay strong, honey. We love you."

The orderlies continue to wheel me away, and I turn my head, seeing the three people I love the most in the world watching me go in for the surgery that could save my life.

Caleb

*F*ive hours.

She's been in there for five hours and we have no clue what's going on. The doctor said the surgery was routine and she should be out within three hours, so why is it taking this long? Maybe the cancer was further along than they thought? Maybe something went wrong? Why the hell isn't anyone telling us anything?

I stand up and being to pace the hallway, stopping when I hear Diane say my name. "Cal, I know you're worried, but please sit down. All that pacing is making me nervous."

"Sorry," I say as I quickly sit down. "It's just that it should be over by now. What's taking them so long?"

Diane reaches out and squeezes my hand, and I turn to look at her. "I'm sure everything is okay. It's a complicated procedure and they need to be sure they get it all. I'd rather they take eight hours and get everything than four hours and risk missing something."

I nod at her, knowing she's right. The doctors are probably just being thorough. The last thing I want is for them to miss something and have to open her up again. Even though the doctor explained the procedure could be done by keyhole surgery, Crissie will still have a scar, even if it is a small one.

I stand again. The pacing has almost become second nature to me now. It's all I've done since they took Crissie to theatre. Patience has never been one of my virtues, and

I can't see it changing anytime soon. I'm about to go ask someone if they can find out what's happening, when I see Crissie's doctor walking towards us.

He nods in acknowledgement when he sees me, but his expression is giving nothing away. I want to go towards him, but my brain isn't sending the message to my feet. I can sense Crissie's parents behind me, as eager to find out about their daughter as I am.

"Caleb, Mr and Mrs Walker, thank you for being so patient. Crissie's operation took slightly longer than expected as the cancerous cells went further into the cervix than we originally thought. We were still able to complete the procedure and we're confident we got everything. Crissie is going to have to have a course of radiotherapy, which we expect to last about six weeks, but after the treatment is complete, I don't see any reason why Crissie can't go on to have a normal life."

I release the breath I didn't know I'd been holding and feel a strong hand on my shoulder, knowing it belongs to Crissie's father.

"Thank you, doctor. Can I ask, do you think we'll still be able to have a family?"

"There are never any guarantees when it comes to conceiving a child, Caleb, even without having had surgery, but Crissie still has her uterus, fallopian tubes and ovaries, so pregnancy is still an option for you both. She just won't be able to have a natural birth."

I nod to confirm I understand, and I hear Crissie's

mum ask if we can see her. I see the doctor's mouth move, but I don't hear what he says. The blood is roaring in my ears, and I suddenly feel like I'm falling. Before I know it, I'm sat down and hear someone telling me to take deep breaths.

Several minutes later, I look up to see Diane, Matthew and a nurse all looking at me, concern evident on their faces.

"You okay, Cal? You went pale and then staggered backwards. I think you started to hyperventilate."

"It looks like you had a panic attack."

I look between Diane and the nurse, then down to my hands. I see they're still shaking, and I clasp them together.

"She's going to be okay," I say to myself, before looking up again. "She's going to be okay."

Even though the doctors told us the procedure Crissie was having was relatively routine, I had convinced myself something would go wrong. When they were wheeling her down that hallway and towards theatre, part of me believed that would be the last time I would see her alive.

I've no idea why I believed that, or why I was so convinced she wouldn't make it. I know I should have put my faith in the doctors and nurses who were looking after her. They do this for a living, it's what they trained for. She was in the best hands possible, and still I thought the worst.

That was usually one of Crissie's traits. No matter what

happened, she always went to the worse case scenario, always preparing for the most negative outcome she could think of. I guess some of that negative energy has rubbed off on me.

"We're going up to see her," Diane tells me. "I assume you want to come too?"

I jump up from my seat and head down the hallway, hearing the chuckles behind me. I stop walking, realising I have no idea where I'm going, before turning to look at Crissie's parents, who are smirking at me.

"She's this way," Matthew says, indicating the opposite direction to where I was headed, and I hurry back over to them.

"So, what are we waiting for?" I ask quickly as I indicate for the nurse to lead the way. Now that I know Crissie is going to be okay, all I want to do is see her, so I can see for myself. It's only been a few hours, but I've missed my girl, and all I want to do is hold her hand and sit by her side, a place I intend to stay for the rest of my life.

Caleb

The nurse shows us to Crissie's room and tells us to take as long as we need. She explains Cris may be a little groggy after the anaesthetic but that she should be able to talk to us. When the nurse leaves us alone, I take a breath before slowly opening the door.

I'm unable to stop the gasp from passing my lips at the sight of her lying in that hospital bed. I see the monitors keeping a check on her heart rate and blood pressure, and the IV drip is by the side to keep her hydrated. She looks so small and fragile, and I feel an overwhelming urge to protect her from everything and everyone.

Her parents move past me and stand either side of her bed, each taking one of her hands in theirs. For several moments, she remains still, until finally her eyes flutter open and her head turns to her dad. From my position by the door, I can see the smile on her face when she sees her dad, and his beaming grin in return.

When she turns her head to look at her mum, our eyes connect. I know I should go to her. I know she needs me right now, but my feet won't move. I feel my heartbeat in my chest as my pulse quickens. Then it hits me.

I could have lost her today. If anything had gone wrong, I'd be alone.

My breathing catches in my throat, and I reach out and grip the doorframe as my body begins to shake. Crissie lifts her head, and I can see the moment she realises what I'm thinking when her eyes tear up and she turns to her mum, speaking quietly. "Mum, I hope you don't mind, but can I have some time with Cal?"

"Of course, honey. We'll wait outside."

Within a few moments, Cris and I are alone, and she

holds out her hand out to me. When I'm sure I can move, I hurry over and grab her hand, holding it tightly between mine, only now realising that tears are slipping down my cheeks.

"I'm okay, Cal. I'm going to be fine. Please don't cry, baby."

"Oh god, Cris. I thought it had taken you. I was sure you weren't coming back to me. I don't think I could go on if I lost you."

Crissie is crying now too, and I feel bad for making her cry, especially when she should be resting.

"No, Cal, please don't say that. I'm not going anywhere." She gently tugs my hand and I lean down, carefully taking her in my arms. Burying my nose in her hair, I breathe out and just let myself hold her, trying my hardest to fight back the tears that are still coming thick and fast.

"Sssh, Cal, it's okay. I promise. I'm here. I won't let it take me."

We hold each other for what seems like hours, when in reality it's been only a few minutes.

"I don't want to let you go in case you're not here when I come back," I reveal to her as I loosen my hold.

"You don't need to," she says, and I feel her begin to move away from me. "There's room on here for two."

I pull away and look down at her, seeing she's freed up some space on her bed, so I can lie next to her. "You sure? I don't want to hurt you."

"I'm sure, Cal. I want you to hold me tonight."

"But the doctors, if they see—"

"Cal, will you just get on here already?"

I resist the urge to salute her as my lips form the first smile I've made in the last few days. My tears have stopped, and all I can do is look at her, my precious girl. I lift my hand to her face and cup her cheek, pleased when she tilts her head into my palm.

"You're so beautiful," I whisper.

"Oh please. I look a mess," she replies with a self-conscious laugh.

"No, you'll always be beautiful to me, no matter what you wear or how you look."

When she pats the space beside her on the bed, I carefully position myself and raise my arm. When she moves alongside me and rests her head on my chest, her arm wrapping around my waist, I fold my arms around her and hold on tight. When I feel her breathing even out, I place a gentle kiss on her head and throw up a silent prayer that we've many more years left together.

CHAPTER 41

Crissie

<u>July 2014</u>

"*T*hat's it, Crissie. All done."

I look up at the nurse and give her my biggest grin, which, considering how tired and worn out I feel, is some achievement.

It's been almost three months since I had surgery to remove cancerous cells from my cervix, and today marks the day when I complete my radiotherapy. I can't tell you how happy I am about that.

The doctors warned me of the possible side effects before I had my first treatment, and I swear, I've never felt so ill. The nausea and lethargy knocked me off my feet ninety percent of the time. I've probably lost a stone in weight, not that I had much to lose in the first place, but thankfully, I've still got a full head of hair.

Yeah, I know it's vain to think that, but come on, I'm a girl. I love my hair and, even though I know it would grow back eventually, it's taken me years to get it to the perfect length.

"Thanks, Penny." I smile my thanks to the nurse who has been administering my treatment since the very first time. She's only a few years older than me and reminds me of Pippa in so many ways. She's been a breath of fresh air while I've been here; always making me laugh and trying to take my mind of what's happening. I swear, if it hadn't been for her, I don't think I'd have made it through the last eight or so weeks.

Cal loves her too. He's been to almost every session with me, and she's had him in stitches as often as she has me. He's mentioned to me many times that he's grateful for a nurse who is as dedicated to her job as Penny is, and I can't deny that she's made this process a whole lot easier for me to get through.

I wait while she unhooks me from the machines, and a huge smile spreads across my face when I see Cal standing in the doorway. I hadn't anticipated seeing him until later this afternoon. He dropped me off this morning then had to go to the garage to see to a rush job. He'd tried to get one of the other mechanics to go in, but they were all busy with other jobs.

I'd been expecting my mum to come and pick me up,

so seeing his handsome face standing there has only made this day even better. Penny sees my smile and looks towards the entrance. She, too, is grinning when she looks back at me.

"You know, I wish I could find a guy who looks at me the way he looks at you."

"Yeah, I guess I am lucky. You know, he told me once that he was happy he could put the smile back in my eyes."

"Wow, he definitely has a way with words," Penny says as she glances over her shoulder at him. "He's handsome, too. Damn girl, you're one lucky bitch."

We both laugh at her words as she finishes up and helps me down off the bed.

"Now, you know the drill; rest up as much as you can for the rest of the day. I'll go grab your prescription for the anti-nausea medication and then you're good to go." She pats my shoulder before she leaves, saying hi to Cal as she passes him. He takes a few steps into the room and falls down in the chair next to the bed. He's only been gone for a few hours, but he looks exhausted, which is how I'll probably look by the time we get home.

After every treatment session I've had, I've always slept like the dead afterwards. Cal told me that once I fell asleep in the car on the way back and he had to carry me to the flat and put me to bed, and I didn't wake up until noon the next day. I had slept for almost twenty hours, yet I still felt like I'd not slept in days.

I know Cal hasn't been sleeping well, especially the nights before I'm due to have treatment. It's almost as if he's expecting me not to come home. He always looks so relieved when we're walking out the hospital after the treatment is over, and it's only when we're back at the flat that I see him relax. I'm guessing tonight will be no different.

Penny returns a few minutes later with my prescription, and 'accidentally' knocks into Cal's outstretched legs. He jolts up at the unexpected contact, and I can't help but laugh at him. I'm the one who's been having radiotherapy and should be half asleep, yet he's the one who dozes off when he's been sat down for less than ten minutes.

He stands quickly and holds out his hand to me, looking sheepishly at Penny as he pulls me to his side. "Thanks for everything, Penny. You've been a great strength to us these last two months."

"It's my pleasure, Cal. You know what you need to do when you leave here so I won't go through it all again with you. You just look after her, you hear me? Don't forget, I know where you live."

Cal nods and leans in to place a kiss on her cheek, and I smile when I see her blush at his action. I've yet to meet a woman who is immune to Cal's charms, and clearly Penny isn't either.

I take my hand from Cal's briefly to give Penny a quick hug, then return to his side as we leave the room and eventually, the hospital itself. I hope I don't have to see that place again any time soon, although I know I'll be back there within a few months. The doctors told me I'll need to have repeat scans every so many months over the next couple of years to ensure that everything's okay and the cancer hasn't returned. If it means I don't have to go through that treatment again, I don't mind in the slightest.

We cross the car park and walk over to Cal's car. When I'm buckled up, he climbs in next to me, and before I know it, we're driving home. I lean my head back against the seat and close my eyes, intending to just rest for a few minutes, but when I open them again, I'm back in the flat wearing one of Cal's old t-shirts, wrapped in our duvet, with no sign of Cal.

How long have I been out?

I throw the duvet off me, almost sighing when the cool air hits my overheated skin. One of the side effects of the radiotherapy I hate is the hot and cold flushes I keep getting. One minute, I feel like I'm about the freeze to death, and minutes later, it's like I'm my own personal radiator. This is one of those moments where even the t-shirt feels like it's burning me.

Swinging my legs over the edge, I plant them on the floor before standing. My head swims for a moment and a wave of nausea hits me before I can stop it. As I've learnt to do over the last few weeks, I close my eyes and take a few deep breaths. The anti-nausea pills haven't kicked in yet, either that or they have, and they've worn off. I've still no idea how long I've been asleep.

When I feel normal again, I cross the room and open the bedroom door, seeing the living room is in darkness, apart from a stream of light coming in through the window from an outside security light. I see Cal stretched out on the sofa, wearing nothing but a pair of boxers. The sheet he had covering him has fallen to the floor and, even though I know I shouldn't, all I want to do is touch him, but I don't.

Touching him will only make me want him, and until I'm fully healed—something that is taking longer than expected—we can't have sex. It's been hard on both of us, but we both agreed to wait until the doctor gave me the all clear, not wanting to risk causing any complications to the healing process.

When we do get the green light, I'll be going back on the pill, seeing as we can't even think about getting pregnant for at least the next twelve months. The doctor explained getting pregnant too soon would put additional strain on my body that, until it's fully healed, it may not be able to cope with and could do more harm, which is the last thing we want.

As if he can sense I'm here, Cal stirs, and in the dim light, I see his eyes open. "Hey, you should be sleeping."

"I have been sleeping. I just woke up. How long have I been out?" I watch as Cal stretches his arms above his head, letting my eyes sweep over his lean torso, before he lowers them to glance at his watch.

"It's just after midnight, so about eight hours."

"Seriously? Where did the day go?"

"You were fast asleep before we left the hospital car park," Cal says as he shifts onto his side and waves me over. I don't hesitate as I take two steps towards him and lie down, his front to my back. He drapes an arm over my waist and pulls me into him.

It never ceases to amaze me how well we fit together. Cal tangles his legs with mine, and I can feel his breath on my neck as he breathes steadily. It's late, and despite having been asleep for almost eight hours, I feel like I've been awake for days on end. I hate that the radiotherapy zaps me of all my energy, and I especially hate that I'm so dependant on Cal until this stuff is out of my system.

I know he doesn't mind taking care of things, and of me, but I hate feeling like I'm a burden to him. He'd slap me silly if he heard me call myself that, but I can't help how I feel. It's only really at times like now, when he's holding me and we're just lying here, that I feel like everything is normal and we're just a regular couple in love. I guess in some ways we are, but we've been through more things in our eight years together than most couples go through in a lifetime, and we're still going strong.

"Sleep, Cris. I've got you." I feel the arm he has wrapped around me tighten, and then he places a gentle kiss on my hair, something he has started doing often, and it makes me smile every time.

"I love you, Cal."

"Love you too, Cris, always and forever."

With his words in my mind and a smile on my lips, I drift off into a peaceful sleep in the arms of the man who is my world.

CHAPTER 42

Crissie

"*A*re you ready? They will be here any minute."

And I thought I was bad. Cal has been driving me crazy all evening, and I've made a mental note to say something if he ever accuses me of nagging again.

It's my birthday weekend, and tonight, I'm going out for cocktails and dancing with Pippa and Lizzie. It's the first weekend I've felt well enough to go out, and as a present, Cal treated me to the works at a local spa, along with a new outfit, seeing as most of my going out dresses are too big for me now, owing to the weight I lost while having treatment.

Actually, it's a double celebration as we had the results from my latest scan this morning and everything looks good. The doctor told us that the first scan after completion of treatment is one of the most important, so the fact it came back clear is a huge weight off our shoulders.

"I'm coming," I call out as I grab my clutch bag and secure it on my wrist before walking out in my brand new four-inch Christian Louboutin heels. I have no idea how Cal got the money together to buy them, but the pink sparkly heels are beautiful, and even if I only wear them the once, I love him for knowing how much I would love them.

I enter the living room just as there is a knock on the door. I can hear the voices from outside and don't need to be psychic to know everyone is out there. While the girls and I go out, Cal, his best man, Gary, Lance, and Lizzie's new boyfriend, Shaun, are having a games night, which will probably involve pizza and numerous bottles of beer.

You say games night to me, and I think back to the ones I used to have with my parents, involving board games, but I think the games the guys have in mind are of the electronic variety, which is confirmed when I see Cal setting up all the controllers.

I shake my head and smile at him as I go to the door. I'm almost knocked off my heels by the noise that greets me as everyone streams into the flat. I'm about to close the door when I hear someone holler, and I see Gary coming towards me. He gives me a quick kiss on the cheek as he walks in before joining the rest of the guys across the room.

They do their usual handshake-back slapping routine as the girls start eyeing up my shoes. I can see the question in Pippa's eyes; we are the same size and she's going to want to borrow them, and as much as I love her, she's not getting her hands on these babies.

"Ready to go, ladies? I think the boys want to get their game on."

We all look over at the guys and see them deep in discussion about which game to start with. Each of them is holding a different game in their hand and clearly each one thinks theirs should be first. What is it about computer games that makes grown men turn into little kids?

"Let's just leave them to it," I say as I open the door again, and we all exit the flat. We're almost to the main doors when I hear my name from behind us. Turning, I see Cal coming up behind us. "Hey, everything okay?"

"Everything's fine, but you forgot something."

I furrow my brow and automatically open my clutch, seeing my phone, money, lipstick and keys. Closing the clasp, I look up at him, just as his mouth closes over mine. My whole body heats up instantly, and I lift my hands to grip his biceps as his tongue plays with mine.

God, I love it when he kisses me. His mouth is so skilled I swear he could push me over the edge with just his lips and his tongue. I pull him closer, our bodies now pressed together. I want to climb his body so badly right now, and the fact that I can't pours a proverbial bucket of cold water over my head.

I loosen my grip on his arms as he slows the kiss. It's only when we break apart that I remember Lizzie and Pippa are with me, but when I turn, they're gone, and I'm grateful they gave us our privacy. I look back at him, knowing my cheeks are flushed. I can feel my pulse beating in my throat and my heart in my chest.

"Have a good night, baby." With one final kiss, Cal releases me and heads back to the flat, throwing one last look over his shoulder, giving me a wink for good measure, something he knows makes me go weak at the knees. I resist the urge to fan myself as I leave the building, seeing Pippa and Lizzie waiting for me by my car.

"My brother finally let you go, then?" Lizzie says with a smile, and I just grin at her.

"Your brother wanted a good night kiss."

"Oh, he wanted more than a kiss. He wanted..." Pippa starts, then stops herself, her face falling, "God, Cris, I'm sorry. I didn't think."

"Don't worry about it, Pip," I say as I shake my head, "It's no big deal. I forget myself sometimes, too. It's so easy to get carried away with Cal."

"La, la, la, la, la, la, la, la." We both turn to Lizzie to see her with her fingers in her ears, making the sounds a child makes when they're trying not to listen to something. When she sees we've stopped talking, she removes her fingers.

"Sorry, Cris, but I really don't want to hear about how much you want to bang my brother. I get it, he's cute, but still, ewww. Now, can we go? I need a drink."

Grabbing the keys from my clutch, I unlock the car and we all pile in. Minutes later, we're on our way into town for the first girl's night we've had in several months.

~

It's almost midnight, and both Lizzie and Pippa are three sheets to the wind. Both of them are wobbling on their heels as we work our way around the dancefloor to cheesy eighties songs. They've worked their way through every cocktail on the menu, and we've never laughed as much as we have tonight.

As designated driver, I've been on soft drinks all evening. I couldn't drink even if I wanted to, not with the medication I'm taking. Just one of the downsides of the treatment I've had.

When Chesney Hawkes' blasts over the club's speakers, all three of us scream the lyrics at the top of our lungs as we raise our hands above our heads. I can't remember the last time I had so much fun with my girls. It's been way too long.

"Look at those three. I'd give the brunette a good seeing to."

"Fuck that, mate. Give me ten minutes and I'll be screwing the blonde's brains out."

"Nah, the chick with the black hair is the one. With a rack like that, she's bound to be a great lay."

It takes me several moments to realise the guys stood to the side of the dancefloor are talking about us. I try to concentrate on dancing and having a good time, but the crude comments from the guys are distracting. Do men seriously talk about women like that? Even with the drinking they've bound to have done tonight, there's no excuse for it.

Pushing their words to the back on my mind, I continue to dance with the girls, stopping suddenly when I feel hands on my hips and a mouth on my neck. It takes me just a moment to realise he's sucking and licking my skin as his hands fist in my dress in an attempt to pull up my skirt.

Without thinking, I whirl round, my hand connecting with his face. I feel the sting in my palm as he staggers back, his hand against his face, his eyes blazing. Everyone around us has stopped dancing, wondering what's going on.

"You fucking bitch."

Before I know what's happening, he's coming at me, only stopping when one of his friends grabs his arm and pulls him back.

"Let me go, you fucking bastard. Did you see what she did? The fucking whore slapped me."

"Yeah, well you were being a dick. You can't just grab a girl like that, Dave. You're lucky slapping you is all she did."

I watch the two men as one glares daggers at me and the other tries to calm him down. By now, Pippa and Lizzie are flanking me, and everyone around us is trying their hardest not to make it obvious they're avidly watching what's happening.

"I'd have kneed him in the balls," Lizzie shouts at him, quickly taking a step back when the guy tries to shake his friend off him.

"I'm sorry about this, girls. My friend has had a few too many to drink."

"Don't fucking apologise for me," the guys shouts. "All of 'em want it. Just look at them, flashing their tits and legs. They all need a good seeing to, and I'm just the guy to give it to them. All fucking three of them. You'd better watch your back, blondie. Fucking you would make my fucking year. Goddamn filthy whore." He grabs at his crotch through his jeans to emphasis the point he's trying to make as his friend finally manages to drag him back off the dancefloor. I shudder as his words sink it, realising he just threatened me, threatened us. A bad feeling descends over me, and I know our night is over.

"Come on, let's go. It's getting late anyway."

The three of us head towards the exit, when I suddenly get the urge to pee. I give Pippa my keys and tell them to go ahead and I'll be there in a few minutes. She grabs Lizzie's hand and tugs her towards the exit when she doesn't move quick enough. Knowing the queue for the ladies' room is going to be longer than my bladder can take, I head in the direction of the men's room.

I open the door and peer in, relieved to see it's empty. I'll be in there for literally a minute. I just need to do my business and get out. Hurrying inside, I dive into a cubicle, deciding to hover over the seat as I lower my knickers and relieve myself. Thirty seconds later, I've wiped and adjusted my dress before opening the stall, stopping dead in my tracks as I come face to face with the guy from the dancefloor.

"Well, well, well. What do we have here? Little Miss Prick Tease."

"Look, just let me go and we'll forget everything that's happened tonight." I go to walk past him, but he grabs my arm. I wince as his fingers dig into my skin as he drags me back and pushes me against the wall. He thrusts his hips forward and pins me there as his hands hold my arms to my side. His eyes are fixed on my chest as I try and pull my arms free, but the only thing my struggles are doing is pulling the dress tighter across my chest.

"Those are some spectacular tits you have there." He licks his lips before lowering his head and licking the swell of my breasts. I shift my body, trying to break his hold on my arms so I can get free, but despite his drunken state, he's surprisingly strong and holds me in place.

"Help!" I scream. "Please, someone help me."

"Oh, there's no point screaming, bitch. It's so loud out there, no one can hear you." When he releases one of my hands, I try and use it to my advantage, but he grabs it again and forces it behind me, holding my wrists together with one hand. With his free hand, he tugs at the neckline of my dress, and I hear the flimsy fabric tear. He laughs as he stares at my exposed breasts, and I struggle again, but that only makes him more eager to make me suffer.

"That's it, keep struggling, bitch. Those tits look fucking great when you struggle."

I close my eyes tightly as I feel his mouth close over my nipple, feeling tears burning a path down my cheeks as he bites and tugs my skin with his teeth. This can't be happening. Please, God, don't let him do this to me.

He's laughing as he continues biting my nipples, before releasing them and sucking hard against the sensitive flesh. I know he's going to mark me. There's going to be no way he won't leave his mark on me. His hand still grips my wrists tightly. I struggle to free them, using all my strength, but he's too strong. He's got me right where he wants me and there's nothing I can do to stop him taking what he wants.

His hand moves lower, and I feel him lift my skirt and tug at my knickers. They come away from my body as he tears through them, tossing them onto the dirty floor. I try to close my legs, but he forces them apart with one of his knees, pushing his hips into mine. I feel sick when I feel his erection pressing into me, and when his fingers rub over me, I cry out, ashamed at how slick I am down there. How the hell can I be wet? I'm in no way turned on. This guy is forcing himself on me and my body is betraying me.

"Let's see how much you fucking want this, you whore. Your tits are so tasty. I bet your pussy tastes just as sweet." He lifts his fingers to his mouth and sucks them, his eyes blazing. "Oh, I was right. My cock is going to feel so good when I ram it in your pussy. You're so fucking wet, bitch. I knew you wanted it. Even out on the dance floor you wanted me to fuck you, didn't you? Right there in front of everyone. Does people knowing you're a little whore turn on you? You like that a stranger is about to fuck you, don't you? Well, newsflash, sweetheart, I'm going to fuck you so hard it'll make you scream."

I hear the metal of his belt buckle and then a zip being lowered, and my whole body freezes. I should be struggling; trying to stop him from what he's about to do. I should be screaming at the top of my voice until my lungs are raw, but all I can do is stand there.

"Hey, Dave, you done with her, man? I can't hold them off any longer."

He lifts his head as he hears the voice and my eyes fly open. Hearing the other voice seems to knock some sense into me, and I look straight at him and lift my knee up hard, connecting with his crotch. He cries out in pain and crumbles to the floor as I pull up my torn dress to cover myself, race out of the bathroom, and through the crowds of people. Before I know it, I'm out in the fresh air, and I hear Pippa calling my name.

"Crissie, there you are. We were beginning to... What the hell happened? Cris? Oh God, Cris, are you okay?"

"Just take me home. Please, Pip, just get me home." I stagger towards my car, only now realising I'm only wearing one shoe. Pippa puts me in the passenger seat before racing round the car. My eyes connect with Lizzie's in the backseat, and needing contact, I reach my hand round, sighing when I feel her take it in hers and squeeze.

"We'll be home soon, Cris. Shit, I can't drive. I've been drinking. I need to call Cal or one of the guys to come get us."

"They've been drinking too," I say quietly, before releasing Lizzie's hand and climbing out the car.

"You can't drive, Cris," I hear Pippa say as I open the driver's side door. "You're in shock."

"I'm fine, Pip. I promise, I'll get us home."

Pippa hesitates only slightly before handing me the keys. Less than ten seconds later, we're on our way home and I'm well on my way to forgetting what turned into one of the worst nights of my life.

Caleb

"*Y*es! I beat your arse again. You guys suck."

I laugh as Lance and Shaun toss their controllers on the floor and both reach for another slice of pizza. Gary just sits there, grinning at me.

"It's your game, mate. You've probably been practicing since we suggested getting together for tonight."

"Yeah yeah, believe that if you want to. Truth is, I'm just better than you two." I lift my hands behind my head and lean back, grinning widely as they both scowl at me. I'll never admit it, but Lance was right. I have been playing this game most nights since Crissie suggested I invite the guys round when they have their girl's night. No way in hell was I losing to these two, not at my own game.

I grab another beer from the cooler and pop the cap, looking up when I hear a key in the door. Glancing at the clock, I see it's half past midnight. I hadn't been expecting the girls back for at least a couple of hours.

When the door opens, Crissie walks in, her hand clutched to her chest, and I don't miss the fact she's only wearing one shoe. She doesn't even look at me as she goes straight into the bedroom and closes the door. I hear the familiar sound of the lock clicking into place and realise something is seriously wrong.

Pippa and Lizzie walk in a few moments later and close the door. I'm on my feet and in their face in an instant, torn between interrogating them and banging on the door for Crissie to open it. "Pippa, what happened? What's wrong with Cris?"

My heart is almost beating out my chest as I look between Pippa and the bedroom door.

"I don't know, Cal. We were about to leave to come home when she said she needed the bathroom. She gave us the car keys and told us to go and wait for her. She was gone for about fifteen minutes, and I was about to go in and look for her when she came out. Her dress was torn, and I could see she'd been crying. She wouldn't say what was wrong but... Cal, something happened when we were dancing. I don't know if it means anything or even if it's related, but someone made a play for her, grabbed at her, and she slapped him. The guy wasn't happy. He actually threatened her, saying she should watch her back."

"What the fuck! Call the police, Pip."

"Cal, I don't think that's—"

"I don't care what you think, Liz. Cris was threatened by some guy who grabbed her on the dancefloor. She then goes to the bathroom and fifteen minutes later, comes out looking like that. You don't need to be a genius to figure out what happened. Now call the fucking police."

I turn away from Pippa and my sister and walk over to the door. I resist the urge to hammer on the wood and demand she open it, knowing that, if what I think happened actually did, aggression isn't going to help.

Reining in my temper, I gently knock on the door,

hearing Pippa on the phone to the police.

"Cris, you okay? Let me in, please, baby." I put my ear to the door but hear nothing, and my imagination about what happened to her starts to go into overdrive.

"The police are on their way. I wasn't sure what to tell them."

I look at Pippa, who is being held by Lance. I can see she's close to tears, as is my sister, who is still stood by the door. She hasn't moved since she walked in with Pippa. Her eyes are fixed on the bedroom door, and she's stock still.

"Liz, you okay there?"

"She was attacked." Her voice is quiet, but there's no mistaking what she said.

"What? How do you know?" When she doesn't respond, just continues to stare at the door, I go over to her and put my hands on her shoulders, forcing her to look at me. "How do you know she was attacked, Lizzie?"

She finally looks up at me, the sheen of tears in her eyes finally beginning to fall. "Because the same guy attacked me three years ago."

～

After my sister's revelation, the whole room fell into silence. Pippa wept in Lance's arms by the window, while Gary was fit to be tied. Shaun didn't know what to do with himself. His relationship with Lizzie was still relatively new, and it was obvious to anyone that he had no idea about what had happened to her.

He looked like a rabbit caught in the headlights, and it had taken him less than five minutes to announce he was leaving, but that he would call Lizzie in the morning. I don't think he was walking out on her, but rather the situation. The last thing a man wants to hear is that his girlfriend was assaulted by another guy.

Yet that's what I'm going to have to do, with not only my fiancée, but my sister too; a sister that I'm now sat next to on the sofa as she shreds a tissue in her hands. I can see she's trying to find the words to explain what happened, and all I can do is be there for her and wait until she's ready to speak.

"It happened three years ago. I'd gone out with a couple of girls from work and we somehow got separated. I was outside the club waiting for a taxi when this guy started talking to me. He was really drunk and started telling me what he wanted to do to me if he got me alone. He gave me the creeps, but I was still polite to him, and made it clear I wasn't interested. He started calling me names, saying I was a tease because of what I was wearing. I continued ignoring him, which only seemed to piss him off even more. His verbal abuse just got worse, until he grabbed me and dragged me into the alley at the side of the club. He was calling me a filthy whore and a slut and telling me he was going to show me what I real man felt like."

I listen to my sister as I hold her hand tightly. How did I not know about this? I'm her big brother. I'm meant to look out for her. Lizzie opens her mouth to speak some more, when we hear the click of the lock on the bedroom door, and Crissie slowly opens it, before stepping into the living room.

"He called me a filthy whore too," she says quietly, pulling the robe she's now wearing close to her chest. "I couldn't stop him. I just froze."

I'm about to get up to go to her when there's a knock at the door. Knowing it's the police, Pippa walks over and opens the door, inviting the two officers inside. I stand up and approach them, seeing Lizzie hold out her hand to Crissie, who quickly goes over and sits next to her.

"Thank you for coming, officers."

"No problem. We don't have much information so would someone like to explain why you needed the police?"

I turn to Crissie, who is sat next to my sister. She looks at me and then at Lizzie, who just nods and takes her hand. Cris looks back towards us, and I see her take a deep breath. "I was sexually assaulted earlier tonight."

"And I was assaulted by the same man three years ago."

CHAPTER 43

Crissie

<u>Present Day</u>

*I*t's was six in the morning before we got back from the hospital. We were both exhausted, and I remember Cal had been ready to kill someone on more than one occasion. It can't have been easy for him to hear me talking about what had happened that night, but he never left my side, always remaining close if he wasn't able to be right by me.

Even when I had the examination, he had stayed close to me, talking at me through the flimsy curtain that shielded me from view. I knew the exam was necessary, but it had been so humiliating all at the same time. They taken samples from all over my body, hoping to find some

DNA other than mine. They'd photographed my entire body to catalogue my injuries, and my hair was brushed to within an inch of its life in case there was any trace evidence hiding in there.

The formal interview had been the hardest. Thankfully, the detective who was interviewing me had been gentle and empathetic, something I remember being grateful for. I knew Cal was on the other side of the two-way mirror, listening in, and I can only imagine how helpless he must have felt as I'd recounted what had happened to me.

Lizzie's ordeal was another story. As her assault had happened so long ago, there would be no physical evidence. She was, however, able to recount her version of events as if it happened yesterday, and as she explained what had happened, I found myself amazed that she managed to keep it hidden from everyone for so long.

The way she explained everything to us, it was done so clinically that anyone would think she was reading from a script; that it had happened to someone else and she was just the person telling the story. The police had explained that women who were victims of sexual assault all deal with it differently, and they all find their own coping mechanisms to help them get through it.

Lizzie had disconnected herself from it all, compartmentalised so she was able to get on with a normal life. Me? I hadn't known how to handle what had happened to me and wound up pushing everyone away.

No one knew how to speak to me, so in the end they stopped trying. Other than my parents, Cal and Pippa were the only two who stuck around

They refused to let me wallow in self pity and bugged me until it pissed me off so much, I wound up shouting at them, which I later found out is what I needed to do. I needed to scream and shout; to release some of the anger I felt towards the man who had done this to me, and they both knew it.

It took me a while to get over what had happened to me. In fact, it was only when the man who attacked us was caught and convicted that I really started to put it all behind me.

They found his DNA on me and soon found out he was in the system, having been convicted of several petty crimes in his teenage years. Once they had him, it soon became clear he was the right guy. He didn't even try and deny it, even admitting to Lizzie's attack three years before mine.

He plead guilty, so neither Lizzie nor I had to testify in court, something I was grateful for. The last thing I wanted to do was go into detail about what he did to me in a roomful of strangers. With his guilty plea, he was sentenced to fifteen years for the assaults on Lizzie and me.

Once his sentence was handed down, we started to move forward with our lives. We set a new date for the wedding, and thankfully, our original venue was able to accommodate us. They were also true to their word and transferred the deposit we had already paid over to the new date. Things were getting back to normal.

I stand up from my position in front of the mirror and smooth my dress down over my stomach and hips. I need to get out there soon or Cal will start to think I've jilted him at the altar. I can just see his face now. He'll be chewing his lip and furrowing his brow. He'll be looking over his shoulder every few seconds without realising he's doing it.

I can't help but smile when I think about how good he must look in his suit. I'll always remember the first time I saw him in one. Men in suits have always been a weakness of mine, but Cal in a suit blows all other men out the water.

To me, the man looks good in mucky jeans and a dirty t-shirt when he's had a hard day at work. When he cleans up and dons a suit, he's downright edible. My heartbeat quickens at the mere thought of it, and within the hour, that man will be my husband.

My husband.

I still can't get used to the sound of those words on my tongue. This day should have arrived four years ago, but fate intervened, and it wasn't to be. Nothing has stopped us getting to this day; we haven't let it. We got there and shall be husband and wife before the day is done.

Fate has done it's worst to try and tear us apart. First, there was the miscarriage, then my cancer, then the assault, but that wasn't the end of it. When we received both the best and the worst news within a week of each other several months ago, we had to make one of the hardest decisions of our lives. A decision that, to this day, I know was the right one.

CHAPTER 44

Crissie

<u>September 2017</u>

"So, your dad was wondering whether you and Cal wanted to come round for dinner tomorrow? Apparently, he hasn't seen in you 'forever' and wants to catch up."

"What?" I laugh. "I saw him last weekend."

"I know, honey. I'm not sure why he feels it's been forever, but he was pretty insistent you come."

I nod and take a sip of my coffee as I look at my mum. We're on our weekly lunch date, something we've been doing since my assault almost three years ago. Mum insisted on getting me out the house for a couple of hours at least once a week, so now it's become almost a ritual for us.

We've not missed a get together since we started, even in the early days when I was still trying to push everyone away and really didn't feel like going out and socialising. Mum badgered me until eventually I gave in just to shut her up. Now, I couldn't imagine a Saturday afternoon when I didn't see her for coffee and cake.

"I wonder why he's being so weird?"

"I have no idea, Cris. Ever since he retired, he's been looking for something to fill his time now that he doesn't have anywhere to be during the day. For the most part, he's home alone as I'm still working. Maybe he's just losing track of time now he has the days to himself."

"Maybe. I guess we'll find out tomorrow."

Mum shrugs and takes a bite out of a piece of Battenberg cake. She's loved that cake for as long as I can remember, so when she saw the new addition on the menu, she made a beeline for it and ordered an extra helping to take home for Dad. I, on the other hand, stuck with a tried and tested lemon drizzle cake, something I have always loved.

"How are you and Cal doing? I know things have been tough with his new job. You two doing okay now?"

Ah yes, Cal's new job. That was a surprise when he told me three months ago that he'd been offered a position as chief mechanic for a local racing club. Only that local racing club was just starting to take off and was now one of the most recognised clubs in the North West, which is why they needed Cal.

He was arguably the best mechanic in our area, so when they approached him with the offer, it was a big deal. He hadn't wanted to accept the offer without discussing it with me first, but I knew he wanted to take it.

It meant he'd be working longer hours, but the increase in salary more than made up for that. What we hadn't planned on, though, was the amount of time he'd be working away from home.

With the club's popularity expanding, they were travelling all over the country with their drivers taking part in any number of races and tournaments and, as chief mechanic, Cal was expected to go too. Sometimes it meant he was away several days in succession, often on weekends and, I'm not gonna lie, it was hard.

I knew it was going to be strange not having Cal home with me in the evenings, but I hadn't realised how difficult it was actually going to be. We spoke most nights, and they weren't just five minutes calls. Often, we'd be on the phone for over and hour just chatting about our days and whatever else came to mind.

When the calls ended, it always left me with a sinking feeling and only made me miss him even more than I already was. It took several weeks for either one of us to get into a routine, and, if I'm honest, I still don't think I'm fully used to it, but Cal is out there doing what he loves, and I love him too much to deny him that. After all, he was there for me when I went away to college, so now it's my turn to do the same for him.

"Yeah, we're doing okay. I miss him every day, but it just makes it even better when he does come home."

"When is he due back?"

"In about three hours," I say as I check my watch, a smile creeping to my lips when I realise my man will be home soon.

I take the last bit of my lemon drizzle cake and lift my cup to my mouth, realising it's now empty.

"Do you want a refill?" my mum asks as she finishes off her coffee.

"No, I'm good. I should get going anyway. I want to spruce up the flat a bit before Cal gets home."

My mum gives me a knowing smile, and I feel my face flush. Jesus, I'm twenty-eight years old and I still blush at the stupidest things. My mum knows Cal and I have sex, so why does her knowing embarrass me?

Shaking my head, I approach the counter to pay our bill and join my mum outside a few minutes later. "Do you want a lift or are you good?"

"No thanks, honey. I think I'm going to do a bit of shopping. I'll grab the bus later. You go on home and spruce up the flat for Cal."

I feel myself flush again, and my mum laughs. With a kiss on the cheek, she heads off into town and I cross the road. I've a quick stop to make before I head home, one I hope goes to plan, or my idea of a perfect welcome home for Cal might go out the window.

After twenty minutes, I've a huge smile on my face and

I'm heading towards the car park. It takes me less than fifteen minutes to drive home and another thirty to shower and wash my hair.

It's been four days since I saw Cal last, and I want to look my best for him when he comes home. I know he loves me in red, so I choose my favourite red silk camisole and pair it with my new black jeans, lying both items out on the bed. I'm undecided how to wear my hair, so I do my makeup first, keeping it simple with a pale pink gloss and a few lashings of mascara.

When that's done, I unwrap my hair from the towel and look at my reflection in the mirror. I comb it through to detangle it before adding a few spritz' of heat protection and a small amount of serum. Grabbing my hairdryer, I decide to go for the straight look, which will be no easy feat as my hair has a natural kink my hairdressers struggle to get rid of.

It takes me over an hour to sort my hair out, but by the time I'm finished, it's poker straight and falls halfway down my back. I think Cal has only ever seen my hair straight once before now, and that was many years ago. I can't wait to see his reaction.

Checking the time, I dress quickly, seeing the text from Cal telling me he's forty minutes away. I smile and plug my phone in to charge when there's a knock at the door. I open it to see the smiling face of the maitre'd from our favourite Italian restaurant.

"Miss Walker, your order, as requested." He hands me two bags filled with food that's making my mouth water.

"Thank you so much, Marco. Please can you pass on my thanks to Giuseppe for me? I know he didn't have to do this, so I'm very grateful."

"I will, Miss Walker, and may I say, Mr Roberts is a very lucky man."

"Thank you. Can you just wait there for one minute? I'll be right back."

He nods, and I hurry through to the kitchen, depositing the bags of food on the counter before coming back through and grabbing my purse. I take out a ten-pound note and head back towards the door, handing the money to Marco.

"You don't have to, Miss Walker. You and Mr Roberts are valued customers. It was no trouble arranging this for you."

"No, I do, Marco. Please, accept it."

"Very well, Miss Walker, if you insist. Have a good evening." Marco reaches out as if to shake my hand but places a gentle kiss on the knuckles before smiling and heading off down the hallway. I close the door and hurry back through to the kitchen. I have twenty minutes to get the table set and everything dished up before Cal gets back, and I do it with just five minutes to spare.

I'm pouring the wine when I hear his key in the door, and when he walks in, drops his duffel bag on the floor and smiles at me, I swear my heart almost leaps out my chest.

Even with a three-hour drive on him, he never fails to make my skin clammy and my pulse quicken. He's wearing faded jeans and a tatty t-shirt, but to me there has never been a more welcome sight.

I pick up the two wine glasses and meet him halfway, handing one to him and watch as he takes a sip.

"What's all this for?" he says as he looks at the table where I've laid out the food. "Is that from—"

"It is. I stopped by there earlier to ask if they could prepare and deliver it, and Giuseppe agreed. I wanted to do something nice for you."

Cal puts the wine glass down on the table and just looks at me. I can see him scrutinising every detail as he starts at my hair, works his way down my face to my chest, lingering a little on the cleavage revealed by the camisole before skimming down my legs and back up again.

"You look amazing," he says as he takes some of my hair and twirls it between his fingers. "I like this. You should wear it straight more often."

"I just might if you're going to look at me like that when I do."

"Oh? And just how am I looking at you?"

"Like you're starving and I'm the main course."

"Really? Is that how I'm looking at you?" When he takes a step closer and licks his lips, I see his eyes darken and the butterflies in my stomach take flight. After eleven years together, the fact he can still cause me to feel this way just by looking at me speaks volumes about our relationship. The man can turn me on like a light switch with just one look; the look he's giving me right now.

As much as I've missed him this week, and as much as I want to drag him into the bedroom, this is not how I planned our evening—well, not this early on anyway. I take a couple of breaths to try and steady my out of control heart before I speak. "I figured you'd be hungry, so I got everything ready. Shall we eat?"

I see a flash of disappointment in his eyes, but it's gone almost as quickly as it arrived. Ever the gentleman, he moves around me and pulls out my chair for me to sit, before joining me at the table. He picks up our wine glasses and hands one to me.

"A toast. To the most beautiful, wonderful and thoughtful woman I have ever met. I love you, Cris, and I can't wait to make you my wife."

All I can do is smile as I toast, knowing that if I try and speak, my voice will break. I swallow a couple of times, trying to get rid of the lump in my throat before we start eating. If he's going to carry on saying sweet things like that, this evening is going to end a lot sooner than I had planned. Not that it would be a bad thing for it to end like that, but I've something I need to share with him, and I need to do it before we tumble into bed. Now, I've just got to find the right time.

Caleb

ood food, good wine and a great girl. What more can a guy ask for? I wasn't expecting any of this when I walked through the door a little over two hours ago. When I set my sights on Cris, I was momentarily speechless. I've always known she was a beautiful woman but seeing her standing there with her hair styled differently and that sexy as hell red top and skinny black jeans, I hadn't known what to say.

This new job has taken me away from her more than I originally thought it would, and I'm lucky that, despite her initial reservations, Cris supports me no matter what. I love my new job, but I love Crissie more, so if at any time she tells me she doesn't want me doing it anymore, then that would be it, no question about it.

She will always come first for me, and after everything we've been through, how could she not?

We've finished eating now and my stomach is stuffed to bursting. I take another sip of my wine, not failing to notice that Crissie has hardly touched hers. When she stands and heads towards the bedroom, I watch the sway of her hips, loving how the black denim moulds over her backside. God, I love that arse. I've missed that arse.

I'm grinning like an idiot when she comes back in and

sits on the sofa, calling me over with a nod of her head and a pat of her hand on the sofa. I stand and walk over; the curiosity must be evident in my expression when she laughs.

"I've got something for you. I hope you like it." She hands me a long, thin, white box with a yellow ribbon wrapped around it. I look at her briefly to see her watching me intently as I remove the ribbon and lift the lid. What I see inside almost takes my breath away, and I look between Cris and the box, seeing the sheen of tears in her eyes.

"Is this really true?" She nods. "You're not having me on? This is real?"

"Yes, Cal, it's real. You're going to be a daddy."

I look down again at the pregnancy test, which shows the word 'pregnant' in the little window. I stare at it a moment longer, feeling something drip onto my hand. It's only then I realise I'm crying, and looking up, I see Crissie is too.

"We're going to have a baby, Cal."

Before I can stop myself, I reach out and grab her, pulling her towards me and pressing my lips to hers. I can taste the saltiness from our tears as I hold her there, not wanting to let her go, but I know I have to when the urgent need to breathe takes over.

"We're finally going to be a family, Cris. After all this time, it's finally happening." I grab her again and pull her into a hug, shifting our position so she's sat on my lap as I hold her. We're going to be parents. After everything that's happened, after everything we've suffered and recovered from, we're finally going to have what we've wanted for so long.

And I couldn't be happier.

CHAPTER 45

Crissie

'm a nervous bundle of excitement as we wait for the doctor to come see us. We're here for my twelve-week scan and it's been one week since I broke the news to Cal that I was expecting.

After what happened with my first pregnancy, we've decided we're going to listen to every piece of advice the doctors and nurses can give us. Even though we were told over and over that what happened to Aria was outside of our control, we've decided we are not going to do anything to increase the chances of that happening again. I don't think we could go through that for a second time. It almost broke us then. Going through it twice would just be too much.

"Crissie Walker?"

I get to my feet when I hear my name called, and Cal and I walk down the hallway towards the nurse. She's young—I'd say early twenties if she's a day—and she reminds me a little of Pippa. She has her brown hair styled in a pixie cut and has a round face and button nose. She's the definition of the word 'cute', so much so that if you looked up the word in the dictionary, you'd probably see her picture.

"If you'd like to come in here and get yourself comfy on the bed, the doctor will be with you shortly. Mr Roberts, you can take a seat over there, so you can see the monitor."

I climb up onto the bed and Cal takes his seat by my side. I glance around the room, realising it's the same room I was in when I had my twelve-week scan for Aria. Apart from a fresh coat of paint, it looks pretty much the same. Taking a deep breath, I look down when I feel Cal take my hand, just as the doctor walks in.

"Crissie, Caleb, how are you today?"

"We're good, thank you, doctor. Eager to get this done so we can make sure everything is okay."

The doctor smiles at me kindly as she flicks through what I assume is my chart. I see the smile fade a little, and I assume she's got to the part about the miscarriage, but she quickly masks her reaction and hangs the chart off the end of the bed.

"Well, I shouldn't keep you too long. If you can just lie

back for me and lift up your top a little, I'll get the machine set up."

I do as she asks as she flicks on a few switches, and I see the monitor flicker to life. She pulls up a stool next to me and tears some tissue paper off a large roll, tucking it into the waistband of my leggings so the gel she will put on my belly in a moment doesn't mess them up.

When she reaches for the gel and squirts a little on my skin, I jump slightly at the coldness, causing the doctor to chuckle. "No matter how many times I do this, I still forget to warn people that the gel is cold."

"Don't worry, doctor. I've done this before."

"So I saw. I'm sorry about that."

I don't respond, just give her a small smile as she picks up the scanner and spreads the gel across my belly, applying a little pressure as she searches for our baby.

We don't hear anything at first, but then we hear it, the steady *thump, thump thump* of a heartbeat. We still see nothing on the monitor, but then it comes into focus and we see it, the outline of our baby, clear as day.

"There you are. We have a healthy heartbeat, and going by the measurements, I'd say you're probably closer to fourteen weeks. So, I calculate your due date to be the twenty-fifth of February 2018."

She gives us both a smile as Cal grips my hand tightly and we both gaze at the monitor. The doctor continues moving the scanner, and I see when her brow furrows. She squirts a little more gel and moves the scanner a little lower, before putting it down and taking off the latex gloves she's wearing.

"Is there something wrong, doctor?"

She smiles at us as she stands, but I can tell it's a forced smile. If there's one thing I've learnt to recognise over the last few years, it's when a smile is genuine, and that one most definitely wasn't.

"I just want to get one of my colleagues to take a look. It's nothing to worry about, Crissie. I'll be right back."

We both watch as she leaves the room, glancing at each other before looking back at the monitor. I can still hear the steady heartbeat and the image is clear as day. Everything looks fine to me, but clearly the doctor saw something she doesn't want to tell us about, and that makes me nervous, something Cal senses.

"Don't worry, Cris. I'm sure everything's okay." I nod at Cal's words, my eyes fixed to the monitor, focussing on our baby, trying to convince myself everything is fine, and nothing is wrong. Moments later, the doctor returns with another doctor, one I recognise immediately, and my hopes fade away rapidly.

"Crissie, Caleb, I understand congratulations are in order."

"Well, we think so, doctor, but we have a feeling there's something we're not being told."

"Well, let me take a look and we'll see what's going on."

The doctor I've not seen in almost eighteen months takes a seat in front of the monitor and squirts some more of the gel on my belly. Despite the 'this will be a little cold' warning, it still makes me jump a little. He angles the monitor away from us and put's the scanner on me, moving it around in much the same way the other doctor did.

He leans in and his brow furrows in concentration as he presses a few buttons, which I know is taking photographs of the images on the screen. He carries on doing this for another five minutes, all the while my anxiety level increases as no one tells us what's going on.

"Doctor, what's wrong? Of all the doctors here, why did she bring you in? I know something's going on and we have a right to know. What's wrong with our baby?"

Cal squeezes my hand in support, and I keep my eyes on the doctor, who finally places the scanner back in its cradle and hands me some tissue. "Crissie, get yourself cleaned up and I'll be back in five minutes. I just need to confer with my colleague here. I promise I'll explain what's going on when I come back."

I wipe the gel off my belly and pull the tissue from the waistband of my leggings. Pulling my top down, I sit up and swing my legs round, looking down at Cal.

"It's back, Cal. I knew there was always a chance, but I'd hoped I'd be the exception."

"You don't know that, Crissie."

"Why else would my oncologist come in here? Of all the doctors, of all the obstetricians in this hospital, why bring him in here?"

Cal opens his mouth to say something but changes his mind and just sighs. "If it has come back, we'll deal with it, just like we dealt with it last time."

"But I'm pregnant, Cal. This is completely different to last time." I hear the tone of my voice and stop talking. The last thing I want is to argue with Cal about this. He's right. We don't know what the doctor saw on the scan. Until we know, there's no point in getting worked up. It could be nothing, but something tells me that isn't the case.

True to his word, my oncologist returns after five minutes and sits next to me on the bed. He looks between Cal and me before speaking. "I'm going to cut to the chase, Crissie. The scan shows your cancer may have returned. We need to get a full scan of the area to know for sure, and I'd like to get that done now, if you're okay with that?"

I knew it.

I turn to Cal, who's still holding my hand tightly. I see him break eye contact and glance down at my belly. My free hand automatically goes to my stomach, and I look back at the doctor. "Our baby. Will the scan hurt the baby?"

"No, Crissie, your baby will be perfectly safe. I'll give you a few minutes to talk, then I'll send a nurse in. Just let her know if you want the scan and she'll take you down."

I give the doctor a small smile as he gets up and leaves the room. I keep my eyes on the door as my shoulders sag, and I let out a long sigh.

"It might not be as bad as it sounds, Cris. You should get the scan, so we know what's happening."

I know he's right; he usually is. This could be the same as it was before, but with one major difference. Now I'm pregnant. Nothing will be the same this time around. How can it be?

Why can't things just go right for a change? There's always something lurking around the corner to knock us down just as things are starting to go our way. I'm about to agree with Cal when there's a knock at the door and a nurse peers round the opening. "Miss Walker, are you ready to go for that scan?"

"Okay. Let's do this." I jump off the bed, and, with Cal by my side, we follow the nurse through the hospital corridors, hoping and praying the doctor is wrong.

CHAPTER 46

Crissie

*H*ere we are again.

I've seen way too much of this hospital over the past few years. I had hoped the last time would be just that: the last. But no such luck.

I've had the scan and we're now waiting for the results. I had expected to be sent home and called back in a few days, but the nurse who took me down to the scan instructed us to wait and the doctor would come get me when he had the results.

That, in and of itself, has made me nervous. Cal is still by my side, as he promised me he would be, and he is still holding my hand in his. My other hand is resting against my belly, something I've only just realised I'm doing.

I'm pregnant now. It's not just me I have to consider.

Whatever the doctor tells us, the options available will be different. We've got to think about how all of this will affect the baby. I'm just hoping the doctor is wrong and there's nothing wrong, or if there is, it's nothing serious.

I'm full of nervous energy as I jump up from my seat, forcing Cal to release my hand as I begin pacing the waiting area. One hand is on my hip, the other on my belly as I walk back and forth. I can feel Cal's eyes on me and glance at him, seeing him leaning forward, his forearms on his knees as he watches me.

The expression on his face is one I've not seen in a long time, and it breaks my heart to see it again. I keep forgetting all this affects him too, and I feel bad that I haven't considered how he must be feeling. Last time I was diagnosed, he took it hard. He kept a brave face because he knew I needed him to be strong, but I heard him crying more than once when he thought I was sleeping.

I start to go back to him when the door opens, and I see the face of my oncologist. His expression is unreadable, and I'm not sure whether that scares me or comforts me.

"Crissie, Cal, you can come in now."

Cal stands and takes my hand as we both walk into the doctor's office and take a seat on the opposite side of his desk. The office hasn't changed much since I was last in here, except there's an extra photograph of a woman and a young baby. He catches me looking and smiles. "That's my daughter, Ellie, and her little boy, Jordan. He's just gone one."

"Your first grandchild?"

"He is, and already has me wrapped around his little finger." He smiles again as he looks at the photograph before turning to his computer. He presses a few keys before linking his fingers together in front of him and turning to us.

"It's what we feared, Crissie. The cancer has returned. From looking at the scans, the cancer has spread to the parametrium, which is the tissue next to your cervix, meaning the cancer is more advanced than before. It's now classed as stage two. Now, like before, we do have options available to us, but with you being pregnant, it does complicate things." The doctor pauses for a moment, giving us time to digest the information he's already given us. Even though I was hoping he was wrong, I knew deep down this disease had come back. It was pretty naïve of me to believe it was something other than cancer, but I needed something to hold onto.

"You said it's stage two? How is that different from stage one?"

"Basically, it means the cancer has spread outside of the area where it originated. Your previous cancer was localised to your cervix, and at the stage we caught it, it was early stage one. As I said, this time it's spread outside the cervix, which makes it stage two. Now, your cancer is also classed as recurrent, as you've already completed a course of treatment. What we need to do now is discuss the options we have and make a decision on now to proceed.

"Do we need to decide today?"

"Not at all. As before, I'll give you all the information and then you can take a few days to decide what you want to do, but, Crissie, I need to tell you, being pregnant is going to complicate things, and you might have to make a difficult decision."

I don't like the way he said that, or the way he's looking at me right now.

"What do you mean?"

"Crissie, for a recurrent cancer, the normal course of treatment is surgery followed by radiotherapy or chemotherapy. Once treatment starts, you will almost certainly miscarry very early on in the process."

I inhale sharply, knowing we wouldn't be able to go through that again. Losing Aria almost ruined our relationship, but we battled through. I'm not sure we'd survive it again.

"I know this is a lot for you to take in, for both of you, and what I'm about to say isn't going to be easy to hear. Crissie, you need to consider terminating the pregnancy before we begin treatment."

I don't remember the journey back from the hospital. I don't remember much about anything after the doctor told me I may have to terminate my pregnancy. He gave us the information we needed, then said he'd call us in a few days. Now, we're back home, and I've no idea what to say or what to think.

Can I really consider ending my pregnancy? The doctor seems to think if I don't, I'll lose the baby anyway when I start treatment, and I need to have treatment.

Don't I?

We've wanted children almost from day one. When we got pregnant with Aria, it was the happiest time in our lives. Losing her was the hardest thing we've had to go through, but we came through it and we are stronger than ever. The cancer pretty much put a stop to us trying again, but even then, we always intended on trying for a family once treatment was complete and I got the all clear.

That time is now.

When I revealed to Cal that I was pregnant again, we were both so happy. Even though the pregnancy is in its early stages, we started making plans, even started looking for a bigger place to live. Now it seems that may have all been for nothing.

"I can't lose another baby, Cal," I say quietly. "It would kill me. I can't go through that again."

I turn to Cal, seeing him with his head in his hands. This is a decision we have to make together. It might be my body, but it's our baby, and any decision made with affect both of us. Cal looks up, and I see in his eyes he's as torn as I am.

"I don't want to lose the baby either, Cris, by miscarriage or termination, but at the same time, the alternative doesn't bear thinking about."

I know what alternative he's talking about is, and in an ideal world, it wouldn't be an option I would ever consider. The problem is, we're not living in an ideal world, and if neither of us wants to lose the baby, it might be the only option available to us.

The doctor gave us all the information, but made it clear it wasn't an option he would recommend due to the risks involved. I'm okay now, but by the time the baby is due, I might be too weak to have the c-section. I'll need to bring the baby into the world. So, what we need to decide is, are we prepared to take that risk?

CHAPTER 47

Caleb

November 2017

"Well, Crissie, we've got the results from your latest scans, and I'm sorry to say it's not good news. The cancer has spread to your pelvis, which explains the pain you've been having in your back and stomach. It's pretty uncommon for this type of cancer to spread this quickly, but it does happen."

Crissie and I absorb what the doctor is telling us, our joined hands resting on her protruding belly. We were expecting him to say something like that. Ever since we decided to forgo treatment in favour of the baby, we always knew the cancer could spread.

The doctor talked us through what kind of things

Crissie could go through, and up until now, we've been quite lucky. She's only been experiencing pain the last week or so, which is why the doctor insisted on having another scan.

He's been monitoring both Crissie and the baby closely since her new diagnosis. So far, the pregnancy is progressing as it should, and the baby is the right size for twenty weeks. We found out earlier in the week that we're expecting another little girl, something Crissie and I were ecstatic about.

We knew deciding to maintain the pregnancy rather than Crissie having treatment for her cancer was a big risk, but after we discussed everything, we both agreed that losing another baby wasn't an option for us.

Her oncologist told us that, as the cancer was stage two, there was still a chance that treatment could begin after Crissie has the baby. That is the hope we're holding on to, even after what he's just told us.

"Okay, doctor, but everything is okay with the baby?"

"The baby is doing well. She is the right size for how far along you are and the heartbeat is strong and steady. Crissie, I'd be remiss if I didn't say this to you, even though I know what your answer will be. At twenty weeks, there is still time to terminate the pregnancy and begin treatment. The sooner we start treatment, the better your chances are."

"I know you're only doing your job, doctor, and I appreciate you giving us all the information, but you're right, you already know what the answer is. Cal and I are keeping this baby. In fact, we'd like to schedule the C-section now, if we can?"

The surprise on the doctor's face is evident, and I hope mine doesn't match his. Cris and I discussed booking in the C-section before we left the flat this morning, but we hadn't decided one way or the other. Seems Cris has decided for us.

"If you want to do that, Crissie, we can do." We watch as he checks Crissie's chart before continuing, "Usually we can't perform a C-section until thirty-nine weeks, which, if the previous doctor calculated your due date correctly, will be the nineteenth of February. Now, I want to advise you again, performing a C-section in your condition has a whole new set of risks. If you're too weak to have the surgery, and judging by the rate your cancer is spreading, that's a very real possibility, it places a higher risk on us losing you or the baby, or even both of you. Are you one hundred percent sure this is what you want to do?"

The doctor looks between both of us, before Crissie turns to me, her eyes asking me the question, and for the first time, uncertainty creeps in. "Can you give us a day, doctor? I think this is something we need to discuss in more detail at home."

My eyes connect with Crissie's, and I see the flash of confusion in them before she turns back to the doctor.

"Of course, Caleb. Just give me a call tomorrow when you've decided, and we can take whatever action is necessary at that time. Do you have any other questions for me right now?"

"No. Cris, do you?"

Crissie shakes her head and we both stand, leaving the doctor's office quickly. I know she is going to fire questions at me as soon as we're outside the hospital and on our way home, and the truth is, I don't know what to say to her.

Surprisingly, she doesn't say a word to me on the drive home, and I don't know whether she's pissed at me, or is just thinking about everything the doctor told us today. I find out which of those is right as soon as we walk into the flat.

"What the hell, Cal? I thought we were on the same page in all of this?"

"We are, Crissie, or at least we were."

"So what's changed? Don't you want the baby now? Our daughter?"

"Of course I do, it's just—"

"Just what, Cal? Please tell me what's going on in that head of yours right now as I'm confused."

"I don't want to lose you, Cris!" I shout the words as loud as I can, before turning away from her and letting my head drop. I bend over and put my hands on my knees, breathing deeply. Just saying the words out loud has made me realise there is a very real chance I may lose Crissie. That thought alone cuts me so deep I can feel it right down to my soul.

When I feel her hand on my back, I straighten and

turn to her, seeing her expression has now softened as she looks at me. "You won't lose me, Cal."

"How do you know that, Cris? The doctor said that if you're too weak when it comes to you having the C-Section, you and the baby could die. I could lose you both, and I don't think—no, I *know* I won't be able to come back from that. You're my everything, Crissie. Losing you would kill me. It would end me." I fall down onto the sofa and Crissie sits next to me. I lower my head into my hands, trying to calm my racing pulse. She's close but doesn't touch me. I can already feel the divide forming between us.

"So you want me to terminate the pregnancy?" I hear her voice crack as she says the words, and I feel the tears building up in my eyes. I don't look at her when I speak the next words. I can't see her reaction to what I'm about to say or it will break me. Part of me doesn't believe I'm about to say it, but if we're going to get through this, I need to be honest with her.

"Cris, if you begin treatment now, there is every chance you'll recover and then we can try again for another baby. We're still young, there's still time for us to have a family, but if you go in for that C-section and don't come out of it..." I pause and take a few deep breaths. "We can try for another baby. I'll never get another you. I don't think I can close my eyes and you're there, but when I open them again, you're gone. I'm not strong enough, Cris. I can't go on if you're not by my side."

God, I feel like a right bastard saying this to her. The last thing I want is to make her feel guilty; for making her think she's putting the baby before me. I want our daughter as much as she does, but I can't risk losing her.

"You're not going to lose me, Cal. I'm not going anywhere."

"How can you say that, Crissie? You don't know what's going to happen in four months time. You might be strong enough now, but the doctor said there's a good chance you won't be by the time you're due to have the baby." I'm breathing quickly now, my heart beating and my pulse racing. How can I make her understand what I'm feeling?

"Cal, I don't know what to say. You know how I feel about this baby. I can't even contemplate killing her, because, let's face it, that's what we'd be doing. I understand your fears, believe me, I do. When the police told me about your attack, I was scared beyond belief. Just the thought of going on without you was enough to make me wonder how I could go on. Cal, look at me, please."

Taking a deep breath, I turn, the expression on her face almost breaking me. She is in just as much pain about this decision as I am.

"You need to believe that I'll be okay; that we'll be okay. With everything we've been through; all the times we could have lost each other and we're still here; we're still together and we're still strong. We're stronger together, Cal. I get that you're scared, Cal, but please, believe in us.

343

Believe that we'll get through this like we've got through everything life has thrown at us."

I inhale deeply and release the breath slowly. God, I hate it when she's right. I can't lose faith now. We've been through so much in the eleven years we've been together, but have come out the other side stronger than when we went in.

"Just promise me one thing, Cris. If, when you have the C-section, the doctor says you're too weak, you fight. You fight for me, you fight for our daughter, and you fight for yourself. Fight for us, Crissie, for our family."

I hold her gaze as I take her hand, squeezing it tightly in mine, almost willing her to feel how much I need her to fight for us.

"I promise, Cal."

CHAPTER 48

Crissie

Christmas Day 2017

*I*t's been one hell of a long day.

We went to Cal's family for Christmas dinner, and then on to my mum's for tea. It's still only eight p.m. but I'm ready to collapse and sleep for the rest of the year. When you add to that my painkillers have started wearing off so I'm in a load of pain with my back, and I'm pretty much ready to be put down.

Cal is in the bathroom running me a hot bath, and while it sounds heavenly, all I want to do is sleep. Stripping out of my clothes, I grab one of Cal's old t-shirts and slip it on, pulling it down over my ever-growing baby bump.

I'm almost twenty-eight weeks now and everything is going well, with the baby anyway. With my cancer, not so much. The doctor says I'm showing more and more signs that my cancer is metastasising, at least I think that's the word he used. I'm get tired really easily, the pain in my back is getting worse, and despite eating like a horse, I'm actually losing weight.

Cal and I are both on the same page now. We had a bit of a blip last month when Cal was actually considering terminating the pregnancy, but once we sat down and talked about how he felt and everything we've been through, we agreed to continue with the pregnancy. We spoke with the doctor the next day, and my C-section is booked in for the nineteenth of February.

Even though we are being as positive as we can, we're not stupid. We know there's a chance something could go wrong, which is why we've brought the wedding forward. Now, instead of getting married in June, we're getting married on the seventeenth of February, two days before our daughter will be brought into this world.

We've been very lucky in that Nunsmere Hall have been brilliant and were willing to transfer everything to the new weekend in February, which happened to be the only weekend they had available. For once, fate was on our side. We're relying on word of mouth to let all the guests know the change of date, and I've contacted the boutique who are holding my dress to explain the change of date, and the change in my figure.

After a round of congratulations from the consultant and her staff, they assured me there would be time for me to come in and choose another dress, and as no alterations had been made to my original choice, they could just put any money I'd already paid towards the new dress. To say I was happy about that would be an understatement.

I've an appointment there once the holidays are over to get everything sorted, and they assured me I could take my time and find the perfect dress to show off both me and my bump, which, due to my weight loss, already looks like I'm full term.

"All ready, Cris. You need any help climbing in?" Cal comes out of the bathroom, drying his hands on a towel. When he sees me already in bed, the covers pulled up to my hips, resting just under my bump, he smiles. "I take it the bath is surplus to requirements?"

"Sorry, Cal, I'm just so tired."

"Don't worry, baby, there's no need to apologise. I'll go drain the bath and then I'll join you. We can watch a movie, if you like?"

"That would be nice."

He smiles at me again and heads back into the bathroom. I hear the gurgle of the water as he pulls the plug and the water starts to drain away. I slide down further into bed and pull the covers up over my belly just as Cal comes back into the bedroom.

I see he's discarded his shirt and jeans and is just wearing his boxers as he crosses the room towards our bed. As soon as our eyes connect, I feel the shift in the air. The charge of electricity that our union creates is present and accounted for, if only we could act upon it.

As my pregnancy is classed as high risk, the doctor has advised against intercourse, which we understand fully. Doesn't mean we have to like it though. I'm still wildly attracted to Cal—that hasn't changed in our eleven years together—and it kills me that I can't show him how much I want him in all the ways we excel at.

I'm lucky Cal feels the same way about me, and we are able to show our love and affection in other ways. We know so many couples who clearly love one another, but have difficulty showing it. We've never had that problem, and it's one of the things I've always been grateful for.

When he climbs into bed, he automatically reaches for me and I slide over, snuggling into him as much as my bump will allow. As usual, Cal rests his hand on my bump and strokes it gently, lulling me off to sleep.

"No movie, Cal. Let's just lie here like this. I like just lying here with you."

"Whatever you want, Cris." He continues to stroke my belly, and I feel him place a soft kiss to my hair, something he has taken to doing every night before we drift off to sleep. Tonight is no exception, and before I know it, I'm fast asleep, wrapped in Cal's arms.

"*C*rissie! It's so good to see you again. You look radiant. Pregnancy suits you."

"Thank you, Wendy. I can't tell you how grateful I am for what you're doing for me."

"No need to thank me, sweetie. When you explained your situation, I was more than happy to help. It's my shop after all, so I can do pretty much what I like."

I laugh at Wendy as she links her arm with mine and leads me towards the back of the store. I don't fail to notice when one of her assistants flips the sign on the door to say closed and puts the latch across. Is she really shutting the shop just for me?

"Now, I took the liberty of pulling out a number of dresses I think will compliment your features, your requirements, and your bump. There are a number of different styles and cuts, but I think a dress that's an empire line will be best for you, and, I was thinking, maybe a Grecian style dress." She stops when she catches me staring, and smiles. "Oh, listen to me. It's your dress, honey. We'll go with whatever you want."

"No, it's okay. I was actually thinking about a Grecian style but didn't know where to start."

"Well, I think I have the perfect dress. It's got wide straps and built in support for your chest, so you don't need to wear a bra. The material is ruched across the bust with a pearl and diamante band underneath. The dress then falls away to the floor with a small train on the back."

"It sounds gorgeous," I say with a smile.

It really does, and if the dress looks anything like what Wendy has just described, I have a feeling I may have found my dress.

When she goes and pulls it from the rail and brings it over to me, I run my fingers across the material, feeling the fabric is soft and silky and absolutely beautiful. I feel the tears already welling in my eyes and quickly banish them, at least until I actually have the dress on.

"No tears yet, Crissie. Let's go through and I can help you into the dress. It's just a step in and zip up the back, so it's not a lace up which will be easier on the bump as there's no additional pressure."

I nod and follow her through, and I'm in the dress less than five minutes later. She was right. The dress shows off my slightly fuller figure and gives me a cleavage I didn't know I had. The soft material floats around my legs and cascades down and over my baby bump. The pearls and diamantes glisten in the light, and the wide straps give me the support I need.

It's beautiful, and I feel beautiful in it.

Now the tears begin to slide down my cheeks, and I feel Wendy come up behind me as her hands go to my shoulders.

"You are a beautiful bride, Crissie. Your man is going to fall in love with you all over again when he sees you in this dress, and I'm not just saying that because I want a sale."

I laugh at Wendy's words and swipe at my eyes with the back of my hand.

"Now, you hadn't decided on a headdress, had you?" When I shake my head, she continues. "Well, I've checked the price on this dress and it's actually less than your original one, so we do have some money left over if you want to take a look at what we have here?"

"Could we?" I exclaim. I hadn't thought about accessories when I left the house this morning, so I have no idea what I'm looking for. Do I want something floral? A tiara maybe?

"Of course we can. I'll ask Sophie if she can go and get a selection ready while you change out of the dress. Can I assume this is the one you want?"

I shoot her a look that says, 'what do you think?' before smiling. Wendy leaves me to change when I reach around to lower the zip on the back of the dress. After, I've hung it up on the rail, I dress in my own clothes and pick up my bag from the stool it's been resting on. Turning, I look at the dress and reach out, running my fingers through the soft fabric.

It's the complete opposite to my original dress, but I love it just as much as I did the other one. The diamantes on the band that sits under my bust are sparkling in the lights, and I feel my eyes well up again as I picture Cal's face when he sees me in it for the first time.

Taking a deep breath, I pull myself back to the present as I walk out of the dressing room. Sophie comes in and smiles at me before collecting the dress and putting it in a protective bag. She drapes it over her arm and follows me out into the main area, where I see she has placed about a dozen headdresses on a long table.

I walk over and take in what she has laid out for me to look at. There're all sorts of designs for me to choose from, but one in particular catches my eye. It's a silver tiara that has an intricate leaf pattern interspersed with tiny pearls and crystals. The design is similar to the band on my dress, and I'm drawn to it right away.

Reaching out, I pick it up and hold it out in front of me. I'd never thought about a tiara before, not wanting something too flashy, but this one is pretty and delicate, but not too ostentatious.

It's perfect.

"Here, let me fix it in for you." Wendy takes the tiara from my hands and stands in front of me. She positions the tiara either side of my head and slides it on, making sure it's level before stepping back and leading me over to a mirror. When I see myself, a fresh batch of tears pool in my eyes and I swipe at them before they have the chance to fall.

"You're going to look like a princess on your big day, Crissie."

I nod at her remark, mainly because that's all I can do. I'm pretty sure if I try and speak, the words will come out a garbled mess. The lump in my throat is pretty much restricting any vocal ability I have right now.

Our wedding is going to be everything we want it to be.

Even though doctors perform C-Sections every day, there's always a chance something could go wrong, and that's with a healthy woman. With my current condition, the risks are higher, and we're not naïve enough to believe everything running smoothly is a guarantee. In fact, with our luck over recent years, I'd say it's more likely something will go wrong.

As I consider the possibility of everything not going to plan, a fresh batch of tears fills my eyes. It's happening more and more often recently, probably due to pregnancy hormones, but I know these tears are for a different reason. The thought of leaving Cal all alone hurts me more than anything else ever could.

Shaking myself out of my thoughts, I remove the tiara and pass it to Wendy. Smiling at her, I pick up my bag. "Thanks for everything, Wendy. I'll come in and collect the dress and tiara the weekend before the wedding. Is that okay?"

"That's fine, Crissie. I hope everything goes okay between now and the wedding. You deserve a break, sweetie, after everything you've been through." The way she is smiling at me, and her words, make me want to cry yet again, so I do the only thing I can think of; I take a step closer to Wendy and pull her into a hug. She pauses only a moment before hugging me back, and I release her after a few moments.

I smile at her again, seeing tears in her eyes, too, as I

hurry out of the store. I have one more stop to make before I head home. Cal's parents are coming round for dinner tonight, and I intend to relax a little before they get there. It doesn't take much to tire me out recently, which is another side affect of the cancer.

Cal is cooking, so all I have to do it sit there and make conversation with his mum and dad. That's something that shouldn't be an issue, considering how well we get on with each other.

Checking the road is clear, I cross when there is a gap in the traffic and head towards my destination. I shouldn't be any longer than half an hour, and then I can head back home, run a bath, and have a nice long soak before Cal's parents come around.

I almost groan at the thought of the bath, pulling myself together when I arrive at my destination. I push through the large glass double doors and head over to the counter, asking to see an account manager. When one comes over, a smile on his face as he greets me and introduces himself, I tell him what I want, and he confirms he is only too happy to oblige.

CHAPTER 49

Crissie

<u>1st February 2018</u>

*I*n less than three weeks time, I'm going to be married, and two days after that, I'll be a mum. Now isn't that a scary thought.

As I dry myself after one of the longest baths I've had in a long time, my thoughts drift to how much our lives are going to change over the next couple of weeks. I'll be Mrs Crissie Roberts, and something tells me it's going to take a while for me to get used to that.

For all intents and purposes, we've been married for a long time. We just haven't had the paperwork to show for it. After twelve years together, we're as good as married anyway. The ceremony we'll have will just formalise it.

When I'm dry, I walk over to the wardrobe and open the doors, seeing Cal's wedding suit hanging on the rail, covered in the protective bag. I can't wait to see him wearing it as he waits for me at the end of the aisle. He's going to look so handsome, even more so than usual.

Tearing my mind up from the gutter, I pull out my black, jersey maxi dress. I hang it over the door before grabbing my favourite black bra and knickers set from the chest of drawers. Once I've put them on, the dress goes on next and I look at my reflection.

I know Cal loves this dress. It was my first item of maternity wear I bought and has seen me through every stage of the pregnancy. We're having our final date night tonight before we get married, and it was the first thing that came to mind when deciding what to wear.

We only planned to go out tonight this morning. It's hard for us to plan anything in advance, as we never know how I'm going to feel. The last few days I've hardly moved from my bed. I've been so tired. When I've not been tired, I've been in pain. Luckily, the painkillers my oncologist prescribed have worked for the most part, but sometimes all they do is dull the pain rather than take it away completely.

The pain is something I've learned to live with over the last couple of months. However, the fatigue is something I can't get used to. I'm used to being so active, both around the house and when I'm out with friends. Now, all I want to do is lie down and sleep. I know it's a side effect, but it still pisses me of that I can't do everything I want to do.

I pull my hair up into a ponytail, apply a little mascara and lip gloss, and then I'm ready to go. Cal is waiting for me in the living room, and I know he's wearing my favourite black jeans and white button-down shirt. I smile as I remember watching him as he'd dressed, the muscles of his arms and legs bunching and relaxing as he'd moved.

I might not be able to make love to him, but that doesn't stop my body reacting in all the ways it should; in all the ways it always has whenever Cal is around. He never fails to elicit a reaction from me. Even with just a smile, the butterflies kick up a storm in my belly.

There are days when I look like death warmed over, lounging around in bed with my pyjamas on, hair scraped back in a messy bun, face free of makeup, but he still tells me I look beautiful to him, no matter what I'm wearing. Every time he says something like that, I fall in love with him all over again.

I slip my feet into my ballet flats, which are the only type of shoe I can wear right now and not be in a whole load of pain. When I've secured my bag on my shoulder, I walk into the living room, seeing Cal on his phone. His free hand is on his hip and his back is to me. I can't see his face, but I can tell from the tension in his shoulders that the call is not a welcome one.

"What the fuck do you mean a technicality! He pled guilty! No, I don't give a damn what you have to do, you fix this, and you fix it before that motherfucker gets out. That bastard raped my sister and assaulted my fiancé. You'd better sort this out and fast. Do you hear me?" Cal ends the call and tosses his phone onto the sofa. Both hands are on his hips now, and I can tell by the way his shoulders are lifting and lowering that he is breathing hard.

"Cal? What's going on?"

He turns when he hears me, his expression instantly softening when he sees me. I know I only heard the end of a conversation, but I can guess what the call was about. I thought this part of my life was over with. It's been four years since my attacker was sent to prison for his assault on me and on Cal's sister three years before that. As I heard Cal say, he pled guilty, so what's going on?

"Cris, I didn't realise you were there. How much of that did you hear?"

"Enough to figure out that the guy who assaulted me is getting out. What's happened?"

Cal walks over and takes my hand, leading me over to the sofa as we both sit down. "He isn't getting out as such, not yet anyway. He has a new legal team who are claiming the verdict was unreasonable given the evidence provided, which they say in no way proves he assaulted you." He squeezes my hand as he continues. "He is saying that everything that went on in the bathroom was consensual; that you followed him in there and came on to him. When his friend came in to see what was keeping him, you got scared, ran, and accused him of the assault to try and cover your own back."

My head starts to spin as I listen to his words. This can't be happening. How can he say all those things? How can he say I wanted what he did to me? "And people actually believed him? But his DNA, it was on my body. That proves what he did."

"The sample they took was from your neck, and he admitted to kissing you there when you were on the dancefloor. He couldn't really deny that as there were dozens of witnesses."

"But Lizzie. She gave a statement confirming it was the same guy."

"The testimony of a girl who was raped over three years before your assault; who didn't report it and just happens to be the future sister-in-law of his latest victim. You, me and everyone close to us knows Lizzie is telling the truth, but his legal team will spin it, so a fresh jury will just see it differently."

"He admitted it, Cal. He said he did it."

"He's saying his solicitor at the time told him that with all the evidence against him, he would be sent down and was looking at life in prison. He only pled guilty to get a reduced sentence. He's now saying he didn't do anything you didn't want him to do. His new solicitor is claiming he had ineffectual counsel."

I close my eyes and lower my head, willing the pain in my heart to go away. I thought this was all over. I thought

Cal and I could move on with our lives without this hanging over our heads. "Will I need to go to court?"

"If his team are successful, then both you and Lizzie will need to testify. I'm so sorry, Cris. I know you thought all this was behind us."

All I can do is nod as I take in all the information. I've not thought about that night in a long time. For months after it happened, it was all I could think about. I hardly slept, and when I did, my dreams were plagued with images of what happened. More than once I woke up kicking and screaming, with Cal trying to calm me down.

For a while, I couldn't let Cal touch me as it brought back images of what that man had done to me. That had hurt us both, as I knew Cal would never do anything like that to me, but I couldn't help my reaction. It was an impulse, and it wasn't just Cal. Any guy who came near me I shied away from, but my worst reaction was when they tried to touch me.

Pippa and Lance had come round for dinner a couple of weeks after it happened. I was in the kitchen getting the drinks when Lance had come in and innocently touched my shoulder to get my attention. In that moment, I was back in the club with his hands on me. Lance's hand became his hand, and I'd grabbed whatever was closest to me, and lashed out. Luckily, my aim had been off, or I could have done some serious damage with the empty wine bottle.

"Would you rather stay in tonight? I can ring and cancel the taxi."

I lift my head when I hear his words, seeing the concern on his face as he watches me. Do I want to stay in tonight? Truth be told, all I want to do is curl up in bed and sleep, forgetting we ever had this conversation, but that's not what I'm going to do. I won't let that bastard ruin our lives any more than he already has tried to.

"No. I want to go out. I want to carry on as normal. We can't let this guy win, Cal. He's not worth it." I stand up and secure my bag, just as a car blasts its horn outside. Cal walks over to the window and glances out.

"Taxi's here. Let's go and celebrate the life we've had together so far, and the life we're going to have together for many years to come."

I smile at him as he holds out his hand for me to take. Just hearing those few words has made me feel ridiculously happy. With Cal by my side, we head out of the flat, all thoughts of the conversation we've just had, gone.

CHAPTER 50

Crissie

Present Day
17 February 2018

ell, there you have it, the story of the life Cal and I have shared together so far. I think you can agree, we've had our ups and our downs, but we still made it here. By here, I mean Nunsmere Hall on our wedding day.

Yeah, I bet you were all thinking we'd never make it here and, truth be told, there were times I felt the same way. We've had to rearrange it three times and know we've been extremely lucky Nunsmere Hall have been able to accommodate us.

While this is the same venue where my parents

married and has been my dream venue ever since I first saw my parents wedding album as a little girl, if I'm honest with myself, I'd have married Cal in our living room. As long as it meant, by the end of it, I became his wife, the location wouldn't have mattered.

As it is, we're here, and all our family and friends are waiting for me to make my entrance on the arm of my father, and I can't tell you how happy I am that I can actually walk down that aisle.

For the last few days, I've been so tired and in so much pain I've hardly moved from my bed. We came close to cancelling the whole thing several times, but I was insistent that we would get married today, even if I had to be pushed down the aisle in a wheelchair.

Luckily, when I woke this morning, the pain in my back was minimal and I was able to get around, unaided. I can't tell you how happy I was to realise I would be able to walk after all. Getting to Cal under my own steam means a lot to me, and now that is about to happen.

I check my hair and makeup one last time and adjust my dress. There's a knock at the door, and I call out to whoever it is to enter, seeing Pippa stick her head around to peer in. As soon as she sees me, she tears up.

"Stop it, Pip. I can't cry, not yet anyway."

"Sorry, Cris, but you look beautiful. But then, there was never any doubt about that."

"Is she ready yet, Pippa?"

"I think so, Mr Walker."

I smile when I hear my dad's voice and Pippa's response. Pippa and I have been friends since primary school, and I've lost count of the number of times my dad has asked her to call him by his first name. She agrees every time, then continues calling him Mr Walker. I'm surprised my dad hasn't given up by now.

"I'm ready," I say as I pick up my bouquet of white roses. "You can come in now, Dad."

Pippa steps aside and opens the door wider as I see my dad step into the room. He stops dead in his tracks when he sees me, and I watch his throat work as he swallows several times. His eyes sweep down my dress before he lifts them to rest on mine.

I've never seen my dad lost for words before, and he opens and closes his mouth a couple of times before a gentle shove from Pippa propels him in my direction. He is stood in front of me a few moments later, his eyes swimming with tears as he finally finds his voice. "You look beautiful, honey. I can't believe my baby girl is getting married."

"Thank you, Dad. We finally made it, huh?"

"I always knew you would, honey. That man out there is perfect for you, and anyone can see how much he loves you. Now, shall we go and get you married?" He holds out his arm for me, and I take it as I smile at him. Pippa is still standing in the doorway. This time, Lizzie is by her side. Both women are holding their matching bouquets with huge grins on their faces as they watch us approach.

. . .

"*D*on't you girls need to go in front of us?" my dad asks them, laughing when they realise everything is starting and scurry off ahead of us.

I slowly make my way down the hallway towards the main hall, grateful the venue put us on the ground floor. I might be able to walk, but it doesn't take long before I start feeling tired, so the shorter distance I have to walk, the longer I can stay upright.

Pippa and Lizzie are both waiting by the huge wooden double doors, smiling as they see me coming closer to them. I watch as Pippa looks into the room and gives a small nod, before music fills the air. My dad and I come to stop just out of sight of everyone in the room, and I take a deep breath as I see Pippa, then Lizzie walk into the room.

I turn and look to my dad. "Here we go."

With one final breath, we walk into the room and towards my future.

~

Caleb

I can't believe today is finally here.

It's taken us almost twelve years to get to this point in our lives, but it's finally happening. By the end of today, Crissie will be my wife and I will be the luckiest man alive.

Gary is stood behind me, only a few feet away, and I can hear him quietly murmuring for me to remember to breathe. I know he's saying it jokingly, but at times, I do have to force myself to exhale.

As I wait for Crissie to make her entrance on her dad's arm, I look around the room, seeing our closest friends and family who have come out to see us pledge our lives to one another. They're all chatting amongst themselves, all dressed in their finery.

I swear I've never seen so many women in hats. I didn't even realised women still wore hats, except if you were royalty or going to ladies day at Ascot. There's a whole array of styles and colours, but the one that stands out the most is my mum's fuchsia pink one. Trust her to go all out to be noticed.

I smile as I look at her chatting animatedly with Crissie's mum, pleased our parents get on well. It makes for happier family functions, that's for sure. I'm about to get their attention when I feel a hand on my shoulder. As I turn to Gary, I see him nod towards the main doors, and see Pippa and Lizzie. They're looking to the left and smiling.

Oh god, this is it. Crissie is just off to the side of those doors. Any minute now, she's going to walk in and I'm going to see my bride for the first time.

When Pippa looks into the room and gives a small

nod, the music kicks in and she begins to walk down the aisle with my sister. They both look beautiful in their ice blue, strapless gowns. I smile at them both as they come nearer, and when they arrive at the front and take their positions, the music changes and I hold my breath.

As Crissie comes into view, I'm floored. I know she had to change her dress because of the pregnancy, and I've no idea what her previous dress looked like, but the one she's wearing now makes her look more beautiful than I've ever seen her. When you add in the fact she's carrying our child, too, there's only one word to describe her.

Perfect.

It was only a couple of days ago that we thought she may not be able to make it down the aisle on her own two feet, but she was determined to make it happen. Now, as she walks towards me, supported by her dad, who has a huge smile on his face, I've never been more proud of her in my life.

Her eyes are locked on mine as she comes closer, and I know I'm close to tears. I promised myself I wouldn't cry; that no matter how perfect the moment was, or how perfect Crissie looked, I would not cry. Yeah, that promise to myself is not going to be kept.

When she comes to stand next to me, I watch her turn to her father as he places a kiss on her cheek. The older man is close to tears too, and when he places his daughter's hand in mine, in that instant, I know he is trusting me to look after her, and I have never felt more humbled.

When he steps back and stands next to his wife, Crissie and I are left on our own, and as we look at each other, everyone else in the room fades away. It's just me and her and the love we have for one another. Suddenly, everything we've been through up to this point seems inconsequential. This is what's important. We've made it this far, and we're finally going to do what we promised to do almost seven years ago:

Become husband and wife.

CHAPTER 51

Crissie

"I now pronounce you husband and wife."

I keep replaying those seven words in my head, still not quite believing it. Cal and I are married. He's my husband and I'm his wife. How the hell did that happen?

I laugh at myself at the silly thought. I know how it happened, but part of me still can't quite believe we actually did it. I look down at my left hand and see the sparkling wedding band next to my engagement ring. When Cal pushed the ring onto my finger, I'd had to swallow the lump that formed in my throat, just as I saw he had to do when I did the same to him.

His ring matches mine, and as I glance over at him as he chats with his dad, I see the ring glint in the light, and, as if I didn't know it before, I know now that he is one hundred percent mine, and that simple platinum band confirms it.

"Hey."

I turn when I hear a familiar voice, smiling when Lizzie sits next to me. She's smiling, but I know behind the happy face is a sad soul. A little over a week ago, we received the news that the guy who had previously been convicted of attacks on us both had won his case and was now awaiting a retrial. That meant both Lizzie and I would now have to testify in court and relive what could possibly be one of the worst nights of our lives.

"Hey, you okay?" I say as I take her hand in mine.

"Yeah, I will be. It was a beautiful ceremony, Cris. I still can't believe my brother actually cried."

This time the smile and laugh are genuine as we both think back to the ceremony. Cal didn't cry; he blubbed like a baby, and only just made it through the vows. I have to admit, it was very endearing to see a man openly show his feelings, and that man is mine.

"Yeah, it only makes me love him even more." I continue watching him, and as if he knows, he turns and his eyes lock with mine. The room is packed with our nearest and dearest, and the noise from the DJ and from friendly chatter is filling the room. It's almost 8:30 p.m. and any minute now, the DJ will call Cal and I to the dancefloor for our first dance.

As if the DJ could read my mind, he does just that and

is met with cheers and applause from our guests. I stand from my seat as Cal approaches and takes my hand, leading me out onto the dancefloor.

When it came to deciding what song would be played for our first dance, there really was no discussion. It's the song that was playing when we declared our love for one another. Amazed will always be a special song for us, and as the strains of the introduction begin, Cal takes me in is arms, which is no easy feat considering the side of my baby bump, and leads me around the dancefloor.

I can see the flashes from cameras in my peripheral vision as everyone captures this special moment between us, but right now, I only have eyes for my husband. As Lonestar sing the words of the song we've come to love so much, I struggle to breathe as I finally accept that this handsome, kind, gentle man is actually mine.

So far, I've managed to keep the tears at bay, but as we move around the floor, they finally break free and slip down my cheeks. When Cal begins singing the words to me, I have to take a few deep breaths as my pulse begins to race.

I love it when he sings. He has a beautiful voice but doesn't like to share it with anyone, except me. I'm the lucky one who gets to hear him sing some of the most beautiful love songs ever written. His voice is deep and rich and always made me go weak at the knees, and right now is no exception.

As the song draws to a close, Cal stops our movement

and leans in to kiss me, just as we're engulfed in a group hug from our friends. I laugh as they hug us both as tightly as they are allowed, then stop suddenly when I feel a twinge in my stomach. When the crowd disperses, I look down, seeing the puddle around my feet.

"Erm, Cal."

"Yeah, baby."

"I think we should get to the hospital. My water just broke."

CHAPTER 52

Caleb

$\mathcal{W}$ ell, this wasn't how I saw us spending our wedding night.

I'm pacing the waiting room as the doctors and nurses work to deliver our baby girl. I've removed my jacket, discarded the tie, and unbuttoned my waistcoat, as has my dad and Crissie's dad, as we wait for news.

After her waters broke at our wedding reception, her mum had called an ambulance, which arrived within five minutes. Because of the procedure Crissie had previously, she couldn't have a natural birth, so she was rushed into surgery for a C-section as soon as we arrived. There hadn't been time to get me ready to go into the room with her, so I was stuck in this dingy waiting room with our families.

It's been almost ninety minutes since they took her in,

which I know is almost twice as long as a C-section should take. I figured it may take a little longer because of Crissie's condition and previous surgery, but I thought she'd be out by now.

I'm about to go in and demand to know what's going on, when the door opens and a nurse walks in. She's holding a pink bundle in her arms, and she has a smile on her face as she approaches me.

"Mr Roberts, would you like to meet your daughter?"

My hand shoots up to my mouth as I gasp at the little bundle being passed to me by the nurse. I remember everything Crissie and I learned and support her head as the nurse places her in my arms.

I gaze at my daughter for a few moments before looking at the nurse. "How's Crissie? When can I see her?"

"The doctors are finishing up with her now. You should be able to see her soon. I'll come and get you when it's time."

I nod at the nurse as she leaves and look down at my daughter. She is so tiny, and I find it hard to believe Crissie and I actually made this little miracle.

"Oh, Cal, she's gorgeous."

"She's a little beauty."

"She has your eyes, honey."

I hear the words from our family, but none of them penetrate my brain. All I can see is the two bright blue eyes that are looking up at me. I thought loving Crissie was the easiest thing I've ever done but seeing our daughter in my arms makes me realise I was wrong. This little bundle is completely dependant on Cris and me for everything now. She is our whole world.

"Do you have a name for her, Cal?" my sister asks as she stands next to me.

"We do. Everyone, I'd like you to meet Hope Elizabeth Roberts."

When Hope lets out a long sigh and her eyes close, the love I have for this little girl almost overwhelms me, and I realise I would go to the ends of the earth to make sure she has everything she ever wants.

~

*I*t's another thirty minutes before the nurse comes and tells us we can see Crissie. She returned to take Hope to the nursery twenty minutes ago, giving us enough time so that everyone here could hold her and get their first cuddle.

When I reach Crissie's room, the doctor is outside waiting for me, and I instantly get a bad feeling.

"Caleb, it's good to see you again. How is your little girl?"

"She's perfect, doctor, thank you. How's Crissie?"

"I wanted to speak with you before you go in to see her. There were some complications during the C-section that resulted in Crissie losing a lot of blood. Her heart stopped once, but we were able to restart it pretty quickly. We managed to stop the bleeding, and provided there are no further issues, she should make a full recovery."

Her heart stopped? I could have lost her? Now that we have little Hope, the thought of losing Cris is twice as painful as it was before. The thought of our daughter growing up without her mother is a pain I don't ever want to experience.

"Now, I know her oncologist wanted to start the treatment for her cancer as soon as possible, but right now, she's too weak to handle another surgery. We'll continue to assess her condition and shall start treatment as soon as we can, but right now, what she needs the most is to rest."

"I understand, doctor. Has she seen our daughter yet?"

"Yes, she did briefly, shortly after she was delivered. If you like, I can ask the nurse to bring her to her room, so you can both spend some time with her?"

"That would be good. Thank you, doctor."

When the doctor smiles and walks off down the corridor, I open the door to Crissie's room. It's not the first time I've seen her in a hospital bed attached to monitors, but it's a sight I'll never get used to seeing. As I approach, she sighs and turns her head towards me.

Her eyes are closed and she's breathing steadily. It looks like she's sleeping, so I decide not to wake her. Instead, I just sit in the chair by her bed and watch her sleep. She looks pale and fragile, and I feel an overwhelming urge to protect her. I reach out to take her hand, and when I do, her eyes flutter open and her lips tilt up in a small smile.

"Hey you. How are you feeling?" I ask her as I pull the chair closer and place and soft kiss on her cheek.

"Tired, and sore." She pauses and winces when she tries to push herself into a sitting position. "Where is she? Where's our baby?"

I hear the panic in her voice as she looks around the room.

"It's okay, Cris. The doctor has gone to ask a nurse to bring her in. She's been in the nursery. Crissie, she's beautiful. Our little Hope is finally here, and she's the most beautiful thing I've ever seen." I see the relief swamp Crissie as she bursts into tears. Moving quickly, I sit by her on the bed and gently pull her into my arms as she cries on my shoulder.

"It's okay, baby." I hold her for several minutes before I hear a gentle knock on the door, seeing the nurse peering in through the small window. I nod to let her know it's okay for her to come in, and when she does, she's pushing a small cart. I see the bundle of pink before Crissie does, but when she lifts her head and her eyes connect with our daughter, the smile that spreads across her face fills my heart with more love than I ever thought possible.

The nurse wheels the cart around to the side of the bed as Crissie watches, never taking her eyes off our daughter. When the nurse carefully picks her up, I move from the bed so Crissie can shift as the nurse places Hope against her chest. I watch my wife holding my daughter as the nurse leaves the room.

These two girls are the most important things in my life. Nothing will stop me from doing everything I can to keep them safe.

I see the tears slipping silently from Crissie's eyes as I sit beside her and wrap my arm around her shoulder.

"She has your eyes, Cal."

"My mum said the same thing," I say with a smile.

"I love her so much. I didn't think it was possible to love someone this much, Cal. I can't believe we made something so perfect."

"I know, baby. We did good."

"I love you, Cal."

I return her words with a soft kiss to her lips before she turns back to Hope. All I can do is watch them, my heart almost stopping when Hope grabs hold of my finger. I always thought it was a myth when they said the moment your child grabs your finger for the first time, you realise everything in your life has changed. I now see everyone who ever said that was right. Crissie and Hope are my world. Nothing else matters now. As long as they're with me, I can do anything.

"Cal, can you take her, please? I don't feel well."

I'm shaken out of my thoughts by her words and take my daughter from her arms just in time to see Crissie's eyes roll back into her head as she falls against the pillows. The machines she is attached to start to beep madly, and before I can call out for help, the door slams open and I'm surrounded by doctors and nurses.

I move to the back of the room as they gather around Crissie. The noise is so loud, Hope starts crying, and I instinctively start rocking her to try and calm her down. Before I know what's happening, a nurse is taking my arm and ushering me out of the room.

The last words I hear are ones that chill me to the bone.

"We're losing her."

CHAPTER 53

Six weeks later

"Hey, Mum. Are you ready to go?"

"Just need to grab my bag and then we're good to go."

I watch as she hurries around the room, stuffing everything she comes across into her black bag before slinging it over her shoulder. I swear she thinks she's Mary Poppins and that bag is bottomless. With the amount of stuff she's throwing it in, I'm starting to think it might just be.

When she starts heading over towards me, I breathe a sigh of relief, exaggerating it for my mum's benefit, before I pick up Hope's car seat and head towards the door. Mum opens it for me and I walk down the path to my car, shifting Hope into the crook of my elbow as I open the rear driver's side door.

I'm a pro at fixing Hope into the car now. For the first few weeks, it took me several attempts to get the damn thing fastened correctly. I've lost my temper more than once and had to stop myself from blowing up. Now, I've done it so often I can do it in my sleep.

"Is everyone else meeting us there?"

I nod at my mum as I secure Hope's blanket around her after checking the restraints one more time. I'm almost OCD about making sure everything is fastened correctly and tightly. No matter how many times I check, I always have to do it one more time, just in case I missed something the previous dozen or so times.

Eventually, I drag myself away and close the door before climbing into the driver's seat. It only a short drive to our destination, and we're there within ten minutes. I park the car and can see a crowd of people waiting for us. A lump forms in my throat when I see how many people are here, and it takes me a few moments before I can get out of the car.

By the time I do, I see my mum has already unbuckled Hope and is holding her granddaughter in her arms as she waves her arms around, something she only started doing this week.

Reaching out, I take Hope from my mum and walk over to the crowd of people, accepting brief hugs and kisses off everyone as we walk. Even though Hope is almost six weeks old, people still coo over her like she was born only yesterday. If I didn't know any better, I'd say my little girl loves the attention as she laughs and bats her lashes at them.

We continue walking for five minutes until we come to where we need to be. The crowd gathers in a large circle as I look down and feel the tears fighting to break free as I read the inscription engraved into the highly polished black granite:

Crissie Elizabeth Roberts
15 August 1989 ~ 17 February 2018
Beloved Wife to Caleb
Adoring Mother to Aria and Hope
Loving Daughter to Matthew and Diane
Miss You Always, Love You Forever

EPILOGUE

Eighteen years later

I can't believe my baby girl is eighteen today.

She's not a baby anymore, and she hates it when I call her that, but she allows me to continue. It's been my pet name for her practically since the day she was born, and no matter how old she gets, it will always be my name for her.

I wait for her to emerge from her bedroom as I drink my tea, glancing across at the TV when a familiar name flashes across the screen. I turn to give the news report my full attention, my ears not quite believing what they're hearing.

"Washford had been convicted of three counts of rape in 2019, having been acquitted of rape and sexual assault the previous year after a jury found the evidence against him to be

insufficient. It is not yet known who took it upon themselves to end his life, but one thing's for sure, this woman, and all women across the country, can sleep peacefully now that this sexual predator is no longer among us."

My chest feels tight as I watch the TV, the realisation that the man who attacked Crissie and my sister is now dead. I was brought up to value all human life, but I'd be lying if I said I hadn't thought of hundreds of ways I could make that man pay for almost ruining the lives of two of the women I care most about in this world.

Crissie hadn't been with us when the bastard who almost raped her went to trial, and part of me is glad she wasn't around to see the charade that is our judicial system, fail her. It would have broken her all over again. She was a strong woman—had to be with everything we went through—but I knew Crissie better than anyone. She would have struggled to cope, had she been here, to see him walk free from that court.

Picking up the remote control, I switch off the TV and turn back to waiting for our daughter to make her grand entrance. Not for the first time this morning, my mind wanders to the past, and I can't help but imagine what Crissie would be doing today. She'd probably be rushing around decorating the house before Hope got up. Fixing banners to the walls and attaching balloons to every surface that would hold them.

Crissie would be so proud of the young woman our daughter has become. She has my eyes—so everyone says anyway—but in all other ways, she's the mirror image of her mother, with the same kind heart and infectious laugh. She's clever too. She got straight A's in all her GCSE's and repeated the feat in her A-Levels. In six months time, she's off to university to study medicine. Yes, Crissie would be one proud momma bear.

Hope will be studying at Chester university. She told me it was the best place for the course she wants to study, but I have a feeling it's because she doesn't want to leave me alone. Being a single parent hasn't been easy. We've had our ups and downs, our screaming matches and an equal number of crying sessions, but the bond between Hope and I has never been stronger.

Losing her mum at just twenty-eight years old was hard; probably the hardest thing I've ever had to go through. The fact it was on our wedding day and Hope's birthday, made it even harder. We never did find that miracle cure I'd dreamt about. When she flatlined in that hospital bed, my heart stopped with hers. Watching the doctors and nurses working on her as I cradled Hope to my chest almost broke me.

The doctors had said it was a cardiac arrest, and her body was just so weak from the C-section and her cancer that there was nothing they could do to save her.

Once the funeral service and memorial were over, I started the process of living my life without her. It took me several months to even contemplate getting back to normal, and if it hadn't been for the support of my parents and Crissie's parents, I don't think I would be here now.

I'm pulled out of my melancholy when I hear Hope's bedroom door open and her feet on the stairs. It took me a while to get used to having stairs. The flat Cris and I lived in was on the ground floor, so everything was on one level. That place held so many memories of Crissie and me that I hadn't wanted to leave. It was my mum who eventually convinced me that my memories of Cris were in my head and I would always have them, no matter where I live.

Hope had just turned one when we moved into the house we now call home. It's just outside Chester and, while it's not big, it suits us just fine. Hope and I have made this little two-up two-down our home. I know Crissie would have loved it here.

As I wait for Hope, I check everything is in place. The birthday breakfast I've prepared includes her favourite: pancakes with maple syrup, a glass of orange juice and a peppermint tea. I hope she doesn't have to run off too early. I know she has plans with Craig, her boyfriend, today, but I'm hoping she has at least a couple of hours to spend with her old dad.

When she walks through the door, I'm briefly taken back to the first time I saw Crissie. She really is the spitting image of her mum, and, in a way, I'm grateful for that. I'll never forget Crissie. How could I? But having Hope makes what we had together last long after she left our lives.

"Happy Birthday, sweetheart." I stand from my place at

the breakfast bar and walk over to her. She gladly accepts my hug as her arms wrap round my back and I kiss her on the cheek.

"Thanks, Daddy."

She has always called me daddy. Even now, at eighteen, she still does, and part of me hopes she always will. Even though she's an adult now, she will always be my little girl.

"I made your favourite breakfast, and, as requested, I've transferred some money into your account, so you can spend it as you like."

At the sound of money, her eyes light up and she smiles at me, giving me another hug before sitting at the breakfast bar and pouring a glass of orange juice. I watch as she devours the food I've prepared for her, wanting her to keep eating, knowing that when she finishes, there's something I need to give her, something I'm not sure what her reaction will be.

I finish my cup of tea just as Hope finishes hers, and she leans back, her hands on her belly.

"Thanks for that, Dad. That was great, as always."

"You're welcome, sweetie." *Here goes nothing.* "Hope, I have something for you. It's from your mum." I watch as her eyes sweep to me and her expression softens. Hope never knew her mum, but our families have done all we can to keep her memory alive and have told her stories of our time together.

There are photographs all over the house, including

one I snapped quickly with my phone, in the hospital when Crissie held Hope for the first time. We've made sure Hope knows the kind of woman her mother was, and that she will never forget her.

"A few weeks before she died, your mum took out a safe deposit box. In it, she left this." I take the envelope out of my back pocket and put it on the table. On the front are two words: 'My Daughter'. "She left a note with it to say this was to be given to you on your eighteenth birthday."

Hope looks at the envelope for a few moments before reaching out, resting her fingertips on the paper. Her eyes are filling with tears, and I see her swallow a few times before she speaks. "This is from Mum?"

Hearing her voice break as she fights tears makes me want to hug her tightly. Crissie left a letter for me, too, and I remember crying for hours after I read it. She told me she loved me, and that I was the first, and will be the last man she ever loves. She said that if she didn't make it, she trusted me to look after our daughter and bring her up with the same values that made her fall in love with me in the first place.

As I read it, only three weeks after her death, I remember thinking she had been preparing for the worst and hadn't said a thing to me. At the time, I couldn't understand why she wouldn't tell me how she was feeling, but as time went on, I realised she had just been thinking of me and not wanting to hurt me.

That was my Crissie, always thinking of others before herself.

"Yes, sweetie. I don't know what it says, but knowing your mum as I did, it's something you'll want to read. I can leave you alone if you want? She left me one, too, and I was a blubbering mess by the time I'd finished reading it."

I give her a small smile as she picks up the envelope and gently brushes her fingers across her mother's handwriting. She takes a deep breath and looks at me.

"No, can you stay while I read it?"

"Of course I can, baby girl."

She nods as she takes another breath before tearing open the envelope and taking out the piece of paper. I can see Crissie's handwriting on the paper and take a shaky breath. Memories of the time I spent with Crissie are never far from the surface, but most of the time I am able to put them to one side for the sake of getting on with my life without breaking down every five minutes. I need to stay strong for Hope.

When Hope starts speaking, I reach out and she grabs my hand, holding on tightly.

Dear Hope,

Yes, you're not even here and I know your name. Your dad and I agreed on it when you were only a few months old. After everything your dad and I went through, it seemed a fitting name.

Anyway, as much as I hope this isn't true, you're reading this on your eighteenth birthday and I'm not there to see the wonderful woman you've become. How do I know how wonderful you are? Well, that's easy, because your dad raised you. Hope, I can't begin to tell you how much the thought of leaving your dad alone to raise you hurts me, but I know he will do a fantastic job.

Your dad is the only man I've ever loved, and I can only pray that you find yourself a man who treats you like a princess, because that's what you deserve, baby girl. Don't settle for anything less than a man who puts you first. I was so lucky when I found your dad. Not every girl finds their prince on the first go, but I did. I know you'll find your prince, too, baby.

You probably know from your dad that I was sick before you were born. You never know when the big guy upstairs is going to take you, so if I die before I get to know you, know that I love you, Hope. I love you so much it actually hurts. I never understood how people could love something with that much devotion, but you're still in my belly and I already know I would do anything for you.

You're my daughter, Hope—you're our daughter—and I know that even though I'm not there with you, your dad will tell you stories about me, none of which you should believe, by the way. Hope, please look after your dad for me. He'll tell you he's okay, but don't believe him. Sometimes you have to push to get him to open up. He'll open up eventually, and he will need you.

I'm going to sign off now. Remember, Hope, I loved you from the moment I became aware of your existence. You are still loved, baby girl. Never forget that.

Love always,
Mum x

By the time Hope finishes, we're both in floods of tears, and she jumps down from her stool and comes over to me. I pull her into a tight hug and we just hold each other for what feels like forever. We've always been close, but right now, I've never felt closer to her. After several minutes, we pull apart and she swipes at her eyes.

"I should go freshen up. Craig will be here soon."

I just nod as she hurries upstairs as I grab a tissue and dab at my eyes. After a few deep breaths, I tuck the paper back in the envelope and place it by Hope's bag. I walk through to the living room and sit down, grabbing my wallet off the coffee table. Flipping it open, I tug one of the folds and pull out a small photograph.

I'll always remember when this was taken. My mum snapped it on our first Christmas Day together, not long after I told Crissie how grateful I was that she was mine. We'd just hugged, and the picture shows us in each other's arms, just looking at each other, smiles on our faces. My mum always said she had never seen a picture that showed a couple so much in love. I've had the picture in my wallet ever since. I'll hold it close to my heart until the day I die.

"We did it, Cris. Hope is perfect. She's so like you, it's uncanny. I hope I've done you proud in how I've raised her. If I have it's because of you. You were it for me, Cris.

There will never be anyone else. I love you, baby. Always and Forever."

I see a droplet fall onto my hand and realise I'm crying again. Tucking the photo back in my wallet, I swipe at the tears and stand. Thinking about Cris always brings out this reaction in me. She taught me so much during our time together, including how it feels to love, and she proved to me that love does exist.

When I see Hope come back downstairs, looking as fresh as she did before our sob fest, I decide that from today, I will live my life to the fullest, for me and our daughter, because what Cris said in her letter is true.

You never know when it will take you.

THE END

38847216R00226

Printed in Poland
by Amazon Fulfillment
Poland Sp. z o.o., Wrocław